Portrait of the artist as a young killer . . .

"How much do you know about our freak, Grace?" Jaworski asked.

"Some."

"I'll give you the quickie on him before I show you something. He calls himself Michaelangelo. Like the artist, but he spells it wrong. He thinks he's an artist, too. He's killed six already." Jaworski stopped suddenly, and sucked in a deep breath of stale air.

"Four men, two women," he went on. "He . . . uses them. Makes 'art' out of them."

"Prints?"

Jaworski stopped again, this time outside a door.

"Oh, he's not afraid of leaving prints. We've got them by the hundred."

"So he's never been arrested, in the military, or had certain jobs."

"He's been a careful boy," Jaworski said, and reached into his pocket for a small ring of keys.

She looked to the door they stood near, and noticed a makeshift sign tacked above it: GALLERY.

Jaworski smiled. "Did you eat breakfast, Agent Grace?"

TOP TEN

RYNE DOUGLAS PEARSON

JOVE BOOKS, NEW YORK

TOP TEN

A Jove Book / published by arrangement with
the author

PRINTING HISTORY
G. P. Putnam's Sons edition / October 1999
Jove edition / September 2000

The Penguin Putnam Inc. World Wide Web site address is
http://www.penguinputnam. com

ISBN: 0-515-12903-8

A JOVE BOOK®
Jove Books are published by The Berkley Publishing Group,
a division of Penguin Putnam Inc.,
375 Hudson Street, New York, New York 10014.
JOVE and the "J" design
are trademarks belonging to Penguin Putnam Inc.

PRINTED IN THE UNITED STATES OF AMERICA

10 9 8 7 6 5 4 3 2 1

Before all others, Mark Canton, Anna DeRoy, Steve Reuther, and everyone at Warner Brothers deserves and receives my utmost gratitude for their belief, their support, and their patience through interminable delays not of their making. Their talent and their passion are boundless. This book would not be without them.

Howard Sanders and Richard Green took a two-sentence idea and made amazing things happen with it. *They* are amazing. And they are decent men who dispel every negative myth ever conjured about "Hollywood" agents. And they are my friends.

Tom Colgan, my editor and champion in New York for a good number of years now, said he thought this idea could be a book. As always, he was right.

David Highfill, my other editor, jumped on board and helped make things happen.

Chuck Verrill, my "New York" agent, is always available to answer my queries on the literary merits of topics as obscure as, oh, *rebar*.

Irene, my wife, mother of the light of my life, is my savior each and every day.

And finally, as always, for helping me realize the joy of telling stories, my thanks to R.H., S.H., and M.G.

For Owen

PROLOGUE:

[PIECES]

He cut the woman to calm her down.

Not deeply, mind you, just a quick flick with the tip of his blade high on her right cheek, something to clear her head, to focus her thoughts, to crystallize the reality of the situation.

As with the others, it worked like a charm.

He had waited most of the day for a few moments with this one, biding his time in the shrubs behind the small post office, listening to the waters of some nameless slough rustle toward Great Sacandaga Lake, occasionally drawing the blade of his knife slowly and silently across the whetstone always with him, watching as carrier after carrier returned from their routes and left for their homes or taverns they fancied or wherever the joy of an ended week might take them on a Friday evening. Waited and watched until just after seven, until the lights inside went low and just one car remained in the gravel lot. Until the building's rear door opened and the pretty clerk from whom he'd earlier purchased a single stamp backed out with her keys in hand and her eyes on the lock, a pleasant tune whistling from her lips. It was then that he'd grabbed her, from behind, initiating the expected struggle, keys and purse falling, arms flailing. But with the fast sting of his knife and the sight of her own blood upon its tip, lit to a creamy blackness by the moon, her struggling ceased. Her muscles grew taut with fear, with *understanding*. The scream that raged against the palm of his hand withered to a flurry of whimpering gasps.

"I'm sorry," he began, drawing her backward against him, the union almost an embrace, his words a warm whisper upon her ear. "I require your assistance for a while."

He kicked her purse and keys aside and forced her back through the door, into a dim and open space populated by mounded sacks of mail and ranks of head-high sorting bins. Surrounded by the tools of this woman's most banal trade, he paused, pulling her close, glove still over her mouth, and asked from behind, "Will we be interrupted?"

Her mind raced at the question, at what *act* it implied, and she stiffened, her chest heaving in a quick and shallow rhythm, the urge to fight, to flee, rising once again.

But there would be none of that. He spun her halfway around, keeping his gloved hand over her mouth and forcing her hard against the bare brick of the inside wall. The impact stunned her, forced her eyes shut for the briefest of moments, and when they fluttered open again it was there. The blade. She stared at it, transfixed, and hardly flinched when he flicked the blade once more and cut the soft flesh beneath her left eye, a slow trickle of blood tears upon both cheeks now, crimson drops that dragged wet red streaks down her face and onto the brown leather wrapping his hand.

"I can cut you in other ways, in other *places*," he assured her, stepping close, his slim and chiseled face in intimate proximity now, half-veiled in a shadow. "Shall I do that?"

Her head shook beneath his grasp.

"Again, then, will there be any interruptions?"

She answered with another shake of her head, weak this time, resigned. He smiled, it seemed, the mask of his face now showing a gleeless baring of teeth. The warning of a predator in sight of its prey.

She wet herself as he pulled her away from the wall.

He drew her close once again, his whole arm around her neck now and her mouth free, and moved toward the front of the building, leaving the sacks and sorting bins behind, traveling a corridor with a room on either side, packing materials filling one and a copy machine the other, its green READY light glowing. Through a doorway next and into the cramped station behind the front counter, where he had first encountered her, had handed over some change with no thought that soon they would be together again, and finally out into the modest public spaces of the post office where his plans for the day had changed in an instant. To the exact spot he took her, the high table against the wall where one could affix stamps to letters, or address an envelope with the pen that was anchored to the countertop with the flimsiest of chains. Almost nine hours earlier he had done both, then dropped his readied letter into the OUT OF TOWN slot next to the table. Those tasks completed, he would have been gone from the Pembry, New York, Post Office those seven hours now, gone from all of zip code 12078 for seven hours now, likely never to return.

Except for that glance.

Innocent, it was. Just the passing of his gaze, really, over the board above the table where notices were posted. The latest issues of interest to philatelists. Bold promises of low prices and on-time delivery of rush packages. And pictures.

Yes, pictures. Photos, actually, but for one. All upon one stiff piece of paper tacked to the board. A medley of faces and that single approximation that one very mediocre artist had rendered (*if only the hack had been required to sign his work . . .*). Ten in all. All men, though those of the fairer sex had been featured in the past, because deed, not gender, was the price of admission, and the deed must be bad. Very, very bad. The act or acts of criminals. The worst of the worst. And stamped upon the paper that bore this gallery of rogues, the very official seal of the entity that determined one's worthiness of such a low (or high) honor, none other than the Federal Bureau of Investigation.

"Look," he said, pressing the flat profile of her stomach to the table's edge and grabbing a bunch of hair with which he aimed her face at the offending scrap of paper. "Would you mind explaining this?"

She gulped air, sucked it fast and tried to understand what it was that he wanted, searching the wall and the notice board for something amiss, something that might need clarification. But she saw nothing. As hard as she tried, she saw nothing except the very, very ordinary. "Explain . . . explain what?"

He released her hair and reached past her face to rip the paper from the board, bringing it right before her eyes so there could be no mistake this time. "Explain. *Now*."

The FBI bulletin filled her field of vision, but still she had no clue as to what it was she was supposed to explain to him. "It's the FBI's Ten Most Wanted poster. It's always on that board."

His breath on her neck grew hot in a few awkward seconds of silence, and when he spoke again the words came out in a growl. "I know what the fuck it is. But what is that on it?"

The blade came to her neck now. Her eyes began to puddle. "What is what?"

"THE FUCKING NUMBERS!"

The scream jolted her, the blade close to slicing her now. "Numbers? Numbers?"

"ON THE FUCKING POSTER! THE NUMBERS! DO YOU SEE THEM?" He ground the paper to her face and pulled it back, the blood beneath her eyes smeared upon it. "DO YOU SEE THEM NOW? DO YOU?"

"Yes!" she cried out, suddenly focused by the sense that worse things than this insane interrogation might be close at hand. "Yes! I see them!"

"There are numbers!" he barked at her.

"Yes. Yes. Numbers."

"Numbers. One two three four five six seven eight nine ten."

"Yes. One through ten. I see them."

"Why are there numbers there?"

Her wide eyes puzzled at his question. "Aren't there always numbers?"

He sneered at her stupidity. "No. No, no, no. There aren't always numbers. There weren't always numbers. There never have been numbers. No numbers. No numbers. It's always been just one big happy family, everybody the same. A club with no officers. No president, no vice president. No rank. No one better than anyone else." His stare probed the terror of her face. "Do you understand what I'm saying? What I'm trying to make clear to you? Do you?"

She didn't, but nodded nonetheless.

"You see, there are numbers on here now," he went on, holding the bulletin close to her wounded face once again. "And everyone has a number. Everyone is *ranked*. Why is that? Why have some people been made to feel special and others . . . WHY ARE THERE NUMBERS?!!"

"I don't know," she told him, the tears dripping from her eyes to sting the cuts upon her cheeks. "I don't know. We just get those and put them up whenever they come in."

He turned her head fully toward the bulletin. "Read me number one."

"Number one?"

He nodded and twisted the bunch of her hair. "His name, his crime. Read it."

Tears blurred her vision, and the ache of his grip upon

her scalp was numbing, but she blinked hard and made herself focus. Made herself do this little thing that he wanted. "Alvaro Camacho . . ."

"Name *and* crime," he prompted.

"Alvaro Camacho, he . . . he killed three agents of the Drug Enforcement Administration."

"And . . ."

"He trafficked narcotics."

"Very good. Number two . . ."

"Desmond Grace. Bank robbery. Murder. Two counts of murder. Flight from persecution."

"Prosecution," he corrected her. "Number three . . ."

"Ahmed Faisal. Destruction of a civilian airliner. Murder."

"Number four . . ."

"Luke Mayweather. Flight from . . . prosecution. Attempted murder of a police officer."

"And five . . ."

"Mills DeVane. Assault on a federal officer. Drug trafficking."

"Six. . . ."

"Rudy 'Rooster' Coletti. Racketeering. Attempted murder."

"Seven. . . ."

"Robert Jack McCormack. Destruction of federal property. Arson. Assault on a federal officer."

"Eight. . . ."

"Lee Tran. Assault. Extortion. Racketeering."

"Nine. . . ."

"Francis Gunther. Bank robbery. Assault. Kidnapping."

"Ten. . . ."

The next recitation was about to slip past her lips when recognition dammed it there. Her eyes angled toward her captor.

"Ten. . . ."

Her lips began to quiver. "Please . . ."

He set the bulletin on the table and turned the woman around so that she faced him, gently guiding her to that position, his manner suddenly calm. "We needn't cover number ten, I suppose. Tell me, what is your name?"

"D-D-Doris."

"Without the stutter, I imagine."

"Please let me go," she begged in the most pitiful of whimpers, groveling most sincerely. "I have a child, and . . . and . . . and . . ."

His head shook silent regret. "You're not going to be able to help me after all, I see."

"My little boy, he's . . . he's . . ."

He touched the knife to her lips and she fell instantly silent. "Don't tell me about your little boy, Doris."

Quiet came over him, a deep and settled stillness as he drifted off, to a better place where hushed corridors smelled of cool grace and sang with mad brilliance. Soon a twinkle danced on his gaze and he was back. Back and savoring the sight of sweet Doris.

"A thousand years ago Therata captured the nymph of Mygoria in marble," he told her, and she shuddered as the knife came suddenly to her left breast, the tip tracing across the thin material over her nipple. "Her mams were magnificent."

"Please . . . Don't . . . Not that . . . Please . . ."

In the silence beyond her pleas he noted an amusing and incorrect assumption. A misconception so laughable that a grin curled one side of his mouth. "Oh, Doris, do you think I am going to *violate* you?"

Her breath wheezed in and out in fast, dry sobs, the point of the blade slowly circling the soft crest beneath her blouse.

"Doris, I am not a rapist," he said, and slipped the blade deep between her fifth and sixth ribs, puncturing her left lung and nicking the vital muscle that was her heart, withdrawing it quick and easy, like a palette knife from gouache. His free hand clamped over her mouth, pinning her to the wall and trapping the scream that rose, a cry for mercy that God might hear, but no one else.

"I am an artist."

"Clusterfuck."

His back was to her, but FBI Special Agent Ariel Grace knew precisely for whom her supervisor's comment was intended.

"Sixty friggin' agents, Lord knows how many blue suits, and to the last they're all just standing around waiting to get rained on." Jack Hale, Assistant Special Agent in Charge of the Bureau's Atlanta field office, lifted his gaze toward the threatening sky and shook his head. "Beautiful. I'd call this a well-executed operation, Grace."

"He was supposed to be here, sir," Ariel told the ASAC, with certainty so firm that he turned sharply toward her. "I'm positive of that."

Hale glared at her. "Then why isn't he?"

"Why don't you ask whoever left their ride parked on the boulevard?" Ariel suggested, gesturing with her head to a gaggle of agents milling about in front of the Proper Peach Motel. "A blind man wouldn't have missed those hubcaps and that antennae."

"There is no Bureau car on the boulevard," Hale challenged her. "I came from that direction."

"There was."

"You saw this?"

"No," she told the ASAC, hands going to her hips, the unbuttoned front of her windbreaker flapping in the stout breeze. "But Atlanta PD reported it. That would have spooked him, easy."

"Did Atlanta PD think enough of it to note the plate?" Hale asked.

"They described a Bureau car, sir," Ariel said, unwilling to give up ground on this.

A disgusted nod moved Hale's sour face. "Wonderful, Grace. Blame another agent. Blame their car, which *you* never eyeballed. Blame every last man or woman with a badge within a mile of here for Mills DeVane not showing up for this meeting you were *sooo* certain of. Blame everyone, Grace. You can even blame me, 'cause I'm the one who apparently was fool enough to let you run this case." He stepped close to her now, his six-five frame towering over her. "But whatever you do, don't blame yourself. No. Don't do *that*."

Ariel seethed, swallowing her desire to spit venom back at the ASAC. "My work on this case was solid."

Hale considered her for a long moment before looking away toward the taped-off front of the Proper Peach. "Solid? We just wasted a whole lot of dollars and time pissing off a motel full of people and busting one very unlucky junkie who chose to shoot up in the wrong place at the wrong time. That's an interesting take on 'solid.'"

Lights from the TV trucks lined up on the boulevard glared suddenly to life. It was one minute 'til eleven.

"Congratulations, Grace," Hale said, giving the electronic vultures a desultory glance. "Looks like your solid police work is going to be the lead on the late news."

The first spots of mist began to brush her face as Hale turned to walk away.

"You're off this case, Grace," Jack Hale informed her, not even affording her a look as he delivered his decision. "Pick up your reassignment in the morning."

The ASAC turned to leave her there, but a hand on his arm stopped him cold. Her hand. He looked at it, then at her.

"Wait one minute, Jack," Ariel said, a weak smile on her face, as if she had just been the victim of some absurdly unfunny joke. "What the hell was that?"

"You want to get your hand off me." the ASAC asked. It was not a question.

Ariel maintained her grip while the last bit of false

smile drained from her face, then her hand slipped off of him. "What is going on, Jack?"

"You heard me."

"You're taking DeVane away from me?"

"Yes."

Was she hearing him right? Was she? "You're booting me all the way off this case?"

"You did hear me," Hale said. He glanced impatiently over his shoulder toward the camera crews. He needed to get to them. He *wanted* to get to them. Anything to get away from her. "So are we done now, Ariel?"

Her head cocked quizzically at him, that uncertain smile again. "Jack." She inched closer to him and spoke in soft, measured tones. She could be reasonable, he could be reasonable. Right? "Jack. Come on. You can't take DeVane away from me. I've worked this case like a dog. You know that. I'm on him, Jack. I'm close. I know it."

Hale stared at her briefly, then surveyed the scene. He looked back to her and shook his head, thinking of what to say. "I can't tolerate 'close,' Ariel. I'm sorry."

"Jack," she called to him as he turned and left her there, alone and on display, the stares of a hundred or so law enforcement brethren hot upon her as he went to the line of cameras and reporters, their mikes stabbing at him like daggers. She watched him for a moment, unable to move. This could not have happened. No way. Jack Hale could not have taken her case away. *Would* not have taken it away.

But he had.

"I was close, you idiot," she muttered to herself as she watched Jack Hale from a distance, doing his PR thing for the newsies, and then she could watch no more. She turned away. Through the front lot of the Proper Peach Motel she walked, toward the knots of agents waiting for the order to stand down, to pack up, to head home, an order she could no longer give, and so she waded through them. Through the debacle her meticulously planned fugitive warrant service had become. Some asked her what was going on; some averted their eyes, having shrewdly guessed exactly what was going on. The rest stepped silently aside as she hurried to her car.

She sat behind the wheel and stared through the skim of new rain sheeting down the windshield, asking herself the thousand whys. Why had Jack Hale done it? Booted her? For nothing? For one warrant service that would have gone down smooth as silk if that damned car hadn't been parked on the . . .

She stopped herself. Because she was starting to hate Jack Hale, and he was not the one who truly deserved the brunt of her enmity. Some, but the lion's share of it belonged to the man who was nowhere to be found. Who should have been in handcuffs in the seat behind her right then, but wasn't. The man whose capture was no longer her concern, but for whom she had a question. A single, simple question that she asked the night.

"Where the hell are you, Mills DeVane?"

The Atlantic night roared, thunder high in the weeping black sky and wind whipping a froth upon the dark and violent sea. Waves rolled at forty feet. The twin-engine Beech was at sixty.

The Beech had fought the storm to make the Florida coast after a fast flight from the north of Georgia, its pilot's departure premature and hasty, but nonetheless successful. The field attendant was on his payroll and would dispose of the stolen car left behind, and would remember nothing of any encounter with anyone remotely resembling the pilot, a generous man he simply called "Buddy."

He'd taken it up fast and kept it low, skimming the trees all the way to the beach. Out to sea, then a turn to the south to parallel the coast forty miles out, all the way to where he was now, giving all he had to a sixty-knot headwind, gusts to almost ninety, throttles fire-walled against the maelstrom. A major and monumental bitch if ever there was one.

But what could one expect flying in a hurricane?

He went feet dry barely above a stall and hopped his way inland just above the trees, beacons left and right of his course telling him that JAX was to his south and TLH was almost due east. But neither Jacksonville nor Tallahassee was his destination, nor any of the smaller fields like Hilliard, which was coming up fast as he crossed the black and desolate strip of pavement below that was I-95. No, the point of termination for this flight was like that for most he had ever flown—just a strip of terra firma long enough to land on and not too short to take off from. All navigation beacons aside, his gut and his fuel gauge told him that he was going to be putting in pretty damn soon, one way or another.

He flipped a switch on the overhead console and an electronic display buzzed to life on the instrument panel before him. The darkened cockpit glowed green.

"Where's the tree?" the pilot asked the display, his eyes moving between it and the windshield as his plane trembled through the storm's weakening fringe. "Come on, tree. Come on."

The earth below was a jumble of featureless blacks and grays occasionally lit by bolts of lightning, but not on the display. The small screen the pilot used to find his way showed the terrain not as it was, but as it might be through the eyes of some nocturnal bird of prey adapted to squeeze even the faintest bit of light from the night, though these eagle eyes had cost seventy thousand dollars. And right then he was wishing for every penny's worth of what it could do to find his landmark. That damn hundred-and-twenty-foot southern yellow—

"Shit!" he screamed, looking up from the night-vision

display just in time to heel the Beech hard over to the right, missing the enormous pine by scant feet, cutting power and lowering flaps and gear as he caught his breath and put his plane wings-level in a shallow descent, his heart thudding, adrenaline stoking it, but everything fine, just fine. The field should be straight ahead now, and his expensive night eyes would have no trouble guiding him there, but a quick glance out the windshield told him that would not be necessary. In the dark distance he could make out a line of flares right where his centerline should be.

Someone was expecting him.

That could be good news or bad, but right then it didn't matter because his right engine began sputtering, its lifeblood almost spent. The pilot cut it all the way back and fought the squirrelly winds toward the beacons, clearing the last of the trees just as his left engine started to hack. That one, too, he cut back, both props deadweight now, the Beech vibrating as he brought it down, down, down, the white-hot flares closer, coming up at him, faster, faster, faster, the earth and he about to meet just as he brought the stick back, nose up, setting the wheels down almost gently in the muddy grass.

Momentum carried the plane almost to the far end of the flare line before it stopped, the pilot turning off his systems before the batteries were drained. He undid his safety harness and had the small side door open just as the flashlight found his face.

"Who the fuck is that?" Mills DeVane asked, shielding his eyes with his hand, hard rain pecking at him.

"Hey there, number five," the voice behind the light said.

"Gareth?"

The light clicked off and Mills could see rain cascading off Gareth Dean Hoag's dark green poncho and gathering in the deep scruff of his gray-black beard. And he could see that the light that had blinded him was fixed beneath the barrel of one substantial scattergun.

"I'm in no mood to get shot, Gareth," Mills said, and the man who paid him handsomely lowered the weapon. "How'd you know I'd be here?"

"Oh, I thought you might be back early after seeing the news," Gareth said, as the night pulsed with lightning. One white-hot finger struck a tree and exploded with a crack. "You are one lucky flyboy."

Mills glanced skyward as he hopped from the Beech and closed its door. "This? I can get it up in any weather."

"I'm not talking 'bout the rain," Gareth told him, cradling the shotgun across his chest as two people approached from a barnlike building and began stamping out the flares in the soupy mud. "I'm talking about the party you missed in the city. It was all over the news."

Mills bent to look under his wings. "Not a big deal, Gareth."

"A lot of people waiting for you at that party," Gareth said. Mills stood and zipped his parka against the rain slanting at him. "Imagine their surprise when the guest of honor didn't show up."

"Imagine," Mills agreed, grinning cautiously.

"Imagine my relief, as well."

Mills nodded, and Gareth raised the shotgun fast and put its barrel against his employee's face, forcing him back against the Beech.

"Jesus, Gareth, take it easy," Mills said, twisting his face away from the weapon as best he could, eyeing the unexpected threat sideways.

"Do not take the Lord's name in vain," Gareth warned him.

"Sorry. Sorry."

"You were in Atlanta."

"Yes."

"You were not in Atlanta on my business."

"No."

"Then why were you in Atlanta?"

"You know I have other customers."

"None who pay you like I do."

"You contracted me two years ago saying you had a year's worth of deliveries. Two years. You think I can't do the math, Gareth? You're not going to be paying me forever."

"Thinking about the future, are you?"

Mills nodded, the muzzle of the shotgun scraping his cheek.

"Who were you flying for tonight?"

Mills swallowed and said nothing. The muzzle pulled back from his face and the light blazed at him once again. He squinted at the glare.

"Who were you flying for?" Gareth repeated.

"I can't tell you that."

"Moreno? Teddy Franks? Who were you flying for?"

How the hell did he know about them? "I'm not going to tell you."

Silence from behind the light, a long silence, then the sound of the safety being thrown. The light went black and the weapon came down.

"Good answer," Gareth said. Mills reached up and touched his cheek. A small round circle indented the flesh. "There were a hundred officers of the law waiting for you tonight, every one of them with a question like that for you, I'd imagine."

"You think I'd talk?" Mills challenged his employer.

"I think I can't afford to take that chance," Gareth said, and the gun he cradled drew a long gaze from Mills.

"You gonna kill me, Gareth?"

"I'm going to *counsel* you," Gareth corrected. "Against the error of your ways."

"I'm not stopping my sidelines, Gareth. Some of those people *would* kill me if I tried."

"Drug dealers are a dangerous lot," Gareth said with a snicker, and again Mills's gaze was drawn to the shotgun.

"Anyone can be, I guess."

To that Gareth nodded. "I suppose."

"You know," Mills began, "you have other pilots."

Thunder shook the night, and Gareth glanced toward its source. "None who can fly in stuff like this. Or would."

Mills looked down the makeshift runway as the last of the flares was stamped out, just the blackening trail of his touchdown and rollout leading back toward the trees. In daylight it could be seen as a field, one where sugar beets had grown some time ago, but long gone fallow now. Gareth Dean Hoag owned it, and the hundred twelve acres around it. Rotten land, the locals said it was. But Gareth had seen some value in it. It and the barn big enough to park a plane in.

"Did they spell my name right this time?" Mills asked. "Big D, big V?"

Gareth nodded. "But that picture they got still doesn't do you justice."

"Good. Make it harder for the *federales*."

"You were lucky tonight, number five. But you need to be careful. Especially now."

"What do you mean?"

"I got another deposit coming up," Gareth explained. "Special things after that. I don't want to lose you."

"Skunky or Lane could take it," Mills suggested, but Gareth shook his head. The two who'd put out the flares joined them now, Nita Berry and Lionel Price, Gareth's "other" halves.

"You can get in and out of anywhere," Gareth told him, and Mills knew he should be pleased. But what he was was tired. "Better than anyone."

"I always told you so."

The night exploded and lit them with white-hot radiance. Gareth cast a joyous face to the raging sky. "Soon, number five. Big things are coming soon."

"He shits you not," Lionel said. Nita tucked her hand in Gareth's front pocket and agreed with a nod.

Mills wiped his eyes, the night spitting hard at him now, a squall line moving through.

"Big things," Gareth repeated, laughing now as the heavens dumped on them.

Troopers Jimmy Nance and Kyle Callahan of the New York State Police were cruising down Roseland Road toward the coffee shop at the Pembry Lanes, the former extolling to his rookie partner of three weeks the utter magnificence of the Lanes' lemon meringue pie and how fantastic it was with a good cup of coffee, when the sweep of their unit's headlights lit up the front of the town post office.

"Ho-ly Moses," Trooper Kyle Callahan exclaimed calmly from behind the wheel, slowing the dark blue Chevy Caprice to a stop at the curb as his partner put a spotlight on the building. "Ain't teenagers got nothing better to do on a Friday night?"

"You call it in," Nance instructed as he swung the passenger-side door open. "I'll have a look-see at what the fine young citizens of Pembry have cooked up this time."

And cooked up was a darn good way to put it, Nance thought as he stepped from the warmth of his cruiser and took his flashlight from its place on his Sam Browne. The last time the kids from Hollister High had gotten some beer and stupidity in them at the start of a weekend, two Dumpsters and an empty shed had gone up in smoke. And though there was nary a hint of smoke or flame coming from inside the Pembry Post Office, there was going to be damage inside. Oh, yes. That Jimmy Nance could tell

quite plainly as he got to the top step and shined his flashlight on the twin glass doors that led into the building.

"Hooligans," he commented, shaking his head and
playing the light over the display that had been plastered
upon the inside of the glass. "Where the hell are your parents when you're pulling this crap?"

"Someone's gonna call the postmaster," Callahan said
as he reached his partner's side. He took his own flashlight in hand and added its beam to the mix. "Creative little buggers."

"It don't take much creativity to photocopy your teat,
Callahan," Nance said, and illuminated one of the three
dozen or so pieces of paper taped to the inside of the
glass doors, each a small section of a human—a very
naked human— body that had been arranged into a gar-
ish mosaic of the female form. "Sick little punks."

"Can you imagine the positions she must've had to get
into to get all her parts on the glass?" Callahan asked,
taking a moment to survey the creation, stepping back to
take it in whole as one might a museum piece, noting the
careful mating of all the sections of the body into a whole
and how the assembled black-and-white image seemed to
him to be of a woman cut out of midair, arms and legs
outstretched as if falling, the picture oddly intriguing and
disturbing. "So how come there's no head, Jimmy?"

Nance shook his head at his trainee's question. "These
kids are stupid, Kyle—not dumb. They're not going to
put a damn photocopy of one of their faces up there."

"True," Callahan agreed, catching the logic he should
never have missed. But then, it was the obvious that
tripped you up sometimes. It was that way with criminals, especially. Folks would do something they
shouldn't in a place they shouldn't be, they'd wipe down
the doorknobs and light switches to get rid of their fingerprints, but they'd forget that they leaned against a doorjamb or a banister or some other thing like—*oh, yes, like*

that! "Jimmy, we might just have a line on these little shits."

"How?"

Callahan shined his light at the weird mosaic's right hand, which was palm and fingerpads down and clear as the October sky above them. "We got ourselves some prints."

"I'll be . . ." Trooper Jimmy Nance never finished the exclamation. Not when his own light shined upon the figure's right hand, from a sharper angle than his partner's, and lit up what was covered by the overlapping piece of the paper above it. His free hand went to his pistol and he said, "Oh, goddamnit, Kyle! Damnit! Look!"

Callahan sidestepped toward his partner and peered under the obscuring flap of paper as best he could, which was plenty good enough to see that when the copy of the hand had been made, the appendage had not been connected to any arm. The ragged cut just at the wrist was indisputable.

This was no case of vandalism. At least none like they'd ever seen.

"Mother, mother, mother, what the hell is this?" Callahan asked himself as he stared wide-eyed at the macabre image.

"Call it in, Kyle," Jimmy Nance instructed, his hand wrapping tight around the grip of his holstered pistol now. Breath puffed from him like the white exhaust of an ancient locomotive at speed, fast and furious.

"What the hell do we call in?" Callahan asked.

"I don't know," Nance answered and put his light close to the captured image of the severed hand. Close enough that it touched the glass and moved the door.

He drew his weapon now and took a step back. "Kyle, it's open."

Callahan stepped back as well, drawing his own weapon and reaching up to the mike attached near his collar. "Trooper Ten, we have an open door, Pembry Post Office. Can you roll us a backup?"

The acknowledgment came from dispatch, and Nance reached for the door.

"Shouldn't we wait, Jimmy?" Callahan reminded his partner.

"I know folks that work here, Kyle. Let's just see what we got."

"Yeah, but backup'll be here in five minutes."

"If there's anything that looks bad, we'll pull back," Nance said, and crouched low next to the right door. "Okay."

Callahan assumed an entry position as well next to the left door. "Okay."

"We go fast and cover the sides," Nance said, and got a nod from his partner. "On me. Ready?" Another nod. And a breath. And another. And another. And . . . "Go."

They pushed each swinging door inward in sync, Nance going right and Callahan left, the aim of their weapons tracking the sweep of their flashlights over the dark inside of the Pembry Post Office's lobby.

"I got nothing, Kyle," Nance told his partner in a hushed tone, the beam of his flashlight scanning the ranks of dull metal PO boxes filling the east wall.

"Jimmy?"

"Yeah?" Nance answered, crouched low still, not advancing yet as he lit up a dark corner behind a waste can.

"Jimmy?"

"What?"

"Jimmy?"

Finally Nance just looked over his shoulder, toward his partner, but saw instead what Kyle Callahan's unmoving flashlight had lit up on the west wall. "No, Jesus. No."

The lettering was stark under the harsh beam. Big and bold and red upon the white wall next to the courtesy table and bulletin board. Four words splashed there. One distressing message born of the grotesque mosaic they had stumbled upon.

she went to pieces

"This is not good," Callahan said so quietly that his partner could barely hear him. "Not good, partner."

"No, not good at all," Nance concurred, and duck-walked the few steps toward his partner. Almost there his boot slipped on something slick. He shined his light on the old linoleum floor and saw thick, red, shoe prints leading both directions from their place at the front entrance to the side of the service counter. "We got a lot of blood, Kyle."

Callahan looked, and lit up a second trail of bloody prints going back and forth from the writing on the wall to the service counter. "Jimmy, let's back off now and wait for backup."

Nance did not reply immediately, though his intention was now to agree with his partner and get some more manpower on scene before pressing their entry any further. But in the near silence before he could reply, he heard something. A soft and rhythmic sound. Maybe a clicking. Definitely mechanical.

"You hear that?" Nance asked.

"Jimmy, let's back off."

"Listen."

Callahan did, and he could hear it, too, but right then he would have still wanted to wait for backup if what he'd heard was the Lord Himself saying "Come on down, Kyle."

"Jimmy . . ."

Nance rose slowly out of his crouch and aimed his light and his weapon north at the far end of the lobby, covering the service counter and the hidden spaces beyond it. Just part of a doorway was visible, leading to a

hallway it seemed from this vantage, and down that hallway there appeared to be . . .

"Kyle, you see that?"

Callahan stood and looked in the direction of his partner's light, just as Nance clicked the beam briefly off. In
the din that followed, he could plainly see what had
caught his partner's eye. "What is that?"

"I don't know," Nance told him, studying the flashing
light coming from the opening on the right side of the
hallway, its rhythm long with but a brief burst of darkness
between sustained pulses. Pulses that seemed synced to
that sound. "But let's find out."

Callahan would have protested again, but his partner
was already moving, his light back on and scouring the
area before him. There was nothing to do but follow.

They made it to the service counter and carefully
checked behind, finding only more footprints there, dark
red under the glow of their flashlights. Nance moved first,
trying to straddle the bloody trail as he stepped behind
the counter and peered down the hall, seeing the pulsing
light more clearly now, and hearing the clicking with near
full clarity, both things mating in a deduction that was
confirmed by what he saw fluttering from the doorway on
the right. Paper.

"Copy machine's running," he told Callahan in a
hushed tone.

"Copy machine?"

Nance nodded and shined his light on the floor outside
the doorway. Hundreds of sheets of paper were piled
there, another one settling atop the uneven mound every
few seconds, enough so that the bloody trail was
obscured from view. Some pure white, and others showing something on their surface, depending on whether
they were landing faceup or facedown.

"It's copying something," Nance told his partner.

"Oh, Jimmy, you don't think . . ."

But he did think, exactly what his partner could not

voice, and for some reason even he did not understand Trooper James Fitzgerald Nance had to know. Had to see. Had to lay his gaze upon what he knew, just *knew,* was in that small room off the right of the hallway. Maybe to convince himself that this was real, or unreal, or something in between, some macabre scene come to life, to *his* life. And so he started down the hallway, his partner hanging back now, covering from where he waited. Stepping with care on either side of the ghastly trail, nearing the pile of papers, new ones shooting out from the doorway one after the other, one floating earthward and slipping down the side of the mound and landing faceup at Trooper Nance's feet. He shined his light down upon it and swallowed hard.

A dead face stared back at him in black and white.

It was what they'd feared, and he'd seen the image captured, but not the truth from which it had been cast, and so he took one more step forward and looked through the doorway and saw the copy machine pushed almost out into the hall, its lid angled half-open and resting upon the severed head of a woman, light flashing beneath it every second or so, blood and tissue dripping from the ragged edge of the neck, pooling in large, slick clumps on the glass.

"Oh, Jesus," Nance said, stepping back, the sight his now for all time. "Oh, dear sweet Jesus."

"Jimmy," Callahan said as he watched his partner back away from the door and through another opposite it. "Jimmy!"

But Trooper Nance wasn't hearing his partner. His senses were tuned to what was across the hall from him now, that face, that head, the machine chugging along, its rhythm seeming the echo of a dead heart's beating, and nothing could have drawn him from his rapt fixation.

Nothing but the hand that brushed his cheek and sent him reeling.

He spun in place in the darkened space, the hand tapping him, and another, the beam of his flashlight slicing the din, tracking fast across the hand, and an arm, and a leg, a breast, all seeming to be floating about his head. He swatted at the passive assault and his hand came back wet with blood.

"NOOOOOOOOOOOOOOOOO!"

He fell to the floor and scooted his way through a slick puddle, driving himself into a corner as his partner made it to the doorway and lit up the space with his own flashlight.

"Oh, my God," was all Trooper Kyle Callahan could say at the sight of his partner. "Oh, my God. God. God."

"He's not here," Trooper Jimmy Nance said, laughing and weeping, hugging himself.

1

[DOTS]

God's gray rain fell on Damascus, New York.

Special Agent Bernard Jaworski, stern and sticklike, bald and yellowed by the chemo and radiation the whitecoats were hopeful would do a number on the tumor raging low in his back, sat at his desk midmorning on Monday, the weather glazing the window behind him, and read the orders just handed to him for a third time.

"I don't get it." He looked up to the person who'd brought the orders with her. "Why is Atlanta sending me personnel?"

"I've been reassigned to you," Ariel Grace told him, though to her a more proper term would be "exiled." She'd thought that from the minute she saw the orders Saturday morning. Expecting Jack Hale to shift her to FEDBOMB for her perceived failure to get DeVane, or maybe have her sitting on a wire, or at worst running background on clearance applications, she'd instead gotten a letter with a plane ticket attached. And here she was, standing before her new boss, pissed as hell and unable to do anything about it but curse Jack Hale under her breath and move on.

"From Atlanta?" Jaworski asked, puzzled. A cough shook his wasting frame. He took a long sip of ice water. Ariel thought his fingers looked like dying twigs wrapped around the sweating glass.

"The orders were approved by Washington," Ariel said. And mustn't that have been a trick for Jack Hale to arrange overnight.

"I can see the signature, Agent Grace, but what I can't see is why I'm getting you from all the way down south. I've requested additional personnel, but usually they get pulled from somewhere close."

"I didn't request this, sir. But I'm here, and I'm ready to work."

"Sit down, Agent Grace." She took the only other seat, a government issue facing Jaworski's desk, stiff and gray, vinyl and metal. He looked at the orders again as she shifted for a comfortable position. "What did you work in Atlanta?"

"I ran Task Force Five," she said, surprised that he didn't know that.

Jaworski looked to her, squinting a bit. "You ran a Most Wanted task force?"

"Looking for Mills DeVane, sir."

He considered her for a moment. Businesslike, she was, in matching blue blazer and slacks. Her hair was brown and fell just below the collar, coiffed very proper. Voice clear, blue gaze steady. She was trying hard to not be something. To not be seen as something.

"How old are you, Agent Grace?"

There was the briefest pause before she replied. "I'll be thirty in December, sir."

"Twenty-nine, then, are you?"

She nodded to his "clarifying" query.

"Twenty-nine and running a task force," he said as comment. "How long have you been with the Bureau?"

"Six years, sir," she told him. No hesitation this time. "I was fully capable of doing the job."

He nodded. "So why aren't you still?"

That pause stalled her again. Jaworski had her number. She wasn't sure she liked that.

"One of my warrant services went bad," she told him. That was one man's opinion, anyway.

Lines cleaved his brow. Hell, he'd been living and breathing his own task force, number ten, night and day, but he hadn't been that disconnected from Bureau happenings, had he? "People get hurt?"

She shook her head.

Now he was really lost. "No one was hurt. So what went bad about it?"

"DeVane wasn't there." *Would have been, except for that car . . . that car that was and wasn't there.*

"Wait," Jaworski said, sitting back, letting the chair's soft cushion nearly swallow him. "You got yanked and spanked because your guy wasn't there? Because you *missed* him?"

That might seem the reason, but Ariel knew better. Knew as soon as she'd read her orders Saturday morning. The orders that also mentioned her replacement.

"ASAC Hale made the call, sir. It's his task force now."

"I see that," Jaworski said. Right there, in the orders, it was spelled out. And wasn't *that* odd? Why in the hell was the number-two agent in Atlanta taking on a task force? There had to be something more to this.

But whatever that might be, it was not Jaworski's concern. He had no time for it. More pressing matters were at hand. Like catching his own freak, who was very much out there and very much active. And now he had one more body to throw at his boy. One more body that he had to get up to speed. Fast.

"You're all squared away, then, Grace?"

"Sir?"

"Ride, place to stay? The FO get you what you need?"

"Yes, sir." She'd flown in on Sunday and had been issued a Bureau Taurus by the Albany Field Office, and vouchers for the Bright I Motor Hotel here in Damascus. She'd spent a restless night there watching an old horror flick on the tube and eating take-out Chinese. When sleep finally dragged her down she dreamt of Jack Hale. He was getting the shit stomped out of him by some Frankensteinish fiend.

"All right, then," Jaworski said, and pushed himself up using both arms of his chair. With a grimace and some difficulty he stood and came around his desk, heading for the door. "Your learning curve here is going to look like the steep side of the Matterhorn."

"I can handle that," Ariel said. She stood and followed her new boss out of his office. They made a quick left through an outer office, and a right after that, heading down a long, dim hallway. Stacks of boxes yet to be unpacked crowded the passage, creating chokepoints through which one had to slip sideways. Jaworski took those walking straight on.

He moved fairly quick, considering, Ariel thought. But then, maybe being up was better than being down. A physical thing. Maybe mental, too.

Her mother had done housework all through her chemo. Called it her "therapy." She did the dishes the day she died, looking better than the man walking ahead of Ariel right then. Walking as he started talking.

"Welcome to Task Force Ten, Agent Grace," Jaworski said. "Around here we call it Base Ten. Someone nicked it that. I don't know why." At an intersection with another passage they turned left. More boxes cramped their way. A lone window in the distance washed the corridor with dim and dirty light. They walked toward it. "The Bureau rented it for our operations when we outgrew the space at the Utica RA." The RA, or resident agency, was the Bureau equivalent of a police substation, a local presence maintained in areas from which a field office was too distant, or where one was deemed necessary. "The building is vacant except for us and the rats."

"How many agents are you running?" Ariel asked. The

bulge of her hip-holstered weapon snagged a box as she squeezed by and almost sent it tumbling.

"Sixteen counting you."

"I only saw one agent at the door when I came in."

"I believe in fieldwork, Grace. Our freak is not going to walk in here and hold out his hands. This ain't Hollywood. People who work for me work leads. Cold, warm, or hot. That's how I run Task Force Ten. I only wish I could get out there more."

"Someone has to run things," Ariel reminded him.

"It's kind of you to put it that way," Jaworski said. "So how many did you run, Agent Grace?"

"Forty full-time."

"How long?"

"Ten months."

"So you were around for this numbering crap."

"I was," Ariel said.

"Tell me, did it 'focus task force efforts' any more by having that number tacked on to DeVane?"

"It was crap, sir, like you said."

Jaworski glanced back at her as he walked. A smile flashed. "Glad to see me and the other five thousand or so people aren't alone in our thinking."

"Washington comes up with some beauts," Ariel said. She knew that now better than most.

They neared the window. It had once been clear but now was filmed opaque with grime. A heavy door was set into the wall to the right of it. Jaworski mustered all his strength and shoved it open, letting them into the stairwell. They started up.

"Did you take the elevator up to three, Grace?"

"Yes, sir."

"Use the stairs from now on. They don't break down twice a week."

"Thanks for the warning." They made it to four and passed through another heavy door and were in another hallway when a question came to Ariel. "Why are you on three, sir? If the building's vacant."

"The rats have one and two. They rarely come to three."

Ariel looked at the ground as they moved down this hallway and wondered how often they came by four.

"How much do you know about our freak, Grace?" Jaworski asked her. His pace had slowed. His breathing hadn't.

"Some."

"I'll give you the quickie on him before I show you something. He calls himself Michaelangelo. Like the artist, but he spells it wrong. One extra 'a.' He thinks he's an artist, too. A master, even. He's killed six already. Two just this last Friday." Jaworski stopped suddenly, half propping himself against one wall with a stiff arm. He sucked a deep breath of stale air. A shallow, wet cough hacked up, and he swallowed its spawn back down again. He looked straight at Ariel. "Let me tell you something, Agent Grace—off the subject. They may save my life, but until the day I do kick I will hate every doctor who ever lived for practically killing me with this cure."

She made no comment to what he'd said. Simply let him take a few more breaths and compose himself.

"Four men, two women," Jaworski went on. "All found in either Jersey, Pennsylvania, or our dear Empire State. He . . . uses them. Makes 'art' out of them. And I'm not talking re-creating the *David*. This freak goes for shock value." He paused, took one more deep breath, and continued on down the hall. "He treats the men and women differently."

"How?"

"Couple of ways. There's mutilation of the males' genitalia. ISU and some outside shrinks have looked at everything and decided either he's gay or not, afraid he's gay or afraid he's not, was abused or was an abuser. You get the picture, Grace?"

"He's not easily profiled."

"I hate that term, Jesus. Sometimes there are just monsters. Freaks. Evil pieces of human garbage that need to be hunted down. The only pigeonhole this guy fits into is fucked up . . . pardon my Polish."

"Pardoned, sir," she said, smiling at his back. "So he doesn't mutilate the women?"

"Oh, hell, he'll mutilate the hell out of them. But he's not interested in their genitalia. Plus we don't get any letters on the women."

"He writes?"

"After each male murder a letter arrives at the Metropolitan Museum of Art addressed to the chief curator. Gives us the 'titles' of his 'works.' " Jaworski shook his head. "Since the first one we've been able to intercept them."

"Prints?"

Jaworski stopped again, this time outside a door just before another intersection of corridors. His breathing was not terribly labored.

"Oh, he's not afraid of leaving prints. We've got them by the hundred."

"So he's never been arrested, in the military, or had certain jobs."

"He's been a careful boy," Jaworski said, and reached into his pocket for a small ring of keys.

Ariel looked to the door they stood at and noticed now a makeshift sign tacked above it: GALLERY.

"Did you eat breakfast, Agent Grace?"

Ariel shook her head.

"That's probably a good thing."

He inserted a key into the lock on the door but didn't turn it. "That agent you saw on your way in . . ."

"Yes . . ."

"That was Vargas. He's the gatekeeper. No one gets into this building unless they have business here. Any tabloid photographer worth his salt would give a limb to get shots of what's behind this door."

"More rats to deal with," she observed, and Jaworski turned the key and opened the door to a darkened room.

"After you."

She stepped in and heard the door close behind her, making the space black for a second before Jaworski switched on the lights and set the walls to screaming.

"Dear God," Ariel exclaimed softly, as though to speak too loudly might stir the madness fixed upon three of the room's four walls to life.

Jaworski himself gave the room a long look, taking it in yet again. It stoked the fire. Helped him to hate the freak that was his to catch.

Ariel was in the center of the room, her eyes tracking from right to left, vibrant and vicious hues assaulting her from dozens upon dozens of stills the Bureau photographers had captured. A visual symphony of horror.

In one a man's penis had been grafted to his forehead, making him a unicorn.

Jaworski saw where she was looking and stepped that way. He tapped the photo holding her rapt. "Calvis Winkler, the one our freak made into a unicorn, was victim number one. Twenty-three years old, an auto mechanic from Shakes Ferry." He pointed to a less-prominent photo of the crime scene. "His body was found on Valentine's Day in a Utica motel room standing before a mirror."

"Standing?" Ariel asked, looking closely at the indicated photo. There was Calvis Winkler, standing at the vanity in a motel room, hands planted on either side of the single-bowl sink, his boxer shorts and white T-shirt wet, red nightmares. He seemed to be intently gazing at the mirror. At the dead perversion of himself.

"Rebar," Jaworski said in response to the question her puzzled expression was asking. "Those metal rods they put in concrete to strengthen it."

Ariel nodded.

"I hope to God he was dead already."

"He sculpted him," Ariel observed. "He made himself a human sculpture on a frame."

Jaworski nodded. "His letter told us he called it 'Reflections of a Myth.' "

"The unicorn is a mythical figure," Ariel said. "But here he gave it a reflection."

"Don't chew on it, Grace," Jaworski warned her. "Don't try and figure him out that way. Let the shrinks and the gurus at Quantico handle that end of it. Focus on the tangible. Be a cop, not a psychoanalyst."

She looked to him. "Those methods have worked, sir."

He allowed a nod and looked to the pictures. "I don't think it's going to be that way with this freak. I just don't."

She turned toward the next set of photos in line as Jaworski moved to them. In all the photos an older man sat naked in a chair, his right hand fixed over his mouth, his left over his eyes. "Ricardo Lomanico, sixty, a retired army master sergeant. Found dead in his house in Jersey City in early March by his painter who was touching up the trim around his bedroom window. His uvula had been removed and the object of their killer's rage attached in its place, blocking his windpipe."

Ariel grimaced, but stayed focused on the photos. "He couldn't have been alive. . . ."

"Traces of a muscle paralyzer called napoxcypharin were found in his system. And in Calvis Winkler's. It was found in all the men. The medical examiner said this drug paralyzes the voluntary muscles, but lets you breathe and lets your heart beat." Jaworski glanced at Ricardo Lomanico's hideously abused face. "It also allows one to still feel pain. But not scream."

A shiver scampered up her spine. Agony without expression. The cry withheld. She wondered if that could drive one mad.

"This creation is called 'Hear My Evil.' Try and pick that one apart."

Jaworski took a step down and was now on a new wall, the one opposite the door. He touched the picture of a heavyset woman whose breasts had been removed. Her head rested on a lamp whose shade had been removed. The burning bulb glowed through her gaping mouth. "Susan Rollins, age forty-one, she was from Trenton, New Jersey, but was found in a motel room just outside of Centre Hall, Pennsylvania. Her body was found in the bathtub, here." Ariel looked where directed. "Fully clothed but drained of blood. We found about four pints in the toilet tank."

Stone, Ariel thought. *Be stone.* It was hard. She felt her stomach churning.

"Like I said, we didn't get a letter for this victim or the other woman, but he did leave what I guess you'd call messages at each scene. This one he left in lipstick on the bathroom mirror."

Ariel saw the photo nearby. " 'Women bleed.' "

"You think that means something other than the disgustingly obvious?"

"It might," Ariel replied.

Jaworski shook his head and tapped the wall in a random succession of spots. "Connect the dots, Grace. Connect the dots."

"When was she found?"

"April second, though we know she was killed on the first."

"April Fools' Day," Ariel said. "The second significant day with Valentine's Day."

"And March fourth, Agent Grace?" Jaworski challenged her. "What day of significance is that, other than the day that Ricardo Lomanico died?"

There was no answer to be had. She was thinking too fast here. Taking in too much all at once and trying to put it in place, without knowing what the places were. She was trying a puzzle without having a picture for reference. That would not work. She had to see all the dots before trying to connect them.

"Who was next?" Ariel asked, signaling her readiness to go on. Jaworski obliged.

"This one is called 'Taken for a Ride,' " Jaworski said. The accompanying photos showed the naked upper torso of a man seemingly grafted to a horse lying on its side, both dead. "The guy was James Ondatter, victim number four. He drove a taxi in Centre Hall, Pennsylvania. He was found in the same area. The mount he's stuck to was called Lady Anne Green Apples. Her owner looked out a window in the morning last April third and saw Lady Anne galloping around the pasture. It looked like someone was riding her. Someone was."

"The horse was alive when he did this?" Ariel exclaimed more than asked.

"Police shot it when they got there. They found Ondatter's lower half attached to another horse wandering through open country outside of town. That one died before they could shoot it. Stress from a too-high dose of a veterinary tranquilizer called equipsyx."

"He has access to drugs."

"And surgical glues, sutures," Jaworski said. "But we've done those dots. Pharmaceutical companies, hospitals, doctors, et cetera, et cetera."

"You couldn't have checked everywhere," she said.

"You can never check everywhere, Agent Grace. And even if you could, there's no guarantee you'd see this guy. I doubt he's walking around drooling and showing off his collection of catgut and equipsyx."

Likely not, she knew, but he had to be getting his toys somewhere.

"He used duct tape on Susan Rollins," Jaworski added. "We ran the lot. It came back as shipping to over eight hundred outlets over a year. Maybe fifty thousand people bought it. Mostly cash transactions."

"Not much chance there," Ariel commented. A thought came to her. "Susan Rollins was from New Jersey—how'd she end up in Centre Hall one day before Ondatter was found?"

Jaworski tipped his head approvingly toward her. "Now, there are some dots, Agent Grace. Susan Rollins was in Centre Hall on business. Real estate business. A company she worked for back home was purchasing a tract of land in the area. She was there for an appraisal. She never showed up."

"So why kill her?"

"Dots, Agent Grace. Dots." Another step down the line, to the last two in the grisly series. "For six months our freak was quiet. Then these next two were killed. Close in proximity and even closer in time." He touched a photo. "Lew Bradford, fifty. A car salesman. Found in a field near Oneida, his hometown, on Friday morning. Not far from here. He was killed Thursday night. Napox-cypharin in his system, as well. Our freak hammered a sharpened piece of scrap iron about an inch thick into the ground so that about six feet of it stood proud like a flag-pole. Then he positioned Lew Bradford on top and let gravity do the rest."

Ariel looked away, and her eyes fell upon the dismembered pieces of a woman suspended from a ceiling.

"Doris May," Jaworski began. "Victim number six. Thirty-eight. A postal worker. She was found cut up, photocopied, and hung like a mobile in a post office in Pembry late Friday night. Pembry's just up the road from Oneida. An hour before you got here this morning the letter concerning Mr. Bradford was flagged at the Metropolitan Museum. It came from this post office."

"He mailed it there, then killed her?" What sense did that make? Ariel wondered. Then again, what sense was there in any of the things she was seeing?

His sense, the answer came to her.

"No drugs, just like the other female victim. But unlike her, he didn't use duct tape."

Ariel was making mental notes as best she could. Later she'd put them on paper. Reduce what she was being shown, being told, to cold words. When this was all done, the next day, the next week, the next year, she could file them away. Or toss them. Make them gone.

If only the memories could be so easily dealt with.

"On the wall he wrote in her own blood 'She Went to Pieces.' " Jaworski showed her the photo. Ariel looked. Made it a memory.

The light above dimmed briefly, then went back to bright. Ariel would have preferred it go black. She had seen enough.

"Someone's on the elevator," Jaworski said. "I have an appointment. Doctor here to give me a shot of insta-sick. Oh joy." He turned and opened the door. "Shall we?"

She was ready to leave. She wanted to leave. But when given the chance right then by the man who was now her boss, she did not. She could not.

"Agent Grace?"

The walls were still screaming at her.

"Agent Grace?"

Making memories.

"Agent *Grace*?"

She turned finally away from the walls.

"I have work for you," he said.

"Right, sir."

The light clicked off. Darkness killed the screams.

2

[IMAGE MAKER]

"We called her DoDo," **Judy** Bryce said between puffs on her smoke out behind the Pembry Post Office. Her eyes were teary. The sleeve of her postal uniform was damp. She'd been crying.

Ariel Grace stood close to her on the gravelly ground with a small notebook in hand. The rain had stopped, but a chilly wind blew.

"It was a joke kind of thing," Judy said, glancing upward and sniffling. She took a hard drag and spit the smoke toward the woods. "'Cause she was blonde, you know? But she wasn't dumb." She put the back of her hand to her mouth and stared at the ground. "She wasn't."

"I'm sorry," Ariel told the woman. The page in her notebook had Judy Bryce's name at the top. She'd written nothing else yet. Her pain was not notable.

"I can't believe she's gone," Judy said, puffing again. "I can't."

"It's difficult, Mrs. Bryce. I can imagine." It was time to move past sympathy. "I understand you were on vacation all last week."

Judy Bryce nodded. "My husband and I took the kids to Disney World." She sniffled. "DoDo always wanted to take Lucas there, but she never had the money. It's hard without a husband, you know."

Ariel nodded. She'd jotted Disney World without looking. "You returned when, Mrs. Bryce?"

"Last night. There was a message on my machine from Mr. Hayes. . . ."

"Hayes?"

"He's the postmaster. He said that Doris had been killed and he needed me in this week."

"You were supposed to be off, then."

Judy Bryce nodded. "So here I am." Dry sobs shook her. "DoDo was working for me last week." Tears streamed down her cheeks. She put her cigarette shakily to her lips and drew on it. After a moment the spasm eased. "I'm sorry."

"It's all right," Ariel said. This was going fast to nowhere. Jaworski had sent her to talk to this woman, to pick up this one last interview of staff at the post office where Doris "DoDo" May had been cut up. But what could this woman possibly offer? She'd been out of town when the crime occurred. Out of town in the week leading up to it. What possible dots could be gleaned from her?

"Do you think she suffered?" Judy Bryce asked. Her wet eyes pleaded for a wanted truth.

"I don't think so," Ariel told her, giving her what she wanted. By any other name it was a lie. "Before you left on vacation, did Doris mention anything about anyone to you? Someone new in her life? A boyfriend? An admirer?"

Judy Bryce shook her head. "She had a steady guy. Mike DeRoy."

Who had been checked and cleared already, Ariel knew from the case notes Jaworski had given her. She'd read them while stopped for lunch en route to Pembry. There'd been no pictures included. She'd been able to finish half a sandwich before the cold words sparked new memories.

"He drives trucks across country," Judy told Ariel. "God, has anyone told him?"

"He's been talked to," Ariel assured her. Agents in Montana intercepted his rig and questioned him for two hours. They ended up taking him to a hospital. "So Doris had no one new in her life. Not even a new friend?"

"Everybody knows everybody around her," Judy said. "There's no one new to know."

Ariel nodded and clicked her pen shut. Tucked her notebook inside her blazer. Judy Bryce was a wash.

"I appreciate you talking to me, Mrs. Bryce. I'll walk you back in."

Judy Bryce took a last draw on her cigarette and tossed it to the ground. She crushed it out with a twist of her foot on the gravel and used her key to open the back door. A new lock had been installed over the weekend. One that locked automatically whenever the door closed.

Ariel followed Judy back through the post office. Through the back room and its mail sacks. Down the hall past the rooms where horrors had been done to Doris "DoDo" May. Both were closed off. The floor was shiny. It had been stripped and cleaned and waxed overnight. The place was spotless. Clean. But it would always be stained.

Judy walked Ariel behind the counter where another postal worker stood at the service window chatting softly with a woman buying stamps and mailing a package. The woman was slowly shaking her head.

"Thanks again," Ariel told Judy Bryce once they were in the main lobby. "I know it's hard to talk about."

"I know I wasn't much help," Judy said. Her arms were crossed tight across her chest as if there were a chill in the room. The heater was running at full bore.

"Everything helps," Ariel reassured her. It wasn't a lie, per se.

Judy Bryce looked around the lobby. The floor gleamed. One spot on the wall near the bulletin board had been scrubbed whiter than that which surrounded it. Word was the whole place was going to be painted. Rumor was it was going to be razed.

Ariel, too, took a look around the sanitized space. Muted afternoon light filled it through the doors that had been part of Michaelangelo's canvas. Only part. The walls, too, where he'd scrawled his message, were integral to the shock value he sought to . . .

Camera.

Her survey of the room stopped cold on the surveillance camera pointing almost directly at her from behind the counter. She turned and looked behind. High above the door another one was mounted. A cable from it snaked through a hole in the ceiling.

Jaworski hadn't said anything about cameras. The case notes he'd given her hadn't mentioned any. But certainly they had been noticed.

"Mrs. Bryce, the cameras there and there . . ."

"Bob said your people took the tapes and the recording decks." Judy Bryce motioned to her coworker commiserating with the customer. Her face went sullen. "I don't know if I want them to have seen anything."

Ariel could understand without agreeing. "Again, Mrs. Bryce, I'm very, very sorry. You'll take care, right?"

Judy nodded. "Oh. Wait. Did you bring a new bulletin for us?"

"Excuse me?"

"When the person from your office called and said you'd be stopping by, I thought maybe you'd be bringing a new Most Wanted bulletin."

Ariel looked over to the bulletin board. A faded spot where something had been posted showed like a sore on the nearly covered corkboard.

"Bob said he asked if you could."

Ariel was still staring at the bare spot.

"Miss?"

She turned quickly back to Judy Bryce. "Yes? No. No,

I didn't bring one. I'm . . ." *Why would that be missing?* ". . . sorry."

"Could you put in a request, or whatever, so we could get one?" Judy Bryce asked.

Spot of blood on it, maybe, Ariel thought. Kept as evidence? Thrown away?

"Miss?"

She was seeing what was before her again, not the stored image of that bare spot off to the left. "I'll request one for you. You try and have a good day, Mrs. Bryce."

"I won't," Judy Bryce told her.

The Bureau Taurus was parked on the street half a block down Roseland Road from the Pembry Post Office. Ariel Grace sat in the passenger seat with the door open and one leg hanging out as she took the cell phone from its holder. She began to dial, then pressed the END button, shaking her head. She was calling the Atlanta field office, less the area code. Likely she would have gotten some pizza place or a confused old woman who'd curse her for not being more careful. She paused, flipped through the case notes that she'd opened atop the dash, and found something with Jaworski's number on it. She dialed and waited through three rings.

"Jaworski."

"Agent Grace, sir."

"What do you want, Grace?" It was five past two, but he sounded as though he'd been waked from a dead sleep.

"There are cameras at the post office," she said. The immediate reply she got was silence.

"If you're calling to tell me that there are cameras, Agent Grace, I have to tell you I'm disappointed in you."

Tired and testy, she thought, then remembered his appointment. The doctor had come and gone, she suspected, but left her boss with a reminder of their time together. She wondered if there was a spare wastebasket close by his desk like the one her mother had kept near the bed.

"No, sir, I know you know about the cameras. I'm wondering about the tapes." She could sense his head shaking during the brief pause before he spoke.

"I've seen them. There's nothing usable on them."

"They didn't get it?"

"They got it all, but they didn't get anything clear of him. Unless you call dark clothing, dark baseball-style cap, and turned-up collar, all things we knew already, clear. We had surveillance pictures of him before, Agent Grace, or didn't you read what I gave you?"

It wasn't him talking. Ariel knew that better than most, though she would have given the world not to. "At the stables, sir, yes. But I'm not thinking about seeing him. I want to see what happened in there."

"I have, Grace. There's nothing useful. Trust me."

He was a wall. She doubted he knew that he was. But still she had to get through. "I would really appreciate it, sir, if you'd let me see the tapes. I know it may be disturbing, but if I'm going to be part of your team then I need to be able to access the evidence."

"The tapes are in Washington, Grace," Jaworski told her. He sounded as if he simply wanted her to go away. "The lab has them. They're going to try for an enhancement. They won't get it."

"Can I see the raw tapes, sir?"

"They're in D.C., I just told you."

Easy push. Easy push. Just like what the doctors would be doing and telling him. *One more, Mr. Jaworski. One more round might just do it. Might just get this sucker.*

"The lab makes copies of the raw tapes, sir. They could send copies of those copies."

A breath hissed over the connection. Exasperated.

Dog tired. "Do you want me to get you copies, Grace? Do you?"

"I would appreciate it."

"Fine," Jaworski said. She was listening to electric silence a split second later.

Clarion Key, a thousand miles from the nearest bit of American soil, save Puerto Rico, had been owned by the Spanish, the British, and long before that by a succession of pirate invaders who fought one another for control of the sliver of Carribean land. Cuba had laid claim to it at one time, as had the Dominican Republic, but the truth be told it belonged to no government. Its status was unclear.

That pleased many people.

One of them stood at the end of the tiny island's only airstrip looking west toward the lightening sky. The sun had risen behind him. It warmed his back through the thin shirt that hung upon him like a rag. His shorts were loose and long. His hair was gray. He looked the part of a wayfarer.

One would not likely guess he was worth two billion dollars, U.S.

Of course, his wealth was not kept at Chase Manhattan or at any other institution where the prying eyes of some legally entitled functionary might locate it. Survey it. Seize it. No, that which made him rich was more transitory in nature. He had access to houses, fabulous estates and villas from Rio to Monaco, flats in London and Lisbon, a cottage in the Swiss Alps, and a ranch in Zimbabwe. He could pick up a phone and have a jet waiting at any airport in the world in an hour, if that were his wish. Said jet could take him to a yacht, moored in Hong Kong, if he suddenly fancied yachting from Hong Kong. None of these things were "his," in the legal sense of the word, of course, but that did not matter. The truth be told, he did not *need* money in the traditional sense. If he required cash, for cigarettes in Paris or a bag of qat in Yemen, it would come. Money truly only "existed" for him if he had a few francs in his pocket, or a lira left by accident in one of the many cars that were at his disposal. He did not need money on him, with him, attached to him in any way. He only needed it to pass through him. He only needed people to need him. And in that lay his value. Middleman. He had become filthy rich doing so.

And was about to become just that much richer, he knew, spotting the glint of light low in the west.

The glint paralleled the long north-south axis of Clarion Key for a minute, then seemed to stop moving. But it wasn't. It was growing larger, coming at the man now. Soon he could hear the fine whine of two engines perfectly tuned.

"It's here," the man said over his shoulder in flawless Russian. He could have said it in French or English or three other languages. But the fat man sweating in a chair beneath the shade of three date trees would not have understood him. "Get your fat ass up and have a look. It's a new plane." He looked back out to sea and muttered in his native French: "The lucky bastard has more planes than me."

The hurricane that had skirted the area only days before was long gone, spinning moisture now up the American east coast and into Canada, leaving tufts of white cloud high in the blue, blue sky. The twin-engine Beech came out of it like a seabird, graceful and quick, skimming the paved but worn runway for nearly half its length before its gear dropped and it touched down with three small puffs of smoke.

Yves Costain laughed at the display of bravado and clapped his hands mightily as the Beech taxied toward him. The fat Russian waddled up behind, a pint bottle of rum held low against his leg. It was half full, the optimistic slob knew.

"He is marvelous," Costain said to the Russian, who nodded and took a sip of rum. "Magnificent."

The Beech slowed, pointing right at Costain and the Russian, and swung hard right just in front of them, leaving its left side to them. Costain waved to the pilot. Mills DeVane waved back through the cockpit's side window.

The engines spun down and stopped. Costain walked behind the wing as the pilot's door tipped up.

"Mills! Mills!" Costain shouted, in perfect if accented English. "My friend!"

"Yves? How are you?" Mills said with some surprise.

"I'm fine. Fine. How are you?"

"Good," Mills said, stepping onto the wing and reaching back into the plane.

The Russian put his free hand on the pistol tucked behind his belt against the small of his back. With the other he brought another touch of rum to his lips and watched the American warily from behind dark glasses.

"Are you thirsty, my friend?" Costain asked.

Mills seemed to be struggling with something, then with one final pull he heaved a large black duffel from behind the pilot's seat and dropped it on the wing. "I am now."

He smiled and hopped down, shouldering the duffel and giving his hand to Costain. "I never get to see you anymore. When I make the trip it's usually that Mexican fellow of yours waiting for me."

"Roberto," Costain said, grasping Mills's hand in both of his. "Like a son to me. If he could speak French, I'd adopt him."

Mills and Costain laughed raucously, like school

chums reunited after too many years. The fat Russian sipped his rum and let his hand come off his pistol.

"Mills, you know my friend, do you not?"

Mills nodded and smiled at the fat Russian. He'd met him once, hadn't heard him utter a word, and had never heard Costain mention his name.

"Come, Mills, good fellow. We will go and get you something to drink and you will tell me about this new plane I see."

New? Mills thought. He guessed it was new to Costain. He'd already used it on four runs, and that was about his limit. Gareth would be wanting to spring for a new one soon. New look, new tail number. Easier to get in and out of "iffy" fields without some gung-ho local cop or customs agent asking the wrong—or the right—questions.

"That, Yves, is a brand-new twenty-five-year-old Beech Baron," Mills said proudly as they began to walk toward a grouping of shacks beyond the date trees. In one, there would be barrels of fuel, he knew, and in another, the one in the center with Costain's bodyguard standing outside, there would be a table. A big table. "Pressurized, electric door seal, M1 coupled, dual DGs, and a hell of a nice interior."

"By that you mean as few seats as possible, eh, my friend?" Costain put his arm around Mills, chuckling knowingly. "More room for other things." He put a finger to his nose and sniffed twice in suggestion. "I am right?"

"I transport needed medical supplies from third world countries to poor souls in my country," Mills told him with a broad smile. Sweat was beading on his forehead already. The Beech's A/C had spoiled him. "I'm a humanitarian."

"Of course. Of course." Costain laughed and thumped Mills twice on the back. "Come, hurry, let's get business done so we may relax a bit."

Mills nodded as he walked. Behind he could hear the

fat Russian's sloppy steps in the sandy earth past the date trees. At the shack where his bodyguard waited, Costain paused outside the door and spoke to his man quietly in Russian. The bodyguard nodded and trotted off. "Raoul will be back with refreshments in a moment. Iced coffee is good?"

"Fine, Yves," Mills said, wondering how in the hell the Frenchman had managed ice on this godforsaken rock a thousand miles out in the Atlantic. Then again, Costain had surprised him before.

"Good. Inside. Come."

They entered the small shack, Mills first, Costain behind him, and finally the fat Russian, who pulled the flimsy door shut behind, likely the most physical thing he'd done in a while, Mills thought. The floor was sand, and there were no windows. Virgin daylight poked through several large holes rusted in the corrugated roof, which even this early was radiating heat downward, setting the space to swelter. There was the familiar table in the center, long and rectangular. It had been crafted out of scrap who knew how many years before, and bore the marks of much use. Mills had often wondered what things had been discussed at this table in his absence. What deals had been done.

And the deal now being done. He wondered about that, too. Wondered as he put the large duffel on the table and unzipped it lengthwise along its top. He spread the opening wide to reveal the contents.

The fat Russian smiled.

Yves, too, though to the expression he added a satisfied little nod.

Mills gave it a look, though he had already seen it. In-flight he had opened the duffel and made a rudimentary assessment of the contents. Stacks of hundred-dollar bills. A hundred to a bundle. Two hundred bundles. Two million dollars, give or take. And that was just this duffel.

"Four more like this one still in the plane, gentlemen,

compliments of Mr. Hoag." Mills smiled with them now. Ten million dollars was a lot to smile about.

"Excellent," Costain said. "Beautiful."

How many dozens of payments like this one had been made already to Costain? Seven that Mills knew of, having made those flights personally. Not all had transferred moneys in this amount, though one had involved nearly fifteen million. And none of that counted the flights Skunky or Lane had made. Yes, Yves Costain was being made an even richer man, here. He was being paid handsomely.

The question that nagged Mills was, *For what?*

Costain reached for the duffel and zipped it slowly up, patting it once when it was closed. "You will convey my thanks to Mr. Hoag for following the payment schedule."

"I will," Mills said. Costain smiled wistfully at him over the bag of money.

"One more payment, Mills. Then I shall see you no more."

One more, Mills thought. Gareth hadn't just been dramatic. It was close. Things were winding down. But down to what?

"Unless . . ." Costain began. "Unless you wish to work for me. . . ."

"Yves . . ."

"I can always use a pilot like you. Have you flown in Africa? A large continent with few radars and a refreshing tolerance toward bribery. You would like it."

"You're kind, Yves." Mills looked to the fat Russian. He had stopped smiling.

"Refreshments by the lagoon?" Costain suggested. "And more talk of your future."

"You're a persistent man, Yves."

"It is one of my more charming qualities," Costain admitted jokingly. He went to the door and let Mills and the fat Russian out, following them into the thin shade of the date palms. "Mills, you will stay for the day, won't you? We are roasting a pig."

"I should go, Yves."

"Should nothing. You will stay and have a meal with us."

What was he to do? In no way did he want to offend this man, because to offend him might sully his relationship with Gareth Dean Hoag. And that was a relationship he would not jeopardize. "All right, Yves."

"Yes," Costain said, pleased. "You see—I am not only persistent, but persuasive."

Mills agreed wholeheartedly with a laugh.

"Refreshments, then. Come."

Mills gestured to the Beech resting at the end of the runway. "Let me get the rest of the bags."

"Raoul will get it," Costain told him, but Mills shook his head.

"They're my responsibility until they're off that plane. I'll only be a minute."

Mills jogged off toward the Beech. Costain and the Fat Russian watched him.

"I don't trust him," the fat Russian said in his native tongue.

"*Ni moi non plus,*" Costain agreed in his.

At nine A.M., heeding the ring of her doorbell, Deandra Waley, fifty-nine, opened the front door of her small house on East Twelfth Street in Raven Cloud, Minnesota, and found a man standing on the leaning porch with a pumpkin under his arm.

She stared at him and kept the screen door shut, her hand on its inner latch.

"Good morning," the man said, smiling. "Would you like to buy a pumpkin?"

Her eyes bugged. "Excuse me, sonny?"

"Halloween is coming," he told her, looking past

where she stood to the room within. Couch, TV—this was the living room. Two windows on the west side. He had come up the street from that direction. There were bushes on that side of the white, craftsman house. Overgrown bushes. That was good. "If you buy early you get the pick of the crop."

Her stare narrowed down on him. "Are you serious?"

"Oh yes, ma'am," he assured her through the screen door. The one just inside that—the one that would be closed at night —was of simple wooden construction. Single lock. Likely a chain as well. As if that would do any good. "A good pumpkin can make the holiday."

"Boy, you are crazy," she told him. "First, you a white boy in a neighborhood that don't much trust white folks. Second, you talkin' about Halloween—*it's a month off, boy!* If I was to buy a pumpkin now, it'd be clean through rotted by then."

"Nineteen days, ma'am," he said. There were no children's toys strewn about the yard. No sign of youngsters at all, in fact. That was good, too. Almost as good as the absence of any disturbed canine barking at his presence now. Yes, that was *very* good. "Almost three weeks. Not a month."

She shook her head at him. "Get yourself the hell off my porch and off my property and back to the nuthouse where you belong."

The inner door slammed in his face. He heard a chain being set as it rattled shut. He smiled and left Deandra Waley's porch, her property, and her street. But he was not going to the nuthouse. Why would he want to go there? That's where crazy people lived.

Why is he angry? Why?

The question nagged Ariel Grace now as she sat on the bed in her room at the Bright I Motor Hotel, back against the headboard, a soda can in one hand and the VCR remote in the other. Nagged her as it had since that morning when the Pembry Post Office tape had arrived by overnight courier from the FBI lab. She'd watched it twenty times at the office already, the first few disturbing her as Doris May was tortured and killed and cut up, but after that she let herself become numb to the carnage, the viciousness. She focused. Watched. Studied.

And now, with Wednesday winding down, she relaxed (if that were possible) in her room with a beverage from the vending machine near the office and with the quaking image of what had happened in the Pembry Post Office last Friday paused on the motel TV. She'd borrowed a VCR from the office, and had hooked it up to the wall-mounted twenty-inch Zenith, certain that some damage had been done in the connection process. That, however, didn't bother her. What did was that she had watched the scenes another ten times or so and still she couldn't get it. Why? Why was Michaelangelo so angry?

She pressed PLAY and the scenes came to flat life once again. The images on screen alternated every two seconds between the post office's four cameras—lobby, counter, sorting room, back lot. The lobby would pop up for a breath, then the counter, then the sort room, and finally the back lot before going back to the lobby in an endless, disjointed loop of what had happened Friday evening. A cost-saving feature, it was, requiring just one recording deck, but damned if it hadn't been maddening at first. By afternoon, though, Ariel had become used to it, having almost memorized the sequence, from his pounce upon Doris May in the back lot, to his taking her at knife point through the sorting room and past the counter to the lobby. There he'd forced her to the table next to the mail slots. There he had begun to berate her. There he had become angry.

There was no sound, but *that* was anger she was seeing, Ariel knew. None of his face was visible—Jaworski had been right about that—but his body language spoke volumes of what was driving him. His quick movements, his abuse of her, grabbing her by the hair, *saying* something to her. And her shaking her head. And finally nodding.

And showing her the thing he'd ripped off the wall—the missing Most Wanted bulletin, Ariel had decided. He'd shoved it in her face. Rubbed her nose in it, at one point. Was he threatening her with it, saying, *"Do you know who I am? Do you know what I am capable of?"* Was he saying that?

If so, why would that make him mad?

Ariel watched the tape 'til it turned to snow, then rewound it again. She rubbed her eyes and went to her stomach, lying with her head at the foot of the bed, hands with soda and remote dangling over the edge. She sipped the soda and listened to the tape machine whir. When a loud and abrupt click signaled its stop, she put the can of soda on the bronzish carpet and pressed PLAY yet again. Time thirty-one or thirty-two or thirty-three. She'd lost count.

It began again, and in a moment she saw him surprising her, then he was gone, and the system cycled through lobby, counter, and sorting room before coming to the back lot again. The cycling continued in two-second snippets. Ariel saw a flash of the knife and then she was back in the lobby again. Counter. Sort room. And back lot again as he held the knife before her, displaying it.

Ariel paused it there. The scene quivered. She came off her stomach and sat cross-legged now on the end of the bed, leaning toward the frozen scene on the motel TV. Toward the image of Michaelangelo showing Doris May his knife. Displaying it for her. Displaying it . . .

. . . calmly.

His stance was steady. There was no animation. She was frightened. He seemed composed. *Experienced.*

And he was that, wasn't he, Ariel realized. So why was he calm here and later . . .

She fast-forwarded the tape to where he appeared to her to become agitated, there at the table, just before he ripped the Most Wanted bulletin from the wall.

She paused again, but was not quick enough on the button and ended up on an empty scene of the counter. She rewound, and found her place this time, stilling the image just right.

There, he was showing it to her. Showing it. Saying something, because . . .

She advanced the tape a bit, through counter, sorting room, and back lot, until she saw Doris May nodding.

She froze it there. There on Doris May, terrified and nodding. Nodding to what, though? A question? *"Do you recognize me?"*

She let it play again through the cycle, and stopped on a more frightened Doris May, her hair bunched in Michaelangelo's fist. He was showing her the bulletin again— no, he was forcing it upon her, angrily, enraged, leaning toward her, over her.

Again she stilled the scene. Stilled it on his rage. And the object of his rage, Doris May, already bleeding and now having a piece of paper shoved in her face. Why?

She had nodded. Counter. Sorting room. Back lot. He was *enraged*. Why? Had her response not been what he wanted?

But her response to what?

Ariel shook her head tiredly and let the tape play again. Let it play through. Through a minute or so at the counter and Doris staring at the bulletin Michaelangelo next to her, just standing there, looking at it together.

Why?

And then there she was, looking back to him. Counter. Sorting room. Back lot. Her head shaking. Saying something. "No"? "Please"? What? Counter. Sorting room. Back lot. And Michaelangelo putting the bulletin on the table, his knife going to her breast. Counter. Sorting room. Back lot. And Doris May slumping to the floor, her life gushing out her chest. Counter. Sorting room. Back lot.

Ariel watched it happen again. The cutting. The butchery. The slaughter of Doris May. The pieces of her being carried one, two, three at a time past the counter. Those pieces being taken into one room off a small hallway visible from the sorting-room camera, then directly across the hall to another as Michaelangelo made himself busy with his art.

Ariel sipped her soda as Michaelangelo came back to the lobby for the last piece of Doris May—her head. He worked it with his feet like a soccer ball, kicking it easily a few feet, then a few more, until he had it behind the counter and down that hall and into the first room. It never left that room.

But he did.

Back to the lobby, with a stack of papers in hand. A roll of tape as well. To the doors he went and arranged them, with great care, adjusting the pieces so that each was just right. Calm again. Working precisely. Just . . .

. . . just like an artist.

But he was not that. He only thought he was.

He flattened his hand and put it into the blood on the floor. He went to the wall near the table and put his message there. *She went to pieces.*

Telling all what to think of this, just like the titles of his more masculine works. He was the master, after all. Above all. Better, more knowledgeable than she or Jaworski or anyone who would be privy to his creations.

He had an ego, Ariel thought. Like most artists, especially, this one had an ego. His work had to be explained to those whose eyes would fall upon it. Those unworthy, incapable of understanding it themselves. Its meaning.

Her thumb came down on the PAUSE button and stopped Michaelangelo as he was leaving the lobby, walking casually, heading toward the counter, one of his hands reaching out. To something. For something.

She let it play again and it jumped through the locations.

"Damn," she swore, wanting a continuous view. When it came back to the lobby he was gone. And so was the bulletin he'd put on the table before cutting Doris May. The Most Wanted bulletin.

Ariel stood from the bed and stepped close to the TV as the next view cycled up. There he was, behind the counter, something in his hand. Flat and thin and light colored. The bulletin. He'd picked it up.

Why would he do that?

Her brow bunched down as she wondered. Wondered and watched as the sorting room came up, and there he was, walking through with the bulletin in hand, though smaller now, and she saw him fold it down to a still-smaller square, and then in the back lot she could not see it anymore but could see very plainly him pushing something down into the front pocket of his dark pants.

The tape went to snow again, and there it stayed, the TV hissing white noise as Ariel turned very slowly away from it, the remote still in her hand but her thoughts a million miles away.

Other thoughts were much, much closer. They ticked off in her head like parts of an equation tumbling toward a sum.

He was angry.

He was enraged.

He has an ego.

He berated Doris May with the bulletin.

He took the bulletin.

He was yelling at Doris May.

Was he angry at Doris May?

Or . . .

Her wonderings ceased suddenly there.

"You were there earlier," Ariel said. That she knew. It was on another tape the Bureau lab had sent. His visit that morning had been captured on tape, though no clearer image of him had been. He'd bought one stamp, from Doris May, had addressed a letter at the table and had mailed it.

Except that wasn't all he had done.

Another image had made a memory.

Ariel retrieved the earlier tape from the top of the low bureau near the TV and ejected the tape of Doris May's slaughter, feeding the earlier one in and setting it to PLAY.

The sequence was five minutes long, stuttering between locations as the latter one did. She watched, this one for the third time maybe. It had meant little, she thought. Until now.

There. There he came. In the front door and to the —

Counter. This switch picked him up as he arrived at the service window. The window staffed by Doris. Doris smiled. Said something. Sorting room—two workers working, flinging letters into stacked bins. Back lot—cars parked, a dog sniffing the gravelly ground. The lobby, empty. The counter again, and Doris sliding a single stamp across the counter as she put some coins in the cash drawer. Michaelangelo turning away and . . .

Ariel breathed hard and deep through the interruption as the sorting room and back lot were visited yet again. And then there he was, at the counter, taking an envelope from inside his jacket. Ariel remembered this, but it hadn't struck her until now what was about to happen. The scenes cycled again. Back in the lobby, Michaelangelo was taking his pen off the envelope. He'd written something on it. Addressing it, likely, since an address was all there was when his letters arrived at the Metropolitan Museum.

"Come on," Ariel implored the cycle of images as counter, and sorting room, and back lot were spied once more. "Come on."

And again to the lobby, his hand coming back from the out-of-town mail slot, hovering for a moment as he became still.

There. There is where it happens.

Through the other spaces and back to the lobby. She looked quickly at her watch, noting the time. Then to Michaelangelo, standing there, his right hand hanging, floating, and then coming down slowly. More interruptions, then on him again, and his hand was at his side, and it was clenched. It was hard to tell from the quality of the image, but Ariel thought the newly made fist might be trembling.

Anger. He was angry there. Hours before he was angry with Doris May—or angry about *something* in the presence of Doris May. And what was he angry about these many hours earlier?

Ariel couldn't jump into his mind, but she could her own, and oddly at this moment she thought there might be some symmetry between his reaction to the small square of paper he was staring at and her own to one that she had just a few days before.

She looked at her watch. One minute. The cycle repeated itself seven more times. He was still standing there, still staring at the bulletin, his fist now thumping gently against his leg. And another cycle, and ten more, and when he finally backed away from the table and from the Most Wanted bulletin posted to the wall, Ariel checked her watch and noted that he had been fixed in position for just under three minutes.

"You weren't angry at Doris," Ariel said as she froze the image one last time, Michaelangelo's dark and murky profile centered on the screen. "You weren't angry at her at all."

Glass? Glass? Was that glass?

The questions interrupted a dream, one of her on a beach as a much younger woman with seven men servicing her every nasty need. Shut the imaginary visit to Deandra Waley's own personal vision of nirvana down cold.

Glass? Was that glass?

The questions came from the rational part of herself. From that little space inside one's brain where a light is always left on . . . just in case. Left on so that things out of the ordinary might register. Might raise alarm. Might rouse.

Things like the sound of breaking glass.

"Glass," she whispered sleepily and hefted herself up to her elbows. She blinked at the darkness. The darkness in her bedroom. The darkness beyond its open door. Nothing. Not a thing to see.

So she listened. Had she heard glass? Breaking glass?

Or had it just been part of the dream. Waves crashing on that beach. Or her rattled screams of ecstasy, baby, yesssss.

Nothing, she thought, listening and looking. Not a damn thing. That pissed her off to no end.

"Come back to me, babies," she said softly, and fell into her pillows. "Come back and do me some more."

She fidgeted around for a moment, wanting sleep to take her back down to that dream, but the sandman was a little too slow in his doings right then, so she thought she might help him along a little. Give him a hint of where he left off.

"Oh, yesss, baby, yesss," she whispered to herself and took a long pillow from beneath her head and worked it under the covers, spreading her legs and pulling her nightgown up as she slipped it between. Her knees came together, clamping the pillow tight. Her hands fisted bunches of its downy mass and moved it, maneuvered it right, yesss, right, oh just so right, yesss bab—

The feel of heavy leather over her mouth snapped her dreamy eyes open. Darkness was above her. And darkness had a knife.

"I'm sorry," the pumpkin salesman said, putting his weight to his hand as she screamed against it. With a flick of his blade he drew a line across her forehead. She screamed more as the line oozed red. "I require your assistance for a while."

Her ragged cry pounded uselessly against his leathered palm. She kept it up until he pointed the wet tip of his blade at her left eye.

"The artisans in primitive cultures used ocular fluid to stain their implements," he told her. "Would you like me to demonstrate?"

She had no idea what ocuwhat fluid was, but that thing was pointing at her *eye*. And he'd cut her already. She shut herself up in one quick hurry.

"Good." He sat on the bed next to her and leaned close, his chest against hers. He felt her nipples poke him through the sheets. "This won't take long, I hope. I just need to speak to you for a while."

He eased his hand from her mouth just a bit.

"About . . . about . . . about what?" Deandra Waley asked the crazy pumpkin salesman with the knife.

"Who," he corrected her, coming closer still, his face a deep shadow over hers now.

"Who?"

He nodded and moved the knife to the side of her head, placing its tip in her left ear. He began to twist it slowly back and forth. "We're going to talk about Francis."

Tears filled her eyes. She shook her head. He moved fast and cut her left earlobe off and clamped off her scream.

For the next two hours she shook her head not once.

The Customs plane had him.

A P3-AEW Airborne Early Warning aircraft out of Florida had picked up the unidentified craft six hundred miles off the coast just after midnight and dispatched a Cessna Citation to intercept and shadow him. The suspect plane had not been squawking, meaning either its transponder had failed or the pilot had turned it conveniently off. The Customs radar crew aboard the P3 had not been born the previous day, and, coupled with the fact that the pilot had his bird very, very low over the water, well, it was a fair guess he wasn't a happy flier just off course and trying to make his way back home.

"Tiger Alpha Nine, you have him?" the pilot of the P3 asked the approaching Citation.

"Got 'em, Tiger Lima Four. He's ours now."

"Roger," the P3 pilot acknowledged, and turned his surveillance plane back toward Florida. It had been a long afternoon and night, and it was time for them to put 'er away for the night. They'd keep a radar eye on things until range made that impractical, but the fix was in for this game already. No way a twin-turboprop Beech was going to get away from the Citation and the two turbojets that drove it. Game, set, match for the Air Interdiction Program yet again. "Hang 'em high, Tiger Alpha Nine."

"With a big assist from Tiger Lima Four," the Citation's pilot said, then put his attention on the Beech that was wave-hopping five hundred feet below and a half mile ahead of him. "Hello there, you kwazy wabbit."

His right-seater chuckled and logged the time that they'd taken over the surveillance. It was still that—just a cautious look-see from a distance, because nothing illegal had yet been overtly done. Of course, once this yahoo landed and the Blackhawk helis swooped in to put a couple SWAT teams on his ass, well, maybe a search of that Beech might turn up some evidence of wrongdoing. Maybe a few hundred kilos of evidence. Until then, it was Tiger Alpha Nine's job to stay back, watch where this guy was going, and call in the Blackhawks and their arrest teams when landfall was imminent.

"Fuck!" Tiger Alpha Nine's pilot swore, and his right-seater looked up.

"What?"

"He made us," the pilot said, and adjusted his course to match the turn the Beech had just made.

"How the fuck did he make us?"

"I don't know, but he just fire-walled it and is scraping those waves." The pilot shook his head. "What's the weather between here and the coast?"

"Clear," the right-seater told him. "He's got nowhere to run, nowhere to hide."

"He's sure as hell trying," the pilot said, knowing his copilot was right on the money. Over land and in clouds, maybe this guy could lose them. Eyeballing had its limits, and even radar didn't like low-flying objects mixed in with ground clutter, but on the open ocean under clear skies, well, all this guy was asking for was —

"Whoa! Whoa!" the right-seater yelled, looking down and right as they came upon the Beech fast. Or what was left of the Beech. "He bought it into a wave. Son of a bitch."

The pilot shook his head. It wasn't the first time he'd seen this, and it wouldn't be the last. He slowed the Citation and put it into a slow orbit around the watery crash site. The foamy point of impact glowed atop the black and barren sea.

"Did he get out?" the pilot asked, concentrating on his own flying. He wasn't going to end up swimming, or sinking, like the stupid bastard two hundred feet below.

"Don't see a thing," the right-seater said. "Not a thing."

The pilot nodded to himself and keyed the radio. "Tiger Lima Four, you on?"

"Do we have a swimmer?" the P3 pilot asked. "We lost radar contact with your boy."

"Negative on the swimmer," the Citation's pilot told him. "Maybe a floater until the sharks get him. Is there any Coast Guard presence close by?"

"Neg-a-tive," the P3 pilot informed him. "Three hundred miles north is about the closest."

"Roger that." The Citation pilot looked past his right-seater now for a gander at the crash site—what there was of it. "He sank like a stone."

"Like a big ol' stone," the right-seater agreed. "So what's the plan?"

Plan? What plan could there be? A Coast Guard cutter would take ten hours to get there. By then the guy would be chum crumbs. Plankton would be bigger than him in ten hours.

Unless, of course, he didn't get out of the Beech, which in that case meant he'd be a meal for a whole different class of sea creatures. The kind that lived in a dark world, say, twelve thousand feet down.

Plan? Did he have a plan? He sure did.

"Wish his sorry ass good riddance and let's see if we can't beat Tiger Lima Four back to Jacksonville," the Citation pilot said. His right-seater gave the water below a wave and the bird as the plane leveled out and headed for home.

4

[DEAD MEN WALKING]

Thirty hours after it had left one field in Florida, the twin-engine Beech was back at another, touching down this time on a strip of wild land in Suwannee County with the sun low behind it in the eastern sky. The rugged earth played havoc with the tires, chewing the right-side main almost to a pulp, and the loose stone thrown up during landing left dozens of pits and nicks in the undercarriage from the wings back to the tail. When it finally came to a stop near where Gareth Dean Hoag and two of his associates stood, chances were it was going to have a hard time taking off again.

Then again, it wasn't going anywhere in any case.

The pilot's door tipped up and Mills DeVane gave the trio a wave. None of them waved back.

Something was wrong.

"Gareth," Mills said, stepping onto the wing. The morning breeze tossed his hair in his eyes. He'd have to remember to get it cut soon.

"Number five," Gareth said, and Mills came down from the wing.

"What's wrong?" Mills asked his employer.

"Skunky never showed up," Nita Berry told him.

Worry settled on Mills's face. His look danced between Gareth and Nita and Lionel Price. Spent a fair amount on

Lionel, actually, because he didn't like the guy one bit. Plus, he was a crazy and dangerous one. Part warrior, part Bible-thumper. In his vision of the Old Testament, Jesus would have carried a MAC-10 in case some Jews needed to be greased. One dangerous mother, oh yes, Mills knew. But then, how un-dangerous were any of them?

"Never showed up?" Mills asked. "What do you mean?"

"I mean the four hundred pounds of nose candy he was flying in for us never showed, along with him, which, if you run that thought out a little, my flyboy friend, you'll realize it means that the money our buyers were going to give us for the product is not coming our way."

Gareth was pissed. In general, but some of anger's shrapnel was coming Mills's way. "Shit."

"Shit is right," Gareth agreed. "Big shit. Because our friend you just spent the night with is expecting another payment. A payment that is going to be *late*. *Late!*"

"He'll understand," Mills said.

"He's a businessman, number five," Gareth said. "And in his business he doesn't have to extend credit."

"We don't," Lionel offered, and Mills knew what he meant. He'd once heard Nita talk about Lionel administering a little 'Bible justice' to a customer who came up short on them. The man didn't need both his thumbs, Nita had told Mills with a smile. Mills had wondered then just what part of the Bible that came from.

"You're gonna have to do some extras for me, number five," Gareth said. "Pick up what Skunky won't be able to."

"I've got other people to service, Gareth." The Moreno Brothers in Nashville, they had some runs coming up. And Tuck Bannerman in Jersey. There were at least two, maybe three pickups for him down in Mexico and maybe a hop out west to one of Bannerman's guys on the coast.

"Of course you do." Gareth leaned close and told him

with cold expectation, "But I want you to make time for me. I need you in Colombia next week. Tuesday. You'll fly back on Wednesday."

Mills nodded. What choice did he have? "A big move?"

"Not big enough," Gareth said with obvious regret. "There'll be a new plane at Crutch Field for you on Monday."

"Make it a twin," Mills reminded him. There was nothing he hated more than flying over open ocean with one engine. "Like this one."

"It's only money. Shall we?"

Gareth and Mills and Nita started away from the Beech, heading toward a line of trees on the far side of the rough. There was a glint of sunlight off metal beyond them. The chrome bumper of a car.

But Lionel did not immediately follow them. Instead of leaving the Beech he went to it, taking something from one of the large cargo pockets on the front of his camouflaged pants. It was small and black, a rectangular something wrapped in electrical tape, with a dial on its face that he adjusted carefully before setting it atop the left wing. Right above a fuel cell. That done, he trotted to catch up with the others. A minute later they were moving. Fifteen and they were on an honest-to-goodness road. Twenty, and they were too far to hear or see the Beech erupt in a ball of orange flame that would consume it.

He'd read her report through once as she stood in his office and had her explain it to him twice after he'd told her to sit, but still Bernard Jaworski was having trouble making the leap that Ariel Grace had made.

"So you think our freak is going to go after Director Weaver because he decided to rank the Ten Most Wanted list?" Jaworski scratched some of the stubble he'd missed on his chin and squinted at his newest agent. "The Director of the Federal Bureau of Investigation?"

She nodded. "He's the logical target, sir. He made the decision that made Michaelangelo angry."

"Supposedly angry," Jaworski said.

"Watch the tapes," Ariel told him. "Watch the parts I've noted. Tell me that you don't think he's angry."

"I've seen the tapes, Grace."

She leaned forward in her chair. "When he's standing for almost three minutes, sir, staring at the Most Wanted bulletin. The new ones with the rankings went out three weeks ago. I checked this morning—the Pembry Post Office had received theirs and put it up."

"Admiration," Jaworski said, remembering the scene on the tape, the period of time Michaelangelo had stood still, staring. Transfixed. Though Jaworski hadn't noticed the fist, as Ariel had described it. "He could have been admiring himself."

Ariel shook her head. "Why, because he placed last in a field of ten?"

"You're making a big leap, here, Grace," Jaworski warned her. He hated to see agents get their thinking locked on one track.

"Dots, sir. I'm just connecting dots. These are things I saw. He was mad. Pissed off. He berated Doris May with the bulletin he then took. Why take it? He's been on the list for five months now. What made that bulletin special? So special that it enraged him to look at it? To stare at it for three solid minutes? To come back and shove it in that clerk's face?" Ariel paused and scooted herself back. She had almost come off the chair. "Sir, in a way, I can understand his reaction."

Jaworski's gaze narrowed at her. At that assertion.

"Both he and I were demoted, you might say. Ranked down."

"Come on, Agent Grace. . . ."

"I'm just telling you that I know the feeling, that initial

punch in the gut, when I read that letter Saturday morning and found out I was being shifted from Task Force Five to Task Force Ten. I had come down from it by the time you met me Monday morning, but that wasn't the case on Saturday. I was livid. I was hot. If Jack Hale had been in the room with me I would have punched him."

"No you wouldn't have," Jaworski told her, and she knew he was right.

"I would have wanted to. It would have taken everything for me not to."

Jaworski glanced down at her report where it lay on his blotter. Two pages. A theory. A prediction, really, if you dared call it that. All after two days' work. He shook his head.

Ariel slid forward again. "Sir, you can think I'm a fool, but if he is as angry as I think, and he goes after the director . . ."

"He'd never get close," Jaworski reminded her. The director had bodyguards. He was not some taxi driver or real estate saleswoman who could be lured to their demise.

"But he might try," Ariel said. "And if he did, we could be there. Or close. This could be the first chance we have to know one of his victims in advance."

"Intended victim," Jaworski corrected her. He didn't like the certainty that had slipped into her premise.

Ariel accepted his revision with a nod, but said nothing more. She let Jaworski taste it for a moment. Chew on it. From the look about him he was.

"You're either crazy or brilliant," Jaworski told her, tapping her report with his finger for a moment after that. A moment of thought. "I'm going to request the Albany SAC forward this to the director's office pronto . . . just in case you're onto something. I like the part about knowing who our freak might go after. I like that a lot."

"Thank you, sir."

He shook his head. "This isn't praise, Agent Grace, and you might not want to thank me just yet. Because if this gets to the director and goes bust, well, it's your name on it. Chances are you'll be looked at as a two-time loser."

She hadn't thought of it that way. Her suddenly slack expression made that apparent to Jaworski.

"Do you still want me to push this through?" he asked her.

"Yes," she affirmed after a split second's consideration.

"Okay, Agent Grace. You've just rolled some big dice." Jaworski took a large envelope from his desk and slipped her report in. He'd add a note atop it once she was gone. "I hope they come up."

Ariel stood to leave. "Thank you, sir."

"Go connect some more dots," he said, waving her out with a flip of his hand.

She noticed the crispness of the gesture. She also noticed that he hadn't coughed once in her presence that morning.

5

[HOME BOYS]

Where the fuck was the call?

Francis Gunther stood in the shadows of the alley off Chippewa Avenue late Wednesday night, a dozen feet from the phone booth out on the street. Two police cars had passed in the ten minutes he'd been there. Neither had shined their lights down the dark and narrow passage between the K-Man Liqueteria and the New 2 U Clothes store. That was good.

What was not good was that damn phone not ringing. Just hanging there silent while he was as exposed as he cared to be. If the damn call would just come he could dash out, get the word, and be on his way to wherever his momma had left the shit for him. Although she'd smack him real good if she ever heard him call her cooking and any clothes she'd picked up for him shit. She didn't go in for the foul talk . . . unless of course it was coming from her. He almost laughed recalling that truth, oh yeah. Almost.

'Cause how could he laugh standing out in the big wide open, which was how he thought of even this dark alley lately. The only good place, the only safe place, was inside. Inside away from the cops and those feds who had plastered a number on him and then plastered his face all over the news. Shit if it didn't make even buying a bottle a major production. And worse than all that was that even his friends, like his old-time buds, no lying, were rumored to be ready to rat him out for the hundred thou the feds and the six or seven banks he robbed were offering in reward. If that didn't fucking burn, he didn't know what did.

Well, this came close, he thought, and took the beeper from his pocket. It belonged to his second cousin, but his momma had borrowed it for him, so they could keep in touch, and since that lawyer she got got a judge to tell the feds and the cops to quit following her all around, well, she'd been able to get things to people who would then get them to places where her phone call would tell him to go. Simple. She'd beep him, with the time, just like it said on there now, the 9:15— nine-fifteen. Yeah, simple as simple got, 'cept shit if it wasn't that plus some, and so, oh yeah, this was beginning to burn. Burn on a burn, man, yeah.

He'd give it just another minute, Francis Gunther decided, putting the beeper back in his pocket just as the phone out on Chippewa Avenue started ringing. He rushed to the end of the alley, gave both up and down the street a good look (the feds were never gonna catch him with some lame-ass phone booth setup, no way), and darted out to snatch the handset up on the third ring.

"Talk to me, Momma."

Momma said a whole lotta nothing back to him.

"Momma?"

Silence. But . . .

. . . not total silence.

Francis Gunther checked his surroundings through the glass sides of the booth and kept the phone to his cheek. "Momma."

Breathing. He heard breathing. Suddenly, he was worried.

"Momma, is that you?"

"I'm trying to reach number nine," a man's voice said over the phone, and Francis Gunther let it drop from his hand. He backed out of the booth and looked up and down Chippewa again, but there was nothing. No feds. No cops. Nothing.

He looked down at the dangling handset and half thought about picking it up again, but decided that he needed to be away from this place fast. Someone was fucking with him, somehow, someway, and he didn't like it. No fucking way did he like it. So with a final glance up and down the street he turned and ran back into the alley, into its darkness, going full bore toward the backstreet side of the Liqueteria where he could hop a fence or two and be in a neighborhood with his pick of cars to boost. And once in a car, it'd be bye bye, Francis.

Except he never even made it to the end of the alley. A hand reached out and clotheslined him as he ran, the bottom half of his body slipping out from under him and his head going back hard against the pavement with a wet crack.

"Unhhh," Francis Gunther groaned to the dark sky above as he opened his eyes. Eyes that went wide when he realized the darkness was not in the sky—it was coming down over his face.

Gareth Dean Hoag pulled the Jeep Wagoneer to the curb a few blocks from Hartsfield International Airport. A 767 roared low overhead as Mills DeVane got out of the dirty old wagon.

They'd dropped Nita and Lionel off in Tallahassee, and Gareth had driven Mills the rest of the way alone. They'd made small talk, mostly. Talked about women. Talked about bread. Talked about how impressed women were by bread. Light stuff for conversation.

But now as Mills leaned his arms in the open window

of the door he'd just closed, Gareth looked at him with full seriousness. "You know Skunky's probably dead."

"There's a lot of water between here and Colombia," Mills said, and Gareth nodded.

"You have to be careful," Gareth told him. It seemed more order than request. "I need you. Especially now."

"I don't plan on going anywhere," Mills assured him.

"Good."

"Thanks for the ride, Gareth."

"Colombia. Tuesday." Gareth put the Wagoneer in gear. "Okay?"

Mills nodded and stepped back and watched Gareth pull away. When he was out of sight Mills jogged across the road and hailed a taxi. He gave the driver directions and sat back, thankful to be alone for a while. Well, not quite alone. There was Nick, license number 60067, up there driving. No, he was glad to be *away*. Away from Gareth. From Nita. From Lionel.

If only he could get away from thoughts of Skunky.

His skin crawled suddenly at the thought of going down in water, though there was no evidence to point to that being the case. But logic and circumstances combined here made a pretty powerful argument, one Mills truly did not want to think about.

And so he wouldn't. There were other things to think about. Other things to do. And as he saw the phone booth ahead aglow with its own lights, he knew that there could be something else to plan. So he told the driver to pull over, right to the curb where the glass box stood. Told him to wait, then he went to the booth and closed the doors. From his pocket he fished some change and dialed a number in Charlotte, North Carolina, getting the evening desk of the *Charlotte Register Democrat*. They transferred him to their automated classified ad system, where he left a message, giving the computerized voice a false but valid name and credit card number to pay for an ad that would run the following day.

That done, he returned to the taxi and told the driver to go, to take him home, though he knew that was a place he could not go. Not yet.

6

[MR. SANDMAN]

Mary Sue Salyers went out to play

It was Saturday morning, early still, one might think, for a girl of eight to be leaving her house and six channels of cartoons, but Mary Sue had been planning this since last Saturday, when Randy Grant came up behind her and shoved her off the swing.

"My turn, runt," he'd told her as she lay on the ground, tears coming to her eyes and sand stinging where it had rubbed into her knee. She'd watched Randy, a seventh-grader at Hubert Humphrey Junior High, climb onto the swing that had been hers and push off, gaining speed and height above her. She'd crawled out of the way, her eyes wet without openly crying, his feet narrowly missing her as she made it into the clear off of the sand. There she'd brushed herself off and stood, and there she'd watched Randy Grant swing, and swing, and swing, and after a while she went to the monkey bars and climbed on top and watched him swing some more, and there, sitting high up there, she'd thought up her plan. Her idea. The super-great idea that would mean she could swing on the middle swing, the one not near the bars that Marcie Moore had been bumped into by Randy Grant's friend Lenny McCallister, and she could do it for as long as she wanted. Or at least until eleven, when it always seemed the big kids showed up at West Side Park.

And so this morning she was off, skipping cartoons to skip across the street and down Maple Drive, wearing tights and a thick sweater to beat back the morning chill. In five minutes, she was at the park and walking now so as not to slip on the dew glistening across the expanse of grass soon to go brown for winter. Walking carefully but quickly toward the swings, running once she reached the sand, because who cared if she fell there? That's what sand was for.

And, boy, didn't it look like Mr. Terrafini, the park's gardener and janitor and just about everything else, had taken a rake to the sand the day before, because it looked clean and flat and almost new. And wasn't Mary Sue delighted that she would be the first to test it out, which she already had, she realized, looking back behind to see her small footsteps pressed into the soft bed of sand. She smiled and stamped her name in it, spelling Mary Sue right in front of the middle swing, the one not near the bars where Marcie Moore had lost two teeth. Right where she could see it whenever she swung back, and right where it would be under her when she swung forward.

"I'm Mary Sue Salyers," she said loudly, "and I get the middle swing today!"

And onto the middle swing she hopped, forgetting the morning dew that might be there. The damp surprised her through her dress and her tights, but only for a second, because after that she was pushing off. Walking the swing back on the pristine sand and getting a good jump. You see, the push-off was the most important part. Her big brother had told her that. Had showed her, actually, how to get that big start, and stick your feet out front and lean waaaaay back as you swung forward, and then how to tuck your feet back under the swing and sit forward as you swung back. He said it got you moving like a pendu-something, and she had to agree, if a pendusomething was something that swung really high, because that's what usually happened when she swung like her big brother showed her.

But not now, because there was a problem.

It wasn't the jump-off, because that went good. She got a big jump, and she pointed her legs straight out and leaned back as she swung forward, but as she started to swing back and tucked her legs under, she found out that Mr. Terrafini had evened the sand out a little too much. There wasn't enough room for her tucked-under feet to make it without scraping the ground, and that was slowing her down. That shallow trench under the swing that had been worn in the sand by a thousand, million kids was gone. Filled in. Smoothed out. Shoot!

So as she swung back a second time, taking a kind of extra jump-off because she used her feet to push off again, she figured she'd have to be just like the first kid ever to get on the swing and tuck her feet up a little bit higher. And that was what she did.

It mostly worked.

But with every backswing, Mary Sue Salyers's little sneakers caught a little bit of sand, brushing some, then some more, and still some more, until the depression that had been worn there by not quite a thousand million kids began to reappear. Layer by layer the sand was swept back, revealing more sand, and more sand, and more sand, and . . .

. . . and then the tip of a nose, and the whole nose after that, and cheeks and open eyes, and a dead mouth that smiled.

7

[MEETINGS]

The phone rang in room twelve of the Bright I Motor Hotel at five o'clock on Sunday. Five in the morning.

Ariel Grace rolled right from where she'd burrowed herself among the covers and pillows and snatched the handset up as it rang a second time.

"Yeah?"

"Get yourself up and dressed, Grace." It was Jaworski. Sounding bright and chipper. Not dragging. "Shower if you have time. Do you remember how to get to Oneida County Airport? Near Utica?"

Ariel looked at the alarm clock on the bedside table. It was early. Dark early, she could tell with a glance at the drape-covered window. The yellow glow of the street-light still lay prominent on it.

"Yes," she answered. Saturday she'd picked up rush copies of the enhanced images the lab had processed from the Pembry Post Office. It had been a wasted trip. "Why?"

"You've got a flight in forty minutes."

"A flight?" Ariel asked, then realization jerked her fast from sleep's bog. "Did Michaelangelo —"

"Yes," Jaworski told her. Over the connection she thought she heard coffee being poured and early-morning news on a radio.

"Where?" she asked him, sitting up now, dragging her

feet from under the covers, the front of her oversized tee bunching on her bare legs. She switched on a light.

"Minnesota. But you're not going there. They want to see you in Washington."

"They who?"

"The order came from the director's office."

The director? Revelation bugged her eyes. "Sir, did he get my report? Is this about that?"

"I would guess it is, since the body they found was Francis Gunther's."

The name was familiar. She might have had it without hesitation if not just roused from sleep. "On the Most Wanted list?"

"Number nine."

"How did Michaelangelo . . .?"

"Find him? I don't know." There was a pause and a quiet slurp as Jaworski sipped his coffee. "The local cops weren't sure what they had when they found him. It took them 'til damn near midnight before they knew what they had."

"What did he do to him?"

"I'm not sure yet. The locals' description wasn't very precise."

"What did they say?"

Another sip. "They said he'd been boned and folded."

"What does that mean?"

"I don't know. But, Grace, this is to be kept quiet. Understand?"

"Yes."

"That comes from the director's office, too."

"Right."

"You've got thirty-nine minutes to get to Oneida."

"Okay," she said, standing with the phone still to her cheek.

"And Grace . . ."

"Yes?"

"You weren't in the ten ring with your report, but you were on the target. That's as close as anybody's gotten trying to predict what this freak will do. It was good work."

She smiled at the handset. "Thank you, sir."

"Now get your butt moving."

The connection clicked off. Ariel held the phone for half a minute, the smile on her lips lingering. She had been right. Michaelangelo had been angered. Angered to the point of reaction. And she had called it. She was struck with the irrational urge to call Jack Hale and let him know how right she'd been on this one, but he'd know. Soon enough he'd know, she figured.

She had no idea how right she was.

He'd had her for a day now, putting her through the paces, some low and slow, and some high-speed maneuvering just to make sure she could give what he might have to ask of her someday. So far she was a beaut. But she wasn't ready. That's why he brought her to Nico.

"Sweet, Mills baby, sweet," Nico Trane commented as he walked around the Cessna, wiping his hands on a rag and leering at the twenty-year-old aircraft as though it were some dancing girl in a halter top. "Seventy-eight?"

"Seventy-seven," Mills answered, and glanced at the clock high on the hangar wall. It was almost noon. He needed to get moving. "So you know what I need?"

"What you need is what you get from Nico," the master mechanic said, stopping at the port crew and cargo door, which was open, top half up, bottom half folded down to steps. He gave a look inside and turned to Mills. "Mills, my friend, when you return tomorrow morning, this Cessna 402B, in as good a condition as it already is, will be decked out and tweaked up like any and all the fine flying machines I have so lovingly modified for you."

"I want the new night stuff. Not that French crap."

"American made," Nico assured him. "New autopilot, radio, RWR, the works. Plus I'm gonna throw in something new."

"New better be useful," Mills told him.

"Oh, it could come in handy," Nico boasted. "Mighty, mighty handy."

Mills checked the time again. "Early Monday, right?"

"Seven in the AM tomorrow. Bright and early. I'll even have her washed."

"You're a prince," Mills complimented him, and Nico gave him a bow. "You got the car for me?"

"Just off the tarmac." Nico reached one semiclean hand into the front of his coveralls and tossed Mills a set of keys. "Fool left them under his back tire. How easy is that? I hope you like Buicks."

"If it will get me to Atlanta I'll like it. Is it hot?"

Nico looked at the clock now. "When the guy gets his boat back in off the lake and finds his trailer sitting there all alone, well, I guess it'll be hot then."

Mills gave Nico a thump on the shoulder and headed for the door.

"I'll do her up nice," Nico shouted after him. Mills had no doubt about that.

He found the car right where Nico said it would be, just off Crutch Field's aging tarmac. He got in, started it up, and spun the tires as he hurried away.

Daniel Weaver, Director of the Federal Bureau of Investigation, rose from the wingback chair to greet Ariel Grace as she was shown into room 404 at the Carrington Hotel in downtown Washington, just three blocks from the J. Edgar Hoover Building where she'd expected to be meeting him. Some bewilderment still showed on her face.

"Agent Grace. Come in. I'm pleased to meet you."

Ariel shook his hand.

"This is Assistant Director Mike Kellerman," the director said, introducing one of the men with him.

"Sir," Ariel said, shaking his hand as well.

"We met in Atlanta once," Kellerman told her. "Retirement party for Terry Harman."

Ariel nodded. "I remember, sir."

"I was Terry's SAC in Dallas. What's he up to now? Do you know?"

"Last I heard he was getting kissed a lot by his grandkids," Ariel said. She looked back to the director and noted that the pleasantness about his face was suddenly tempered as he gestured behind her.

"You already know Jack Hale," the director said, and Ariel turned slowly to see him standing behind the suite's well-stocked wet bar.

"Hello, Ariel," he said, and poured himself a glass of ginger ale.

She could only stare at him for the longest moment, not knowing what to say. Not knowing whether to say what she wanted to say. In the end the director didn't give her the chance.

"You're probably wondering what the heck is going on," Weaver said to her.

She kept her gaze fixed on Jack Hale as he came from behind the bar to join them. "Yes, sir. You could say I'm at a little loss here."

"We'll try to explain it all. Have a seat." The director looked to the agent who'd brought Ariel from the airport. "Pete, that's all for now."

Pete nodded and dutifully left. He'd stand outside the door until the meeting was over.

The director and assistant director took the two wingbacks in the suite's sitting area, while Jack Hale positioned himself on the small couch across from them. Ariel was left with no choice but to sit next to him.

"I'm sorry, Agent Grace," Director Weaver said. "We didn't offer you anything to drink."

Shot of vodka, she wanted to say, but obviously couldn't. In reply she simply shook her head.

"There's fizzy water," Jack Hale informed her, smiling at her profile. "With lime."

"No, thank you, Agent Hale," she said without looking at him, hating that he remembered her favorite drink from the Atlanta office. Hating and wondering what his game was now. What the hell this whole thing was now.

Director Weaver sensed her discomfort and started to talk. "We're meeting here, Agent Grace, because we can't chance being seen together at Hoover. You'll understand soon."

Glancing at Jack Hale out of the corner of her eye, she sure as hell hoped she would. Because some explaining was needed.

"Mike here knows more about the situation as it stands, so I'll let him proceed."

"What situation, sir?" Ariel asked.

"You heard about Task Force Ten's fugitive striking again?" Kellerman said.

"Michaelangelo, yes sir."

"You know who he killed?"

"Francis Gunther."

"Number nine on the Most Wanted list," Jack Hale said. Ariel gave him a quick look and a bare nod. "The police in Raven Cloud, Minnesota, went to inform his mother a few hours ago and found her carved up like a pumpkin in her kitchen. Michaelangelo had painted the walls with her blood."

"That's how he got to Francis," Ariel observed softly, almost a thought spun aloud. "Through his mother." She looked to all three senior Bureau men. "He doesn't have to follow rules like we do to find someone."

"Did Agent Jaworski tell you anything more?" Kellerman asked her, but before she could answer the director jumped in.

"How is Bernie, Agent Grace? How's he looking?"

She'd known Jaworski only just shy of a week and she

was being asked to offer judgment on his condition. "Bad earlier this week, sir, but he sounded good this morning on the phone."

The director nodded with hopeful concern and signaled the AD to go on.

"Did he tell you anything else, Agent Grace?"

"Just something about the local police finding him boned and folded."

The director put his hand to his mouth and shook his head.

"I don't know what that means, sir," Ariel admitted. "I haven't seen any photos."

On the small coffee table between the couch and the wingbacks there was a file folder. Kellerman reached into it and laid a photo on top. "Here it is."

Ariel looked. In a shallow hole in soft earth, it appeared, Francis Gunther's flattened face lay atop a pile of something. She bent to inspect it closer and saw that the pile was the rest of Francis Gunther sandwiched upon itself.

"Those came in from Minnesota an hour ago," Kellerman said. "Francis Gunther had every bone removed from his body and what was left was folded up like an accordion and buried in the sand beneath a playground. A little girl on a swing accidentally discovered him."

Ariel shook her head. "Not accidental, sir. This is what he does. His art goes for shock value."

"This isn't art," the director observed with disgust.

"To him it is, sir," Ariel said.

"Whatever he thinks it is, his killing Francis Gunther seems to prove a theory, Agent Grace." Kellerman pointed to her. "Your theory."

"I wasn't completely right."

"You were damn close," Director Weaver said.

"All but on the money," Kellerman said, then added, "And this is the second time."

His addendum zinged her. "Pardon me, sir . . ."

"Tell us, Agent Grace," Director Weaver began, "how did you find Mills DeVane?"

The second time? DeVane? What was this about? "Sir, I didn't find him."

"Well, tell us how you *thought* you'd found him."

She'd tried to forget all about Atlanta. All about Mills DeVane. But now he was back, dredged up for some reason. And she was being made to talk about him. "It was the newspaper, sir."

"What newspaper?"

Jack Hale already knew the story, and she had the suspicion that the other two men in the room knew it as well. For some reason, though, they wanted to hear it from her. "We had two chance surveillance photos of DeVane from a liquor store where he was spotted and one a month later at a gas station. There were witnesses at both locations who identified him and called in the sightings. That's how we got the pictures. In each of the photos he had a newspaper under his arm. One woman recalled that it was an *Atlanta Journal*."

The director's face shrugged. "And . . ."

"I wondered why Mills DeVane would be walking around Atlanta with a newspaper under his arm. Why? And then I remembered a sighting with no corroborating surveillance photos about three months earlier. Someone had thought they'd seen DeVane walking through a motel parking lot with a newspaper under his arm."

"You thought it was a meet signal."

They hadn't heard, Ariel realized, and gave Jack Hale a look. The oddest, faintest smile was barely twisting his lips.

"No, sir. I thought it might be more than just a flag to alert someone, maybe a contact, that he was there. I thought the newspaper itself might hold the instructions for a meeting."

"Classifieds?" Kellerman asked, and Ariel nodded.

"From that earlier sighting we knew where he likely was for a meeting, and we knew what paper he had from the later witness reports, so I had the classified ads for the days leading up to the earliest sighting scrutinized. And we found something in the previous day's paper." She still remembered it. "Four seven twelve Natalie. Seven."

Kellerman was nodding and smiling. "The address."

"Four seven one two Natalie Way," Ariel confirmed. "The location of the Grand View Motel, where Mills DeVane was sighted at approximately seven PM After we had that, we went back to the classifieds for the times near the two documented sightings and we found similar ads. And there were two motels in the two areas with address numbers mentioned in the ads, on streets mentioned in the ads."

"So you took his picture there," Director Weaver surmised quite correctly.

"And we found witnesses. Desk clerks, customers from those days."

"And from that day on you watched the classifieds," Kellerman said.

"Like a hawk."

Kellerman nodded and shared a look with Jack Hale.

"You were surprised when he wasn't there," the AD suggested.

"Very," Ariel said. "Because the ad was in the paper." She shot a look Hale's way. "But someone made a mistake and he was spooked."

"There was no mistake, Agent Grace," Kellerman said, the statement more confirmation than denial.

"What do you mean?"

It was not Kellerman who explained his remark. It was Jack Hale. "What he's saying, Ariel, is that there was a car on the boulevard that night."

"*What?*" she asked, dumbstruck.

"It was my car," Hale told her, and her mouth hung open.

Director Weaver sat forward and drew her attention. "Agent Grace, I didn't approve your being removed from the DeVane case because you were off the mark. The fact of the matter is you were getting too close."

"You would have caught him that night if Agent Hale hadn't scared him off," Kellerman said.

Ariel looked to each of them. Her head was shaking. She was at a loss. "Why in the world would you want to let Mills DeVane get away?"

"Because he's one of us," Director Weaver said. "He's an FBI agent. Undercover."

Ariel stared slack-jawed at him, then asked, "Can I have that drink now?"

Jack Hale got it for her, lime fizzy water, and sat next to her again, his arm on the back of the couch behind her. She sipped her drink and looked at him and saw something different in his face. Something that seemed out of place there, in him, on him, part of him: apology.

"I didn't want to pull you, Ariel. I didn't want to cut you down in front of everybody. But I had no choice. It had to look real."

"It felt real," she said, then the weight of what they were telling her hit. Another long sip half drained the bottle and she set it on the coffee table. "Jesus, what is he doing on the Most Wanted list if he's UC?"

"Credibility," Jack Hale said.

Director Weaver spoke next, all things about him right then exuding seriousness. Danger. "Agent Grace, you're one of a select few to know anything about this operation. I don't need to say the obvious."

That Mills DeVane would be a dead man if the truth ever leaked out or was surmised upon. "No, sir."

Kellerman was the one to continue the explanation. "Three years ago we created Mills DeVane. That isn't his real name. I won't tell you what is. He may yet have a life after this operation is complete."

Ariel didn't like his use of the "may" word.

"The plan was actually quite simple," Kellerman went on, his admiration apparent for what he, or someone, had conceived. "First we erased the man that Mills DeVane was, but we got to keep his skills."

"Four years Air Force," Jack Hale offered.

"Six years in the Bureau. No wife. No children. Low profile. No press on anything he'd done. Minimal interaction with agents, and those that might have recognized him wouldn't after some minor cosmetic surgery. He has that kind of face. Chameleonlike."

"And the lousy picture," Ariel suggested.

"Planned," Kellerman confirmed. "Anyone who knew the man that Mills DeVane used to be would not be able to look at that shot we got and make him."

Ariel was shaking her head in minor awe. "And his record? Fabricated?"

"Retiring U.S. Marshal Trevor Noonan was more than cooperative to lend his name to the operation," Kellerman explained. "A few, fake days in Walter Reed and some dramatic bandaging . . ."

"And you have a federal offense," Ariel completed the line of thought. That was a requirement for being on the Bureau's Ten Most Wanted list. DeVane had "assaulted" a federal officer. They'd put Michaelangelo on after urging from New York State and Pennsylvania officials, using a statute concerning the interstate transport of controlled substances—his use of napoxcypharin on his victims in three states. It was a stretch, but the jurisdictional nightmare of a tri-state investigation made this the best approach, the thinking had gone. Though it was four states now, Ariel reminded herself. And likely to grow beyond that, she feared. Though that wasn't the greatest fear in this room, and she knew it.

"He's wanted, he can fly," Kellerman said.

"Air Force records?" Ariel asked.

"Washed clean," Kellerman answered. "Mills DeVane has his own Air Force records. With disciplinary and drug problems."

"Clever," Ariel commented.

"Agent Hale's idea." Kellerman tipped his head to the Atlanta ASAC.

"So you were in on the planning of this?" Ariel asked Hale. "From the beginning?"

"Agent Hale 'runs' Mills DeVane," Kellerman said. "As much as anyone can run a UC as deep as he is."

The picture was starting to form now for Ariel. She had to admit, it was beautiful. "So DeVane puts his piloting skills to use and starts hauling drugs in for dealers."

"And major suppliers," Kellerman clarified. "We get enough info from him to build information on the supply and distribution operations of the cartels, the major dealers. And from that we run other, completely separate operations to interdict a portion of what comes in. By doing things right we can stop enough of the stuff from hitting the streets to make a difference."

"Without giving him away," Jack Hale added. "That's the trick."

"That was the plan," Kellerman said. His words reeked of prelude. "Things changed after about a year."

Ariel's look said that she was listening.

"Jack . . ." Kellerman knew this was Hale's thing. He'd had to deal with it from the get-go. Had made the call to let Mills shift gears, if you will, to see if something big developed. And had it ever.

Ariel turned toward the man she had almost let herself loathe. She didn't know yet what to feel about Jack Hale, but it certainly couldn't be enmity anymore, could it? He was simply doing his job. Protecting another agent.

"Two years ago a man who Mills DeVane had been

pulling shipments for, Gareth Dean Hoag, asked him to do something a little different: deliver some money out of the country."

"Laundering?" Ariel asked. That could be big. Far-reaching implications to other organizations, governments. Bribes. You name it. That made sense.

But Jack Hale was shaking his head.

"Payments," Hale told her.

"Big payments, Agent Grace," Director Weaver said, offering a word after mostly listening to his AD give her the low-down. "We're talking in the millions of dollars."

"Tens of millions," Hale expanded. "Over many months and many payments. DeVane and other pilots contracted by Hoag would fly bags of cash out to an island in the Carribean and hand it over to a man we were able to identify as Yves Costain."

"Arms merchant," Ariel said. "There was an Interpol notice about him in *Law Enforcement Bulletin*. So Hoag was paying Costain for what? Weapons?"

"More like advance payment for large-ticket items," Hale said. "We didn't really have a good idea of what that might be until about nine months ago when Costain was joined by another man at this payday. Valentin Gryoko. Russian. An arms merchant himself who has, over the past few years, made a name with his ability to procure and deliver shoulder-fired surface-to-air missiles to any-one who can pay the price. And not Afghan-era crap. We're talking top-of-the-line Russian models."

"You don't have to be told what just one of those things could do in this country," Director Weaver said.

"Going price on the black market for top-of-the-line SAMs is one million, Ariel." Jack Hale smiled nervously. "Hoag has paid these two close to seventy-five million already."

"My God," Ariel reacted.

"My God is right," Kellerman agreed. "Hoag has ties

to some far-flung groups, Agent Grace. Some bad boys and girls who'd like nothing better than to take out some aircraft over some cities. Put on a show. Scare people."

"Maybe take some shots at Air Force One," Director Weaver suggested.

"Isn't it protected against that kind of attack?" Ariel asked.

Director Weaver gave her a most unsettling answer. "That's the theory."

"So you can see, Ariel," Jack Hale continued, "how important it is that Mills DeVane complete this mission. This new thing that his mission has become. We have to know where and how whatever Costain is selling Hoag is coming into the country. The best way to do that is to see that DeVane is the one bringing them in."

"They're SAMs," Kellerman told the group. "I'll lay money on it."

"Whatever it is," Director Weaver began, "we've put a lot into this operation. We've given DeVane added credibility by numbering the Most Wanted list —"

"That was why it was done," Ariel said, the realization hitting her hard. The realization and the irony. "And doing so might just have put him in jeopardy from Michaelangelo."

Director Weaver looked to each of the three agents with him, his gaze settling finally on Ariel. "I will not be the man who has to tell the President that airplanes are being shot out of American skies because a Bureau operation failed. I will not. Under no circumstances can we allow Mills DeVane to be captured inadvertently by our own people, compromised by inaction or incompetence, or killed by some lunatic who is out to right some wrong he sees us as having done to him by putting him last on the Most Wanted list. Is that understood?"

Hale and Kellerman nodded. Ariel verbalized her acknowledgment with, "Yes, sir."

Hale touched her on the arm to get her attention. "It's only by blind luck that you're involved in both cases. DeVane and Michaelangelo. That's fortunate for us, but it's going to be a heavy load for you."

Ariel coughed a shallow breath. "I'm one person."

"You're one person who's going to have to guard a secret and protect an asset," Kellerman told her. "Mills DeVane is that asset."

"The best course of action is to stop that lunatic and let DeVane complete his mission," Director Weaver said to the group. There could be no disagreement with that.

"Two things you're going to have to do, Ariel," Jack Hale said. "Without letting on why, you need to accelerate Task Force Ten to max speed."

"I don't run Task Force Ten," she reminded Hale.

"It's going to be difficult, I know, but Bernie Jaworski respects you, otherwise he wouldn't have forwarded your report to the director after having worked with you only a few days."

Director Weaver chimed in on this point. "Plus, if he becomes unable to carry out his duties . . ."

She knew what was being said, and she didn't want to hear it. Not even under these circumstances. "I can push from where I'm at. Special Agent Jaworski isn't going anywhere."

They were forceful words. Kellerman and Weaver both thought there might be command material in there, somewhere.

"What else do you need me to do?" Ariel asked Jack Hale.

"We need you to get to Mills DeVane and fill him in on the situation."

"We're going to try and keep Michaelangelo's dalliance to the Most Wanted list under wraps as long as we can," Kellerman said. He sounded less than sure of that possibility.

"I repeat my belief," Director Weaver began, "that stopping Michaelangelo, that focusing efforts on him, is the best way to resolve this situation without risking compromise of Mills DeVane."

"I agree, sir," Kellerman said. "But we have to be prepared for the instance that that might not happen fast enough. We need to get to DeVane and brief him on what we're doing to stay between him and Michaelangelo."

Ariel thought briefly. "Is he still using the classifieds?"

Hale shook his head. "He changed pattern right away. You won't be able to find him that way."

"There's his father," Kellerman suggested.

Jack Hale seemed to consider that for a moment before dismissing the possibility with a shake of his head. "DeVane said he'd pull out without hesitation if we ever involved his father."

"Do you know any other way, Jack?" Kellerman pressed him. Hale didn't.

"It's your call, Jack," Director Weaver said.

"It can't be me who tries to convince him," Hale said.

All eyes fell on Ariel. "How does his father know how to find him?"

Jack Hale was the one to answer her question. "When he began this operation, Mills DeVane had one condition. Only one. That he be able to keep some connection to his old life. To his true self. His father."

"How does he stay in contact?" Ariel asked.

"He used to do it through the *Atlanta Journal*'s classifieds," Hale explained.

"The motels," Ariel said, and Hale nodded.

"His father is precious to him, Ariel. Putting him at risk could make DeVane give it up. So you have to be careful."

"And you should probably hurry," Kellerman said.

"Why?"

"Because Lee Tran, the number eight man on the list, his lawyer went missing late last night."

"He's killing his way up the list." Director Weaver shook his head at those with him. "If he gets Tran, that only leaves two between him and DeVane."

It was a sobering thought. But it was not what Ariel was going to let herself dwell on. She turned to Jack Hale. "How do I get in touch with his father?"

Arlo Donovan looked through the peephole after the knock on the door. All he saw was newsprint, and, as that came down, the smiling face of his boy.

He opened the door and had his arms around Mills before he was all the way in.

"God, God, God, I had a scare when you didn't show up the other night," Arlo said, clutching his son tight, hands spread across his back, holding him there, just holding him, not wanting to ever let him go again. Wanting to entertain that impossibility as long as he could. "I didn't know what had happened."

"I got warned off, Pop," Mills told him.

Arlo released the hug and held his boy's face in his hands. "Warned off. By who?"

"Probably Jack Hale," Mills told him.

Arlo Donovan did not want to afford much thanks to Jack Hale. Did not want to think much about him at all, and so he would not. "I'm just glad you're here. That you're okay."

"So am I," Mills said, though one day he would ask Jack Hale just why he'd let his agents get so close. And how had they in the first place? "You feeling good, Pop?"

Arlo let go his son's face and sat himself on the bed. Mills sat next to him. "I'm good. Just fine. How are you?"

Mills nodded and managed a smile. "I'm hanging in there."

Arlo studied his son's face. "How much longer you gonna have to hang in there, Sonny?"

"Not long, I think," Mills said. His father noticed no joy, no relief in his son's answer.

"Yeah. Well, that's good. Not much longer." Arlo stood from his place on the edge of the full-size bed and walked to room 124's small, round table. He already had two chairs pulled up to it. Already had the deck of cards shuffled and cut. But he neither sat nor paid attention to the cards. He simply stood there with his back to his son, to his boy whom he could not call by name, and fiddled with the buttons on the front of his sweater.

Mills could only stand to watch it for a few seconds before his heart began to break. He stood and came up behind his father, putting a hand on his shoulder. "Pop . . ."

"Not much longer," Arlo Donovan told his son before stepping away to the other side of the table. There he stood behind the chair he'd placed for himself. "Soon no more newspaper ads, and precautions, and . . ." He put his hands up and smiled at his son with wet eyes. "It'll just be over soon. Soon."

Mills nodded. He could not smile.

After a moment, Arlo Donovan was able to compose himself, sniffling the threat of tears away and sitting himself down at the table. Things would be fine. It would all be over soon. Soon. He reached for the cards and began to shuffle them.

"Did you have any trouble with the new paper, Pop?" Mills asked his father.

"Nah. Just like we planned it. One paper don't work no more, switch to the next. No trouble." The cards slipped from his hands and he hurriedly tried to gather them up.

"Let me get those, Pop," Mills said, and took his own seat. His hands found his father's and he eased the jumbled cards from them. "I'll shuffle."

Arlo Donovan put his hands to his lap and watched his son put a mix on the cards just as he'd shown him when he was twelve. Fast and smooth, the boy had the touch, didn't he?

"Pretty good, Pop, eh?"

"You always did remember the important lessons," Arlo Donovan said, drawing a chuckle from his son.

Mills fanned the cards one way, then another, and his father applauded.

"What's your game gonna be, Father old boy, old chum, old pal?"

Arlo held up a full hand, fingers spread.

"Stud or draw?" Mills inquired.

"Stud is for imbeciles."

"Stud it is," Mills said, and began to deal the cards. They would play for hours. And they would laugh. And they would pretend they had forgotten that it was all going to end.

8

[THE FIX]

Arlo Donovan stood with hands on hips at the front of his
'85 Reliant K and frowned at the uncooperative engine.
His back to the street, he never saw the woman approach
through the open garage door.

"Mr. Donovan?"

Arlo spun quickly around. She had that official sound
to her voice. To him "official" could mean nothing good.

This Monday evening he wasn't far wrong in that belief.

"What? Who are you?"

Ariel approached him and pulled back the left side of
her blazer. Her Bureau shield was clipped to her belt.

Arlo's eyes flared upon seeing it. "Wha— What are
you —"

"He's all right, sir," Ariel said, sensing his worry,
though she also realized that she was not being truthful.
He might not be all right. She had no way of knowing.
Which was a problem she was here to fix. "As far as I
know, everything is fine, sir."

Arlo backed warily away from her, down the rust-
stained side of his vehicle. A plane descending toward
Charlotte International roared low overhead. Ariel waited
for the sound to fade but did not advance. "Who's all
right? Who are you talking about?"

"You know who I'm talking about," Ariel said. His

backward progress was stopped by a pile of boxes marked in childish script "x-mas decorashuns." "Jack Hale told me where to find you."

His head cocked quizzically to one side. "I don't . . ."

Ariel came closer now. "I'm here about your son, Mr. Donovan. He could be in great danger, and I need to get to him."

"I don't know who you're —"

"Mills, sir," she said. "I'm here about Mills."

His hand reached over toward the door to the house and pressed a button on the wall. The garage door tipped slowly down, locking in place with a thud, closing them off from the street.

"Who are you?" Arlo Donovan demanded. "How do you know about my son?"

"My name is Ariel Grace," she said, stepping right up to him now and showing her Bureau ID. "Jack Hale sent me."

"He wouldn't do that. Ted — Mills told him that I was not to be contacted."

"Something's happened, sir," Ariel told him, slipping her ID back inside her blazer. "Something extraordinary that makes it necessary that we contact your son."

Arlo Donovan rubbed his hand over his head and walked past her, his fingers kneading the back of his neck. He stopped and stood at the front of his car, thinking.

Thinking.

"What kind of danger?" he asked her.

"It's better you don't know."

He shook his head as he looked at her. "I can't believe you people."

Ariel approached him again, but he moved around the car. He looked at her across the Reliant K's open engine compartment.

"I need your help, Mr. Donovan. I need your help because I need to help your son."

"How can you help Teddy . . . Mills?" He stopped there, tripped up by words. By a name. He balled a fist and held it before himself as if to strike, to strike something, anything, was his wish, his most fervent desire right then. "Damnit, I don't even know who he is or what I should . . ."

"Sir, he needs my help."

Arlo Donovan relaxed his fist and nodded his head derisively. "All anybody from the FBI has ever done is push him in deeper. A little farther. Go a little bit more, Mills." His angry eyes began to glisten. "He's my Teddy. My son. He's not Mills DeVane. He's Teddy Donovan."

Obviously it was hard for this man, but the operation was important. What she'd heard from the director and assistant director made that clear. "Sir, he volunteered for this. He was qualified. His situation was right. His —"

"His situation?" Donovan said, nodding sharply, angrily. "They told you about his situation, did they, that Jack Hale and his bunch? What was his situation that they told you about, Ms. Grace?"

"Experienced pilot. Not married. No children."

Donovan shook his head and sniffed back tears. "Ms. Grace, he *was* married."

Her expression asked *What?*

"He had a wife, Ms. Grace. A beautiful wife. A good woman." Memory choked his words briefly. "They would have had a family. I would have had grandchildren. He would have . . . would have . . ."

Something stirred in her chest. It was warm and sour, like the prelude to sickness. It wasn't a lie what they had told her about this man's son, but it also was not the truth.

Arlo Donovan composed himself after a moment. "She died, Ms. Grace. Died in a stupid accident. And my . . . my Teddy, his world was gone. He was devastated. He had nothing." And the sorrow that had tinged the man's expression changed right then. Changed as though something inside, deep inside him, had been set to burn. Smoldering hate fanned to full flame by the winds of memory. "And you know what Jack Hale and his bunch did? They said, 'Here, Teddy, give yourself over to a mission. Engross yourself in *this* mission. Focus on *your* mission.'" Tears flowed now down Arlo Donovan's aging face. Tears of loss, tears of anger. "He lost his wife, the light of his life, and they gave him a *mission*." What came next Arlo Donovan practically growled. "And they knew he'd take it! They knew he'd give himself over to their mission if for no other reason than he might die carrying it out."

"But he didn't, sir," Ariel reminded him. Reminded the father about his son. She had to try and get this on track. She had a mission, too, and though this man did not want to trust her, he would have to. Would have to if he wanted to protect his son. His Teddy. "And I don't want him to. I know you don't. I have to talk to him to see that that doesn't happen."

Arlo Donovan reached up and rested his hands on the open hood of his car, his head hanging. Teardrops spattered on the fender's old paint.

"Help me, sir," Ariel repeated. "I wouldn't be here if it wasn't imperative."

He slammed the hood down suddenly and looked up at her, his pained eyes raging. "What's imperative is that I get my son back! MY SON TEDDY!" He clutched his hands to his head as if in agony. "My, God, I just want to be able to call him that again. I just want to be able to call him by name. I don't want to pretend that he's someone named Mills DeVane. That's not his name. His name is Teddy Donovan! That's important. It's who he is."

He stopped and half collapsed forward to the cold steel hood, his hands planted wide for support.

"Sir, please . . ."

"This has to end, Ms. Grace. My son said it would be over soon. It has to be."

"I want to help him get back to you," she said. "The only way I can do that is to protect him."

"From what, Ms. Grace? From what?"

She thought "what" was the proper term, but she could not explain that to Arlo Donovan, grieving father. Grieving for a son not dead. For a son she did not want to see end up dead.

"I wish I could tell you, sir, but just believe me that he could be in danger."

"He's always in danger, Ms. Grace."

"He could be in more now. Much more."

Arlo Donovan looked at her. At this new person. She seemed unlike Jack Hale. Unlike any of his kind. The suits, the functionaries, the "rules of engagement" types. Unlike them, yes. She seemed a human being.

"Please, sir, help me."

He wiped his eyes on the sleeve of his sweater. "I don't know where he is."

Her shoulders sagged.

"But I will, soon. I will soon."

She looked at him and smiled a thank-you. He came around and walked past her, opening the garage door as he went in the house.

She left her card on the hood of his car and trotted back to hers. When she looked back toward Arlo Donovan's house from behind the wheel of her rental, she could see him back in the garage, taking her card in hand and slipping it in his shirt pocket.

Her agency quoted him two hundred dollars. When Passion got there she wanted an extra hundred to take off her clothes. Another hundred for sex. She took off her top and took her purse to the bathroom to pee and lube up.

When she came back out, the room was almost black.

"Hey, what gives?"

"I like the dark," the man said from the direction of the room's queen-size bed. Passion smiled in the dark and walked that way. Her feet kicked his piled clothes. He was already naked and under the covers. This boy was ready.

She kicked off her shoes and stepped out of her jeans and slipped into bed with him. Her bare leg went over his and rubbed up and down. Her hand went to his chest and plowed through its fur. She put her face close to his and said, "How come you want me naked if you can't see me?"

"I can feel you."

"That's for sure, baby," she agreed, and nuzzled her knee up toward his crotch. He breathed deep as her skin slid over him. There. Over him there. "Ooh, baby, we gotta get you more excited than *that*."

He sucked another breath slow and let his fingers trace up her back to the back of her neck. Into her hair. Over her ear. To her cheek. Her face. Her mouth. She sucked his thumb between her lips and worked him with her leg. He was not getting hard. She scooted over, halfway on top of him, and let the soft skin of her inner thigh caress his crotch. After a minute of that, with his breaths coming faster, his condition had still not improved. Her hand began to slide up his leg and over his thigh.

"Ride me," he said, and grabbed her hand, stopping its advance and pulling her atop him.

"But you . . ."

"Ride me," he repeated, and *helped* her to straddle him.

"Okay," she said, astride him now in the dark, just a faint glow upon the motel room's heavy drapes. She wished she'd left the bathroom light on as he began to move beneath her.

"Yes. Yes. Ride me. *Riiiide* me."

She thrust herself on him, the sheet bunched around her ass now, feeling him under her but not in her. He was still not hard. But he was panting, and moaning, and moving like the fire was building in him.

"Baby, go, baby, go, yeah, yeah, baby, go . . ."

He was driving himself up to her, but she couldn't feel him there.

"God. God. Yes. God."

His hands reached up and grabbed her breasts, squeezing them, mashing them, pinching her nipples, making them hard. Harder even than he.

"Baby-where-are-you?" Passion asked him, her breathing stuttered. Though he wasn't inside her, the motion was working her. "Where-are-you?"

"I'm almost . . . almost there."

His grip bore down on her tits. Painfully down.

"Hey . . ."

"Shut up and ride me . . ."

She swung her hand at him, swatting at his hands, his fists that were hurting her. Hurting her perfect 36Cs. "I don't do pain."

•

"Do *meeee*."

He bucked beneath her and held her on him. "Do me. Do me. Close. Close. . . ."

"STOP IT!" she yelled, and swung at his face, making contact with the palm of her hand with a loud *slap*.

"Bitch!"

She twisted herself off of him, off of the bed, and fell to the floor. She heard him move, saw his darkness come up before the drapes, and she scrambled for the light switch, finding it on the second try. When the darkness fell away she saw him upright on the bed, sitting there, the covers down at his feet. He was exposed.

She looked between his legs.

"Oh, my God!"

She grabbed her clothes from the floor and backed away from him. Backed toward the door.

She stepped into her shoes, one by the dresser, the other by the TV, and went for the door.

"Please . . ." he implored her, sadness in his face.

But she was gone. Out the door, which slammed behind her. Gone with his money.

Gone with the moment. The release.

He would have to be selfish. He had not wanted to be selfish. He had wanted her. But she had not wanted him.

It was not her fault. It was not his fault.

He slipped his hand under the sheet and closed his eyes.

He felt himself. He tingled. He began to cry.

They had paid. He shouldn't feel this way. But he did.

He might have to revisit their trespasses.

But a larger wrong had been done him. A different wrong. That was the path he was on now. He had been *insulted*. He had been *degraded*.

The whore had been . . . surprised. She had not insulted. She had not degraded. If she had . . .

Already the next one was waiting. Still and quiet in a napoxcypherin haze. Breathing. Fearing. Ready to be made into something more beautiful. Something *of* him. *By* him.

The next day. Tuesday. In the evening, possibly. He had things to get. Things to do. He had to prepare. It had to be *right*.

Yes, right.

The whore had been unable to, but Mickey Strange could feel himself stiffening. It was her loss. Her loss.

He thought of tomorrow. He thought of tomorrow. He worked himself and thought of tomorrow.

When he came he shoved his fist into his mouth and screamed against it.

That gave him ideas.

An ocean and half a sea away, a call was being placed.

Valentin Gryoko sat in a wide chair in the grand parlor of the colonial-era house in Tunis sipping hazelnut liqueur and waiting for the satellite phone to ring through. In between sips he slipped slivers of pickled turnip into his mouth. Bitter meeting sweet. Food like life. He almost sighed.

From where he sat presently he could see the soft waters of the Mediterranean lapping at the shore, and it made him think how far he'd come in so short a time. Ten of his fifty years he considered a small enough span, for it seemed only the day before the day before yesterday that instead of warm breezes and cool waters his life was one of snow and ice and endless reports to the *apparatchiks* in Moscow. A colonel then, he had served the Motherland for half his life. Had fought the mongrel Afghans. The petulant Chinese at their border. Would have fought the Americans if it had come to that, but then thankfully it had not. Thankfully, because from America he was gaining his riches. Other lands as well, but presently it was Yankee Doodle and Uncle Sam who were keeping him in silk sheets and easily impressed women.

But the money, and the things that came of the money, would not be his if it were not for his past in climes so godforsaken he often wondered what the Great Mother Russia wanted with them. In those conditions, those testing and trying times where true civilization was thousands of miles across the wastes, he had come to know many men. Know them well. Know them true. He remembered them. And some remembered him.

The call rang through finally and was answered in an office high above Mozhinskiy Prospekt outside of Moscow proper. A secretary asked Valentin to wait. He rested his petite liqueur glass on the bulge of his stomach and watched a pair of birds skim above the water. He smiled to himself with the cold, Russian static in his ear.

"Valentin?" a voice said, breaking the hollow wash of electric noise. "Valentin Yevgenovich?"

"Pavel Yurievich," Gryoko said, nodding to the phone. "How long has it been?"

"Too long, you fat bastard!"

The two men laughed. A half-dozen years melted away in that burst of joviality.

"I am warm, Pavel. Are you freezing your ass off?"

"Among other things." A quiet pause, and then: "Is that water I hear? Water moving? Not frozen?"

"Your rivers aren't frozen yet," Gryoko told him.

"Today. A month from today. Does it matter? You are at the ocean, aren't you?"

"I'm tanning. Ha!"

"Hmmmm," Pavel grunted. "It is too good for you."

"Too good for both of us," Gryoko said. "But I am not complaining."

"I would not either. So, Valentin, what brings you to call me from warmer places?"

"You are still involved with matters of intelligence?"

"It is the intelligence *business* now, my friend."

Gryoko nodded at the water. Some might call it the

intelligence racket. But never the intelligence game. It had never been that. Would never be that. The stakes were too serious. Lives could depend upon it. Or, as in this case, a single life. "I am pleased to hear that."

"So this is a business call, my friend?"

Pavel understood well, Gryoko knew. His KGB days weren't so far gone. "I propose a transaction, Pavel. You still have your contacts?"

"Many."

"Good," Gryoko said, and lifted the picture from where it had rested on the table beside his chair. It was clear and crisp. His man had used top-quality equipment, and had waited until the American was facing almost into the sun. From a grove of date palms he had taken it, just as the American emerged from the shack. He had been happy then, Gryoko recalled. Smiling. But his man with the camera had wisely captured the image of Mills DeVane sans smile. That was good. In military identity-card photos one rarely smiled. "There is a man I want you to investigate. An American. I am going to transmit you a picture very soon."

"Very good. What do you know about him?"

"He says he was once an officer in the American Air Force." Gryoko heard his old friend scribbling notes over the remarkably clear connection.

"Is this man a problem to you?"

Gryoko stared at the picture. "That is what you are going to tell me."

The Royal Pet Center in Baton Rouge closed at nine every Monday evening. The phone rang at three minutes 'til.

"Royal Pets," the clerk on duty answered. She listened to the caller. Nodding. Then her whole face frowned. "Yeah, we have rats, but what do you need to know?" She listened further, and the caller seemed to repeat the same question. Her unsoured expression made that seem clear. "We feed them in the morning."

She listened. "Only in the morning."

She listened again. "We don't feed them after that."

She listened still more. "Yeah, you can probably feed them tomorrow night if you buy them in the morning."

And listened. "We feed them at ten."

Listened. "We open at nine."

The caller said he'd be in at nine-thirty and hung up.

10

[ORIFICE]

Donald Jackson, Esq., deceased, had had some good suggestions, and the previous day outside a smoke shop in the French Quarter, Lee Tran had made himself visible. That was his only mistake, exceeding his allowance by one.

And now he lay on a board stretched between two sawhorses, hands tied above his head at one end, feet to the other. Only his boxers covered him. A shred of his T-shirt was shoved in his mouth. He gurgled and screamed against it now, finally able to do so after long hours where he could do not a thing. Just listen to his heart beat and feel his chest fall and rise. And wait. Wait for the madman who'd jumped him going out the back of a bar.

But that madman had come back. Stood over him now, actually, next to the bare bulb that burned from the center of the ceiling in the oddly shaped room. Long and thin. Concrete walls. A roll-up door. Lee Tran's panicked eyes tracked all over the room so that he would not have to look at the madman.

But the madman made him.

"You are not worthy," Michaelangelo told him, and Lee Tran's small, dark eyes bugged in terror. He thrashed against his bindings. Tried to spit the gag out. None of these were successful endeavors. "But I will make you worthy through creation."

The board rocked atop the sawhorses. Lee Tran began to weep.

Michaelangelo lifted a small bowl from the floor, shiny metal and deep, and placed it on Lee Tran's bucking stomach. Tested it there. Centered it, then pulled it away. Lee Tran stilled for a moment, and that was when he heard the squealing. Tiny animal squealing.

Michaelangelo brought the bowl up again and there were large, gray rats clawing at the lip, desperate to escape. He wondered if they knew something. Stilled by shock, Lee Tran did not react immediately when the bowl was flipped and put upside down on his abdomen in one quick motion.

He felt the rats' spiky claws skitter about his navel and was then screaming again into the gag. Screaming and bucking.

Michaelangelo pressed it down, held it in place until he could get the metal tape looped over it and Lee Tran and the board. Several times he worked the shiny adhesive strip around, locking the bowl and the rats trapped within in place. In vain, Lee Tran tried to shake them off. Tried all that he could to get the rats off of him. After a few minutes, he was sweating and wearing down.

That was when Michaelangelo raised the propane torch from where it had sat on the hard floor and flicked it to life. A jet of blue misery fired from its end. Michaelangelo adjusted it. Lee Tran stared at it.

"Heretics were dealt with in this fashion," Michaelangelo said. He twisted the propane bottle and torch this way and that, making the blue flame dance in the dim light. "The procedure was known as the cauldron."

Lee Tran shook his head at the flame. Michaelangelo wondered if he knew what was about to happen. Or if he was just afraid of fire.

He lowered the blue flame to the bowl and began to work it around. Lee Tran screamed. Michaelangelo held him somewhat still with his free hand.

"You'll feel them in a minute."

He was right sooner than expected.

Lee Tran stopped his thrashing very suddenly and raised his head to look at the bowl fixed securely to his abdomen. Little gray paws and claws were trying to slip between the bowl and his skin, but the space was not big enough for escape. There was nowhere for them to go as their makeshift prison heated up.

Except, of course, there was.

"It's the creation that is art's glory," Michaelangelo said, just as Lee Tran felt the first rat start to gnaw through the skin of his abdomen. His cries against the pain, the agony rising, beat against the gag, but could not dislodge it. "The 'after' is the piece. It's the 'during' that determines greatness."

There were five small rats trapped in the upturned bowl, and the world that was theirs at the moment was setting to burn. As blue flame washed over the bowl's silvery surface, it began to change, to glow, to shift between glorious blacks and blues and reds, and within the confines of its miniature hell the rats were driven to frenzy. By the heat, the smell, the sound, the *pain*. They had to get out.

And out meant down.

Out meant *through*.

11

[BLINDMAN'S BLUFF]

Mills looked back over his shoulder to what Ricardo's crew in Medellín had loaded and thought Gareth must be truly desperate.

One hundred pounds. That was what Gareth had sent him down for. That was *all* Gareth had sent him down for. A hundred lousy pounds of cocaine. Mills shook his head and looked back out the Cessna's windscreen.

The sun was a thin line of blue far off to his right on the eastern horizon. Wednesday had come. Another day. Just another day.

Tomorrow would come, too, he knew. And the day after that. And the day after that. One by one by one the days would come and time would pass and he would get closer, and closer, and closer to being done with this life. Soon. As he had told his pop, had promised his pop, it would be soon.

But it would never be soon enough.

He put his sunglasses on as a spark of yellow rose above the eastern horizon. Some distance ahead there was weather to think of. He was nearing the southern coast of Louisiana. There would be air traffic to deal with. Radars were beginning to paint him. He must be conscious of those. So much to do. So much to occupy him. Being busy was good.

But not always.

"Cessna Three Three Niner Papa Edward, respond."

He heard the radio call in his headset and looked quickly out the left-side window. Nothing abeam or behind. And out the right-side window next to see if—

"Damn," Mills swore when he saw the blue-and-white Citation shadowing him above and slightly to the east. He didn't need to be close enough to see the seal on its side to know it was a Customs interdictor. Fast, maneuverable, and on him like a hawk.

Shit. How long has he been there?

"Cessna aircraft displaying tail number Three Three Niner Papa Edward, a response is demanded. This is Tango Alpha Seven, United States Customs Service."

Damn. Fuck. Fuck. Fuck and damn. He was ten minutes from the coast, just ten fucking minutes! And this! He thought. Ran through his head what they'd be doing right now. They were close enough in that the crew would be calling in the cavalry, probably a pair of UH-60 Blackhawk helicopters, fast and maneuverable and loaded with men with guns. Lots of men with guns. Men with guns who could be on top of him before he stopped his rollout—assuming he made it down in one piece.

"Shit!" Mills swore once more, and gave the Citation another glance. Then he turned his attention ahead. The Shell Keys were beginning to shimmer under the day's new light. Beyond them, though, Marsh Island was just a ghost of its fog-shrouded self. He would have to get down. Down and fast. Lost in the soup before the Blackhawks could get on him. If he could lose the Citation—correction, make *it* lose *him*—then he had a shot at getting out of this. A shot.

"Cessna Three Three Niner Papa Edward, this is you —"

Mills shut the radio off and fire-walled the throttles, pointing his aircraft at the water between the Shell Keys and Marsh Island. He had to break their visual on him. Then he could worry about their radar.

• • •

"There he goes," Tango Alpha Seven's pilot commented as the Cessna 402 just ahead and below him to port began to dive. "Are the tac teams airborne?"

In the seat behind him, the communications officer keyed his intercom. "Be on him in ten."

"All right, let's watch this guy," the pilot said and put his plane in a slight dive. "He's heading for the clouds."

"Good luck," the right-seater wished the pilot of the Cessna, though he doubted luck was going to help him any. Luck *or* clouds, not with the picture they had of him on the cockpit radar screen. And he couldn't outrun that, or outsmart it. No, the radar unit humming away in the nose of their bird was just about as good as what the military used, and to his way of thinking, that was plenty good enough to bag them a twin-engine Cessna with a drug-running scum at the stick. Oh yeah.

Two thousand feet, nineteen hundred feet. . . . Mills watched the altimeter spin down. At a thousand feet he began to level off. By six hundred he was wings level just shy of Marsh Island. He took a quick look back and saw the Citation disappear as he flew into the clouds.

When he looked back to the front, the world was a wall of white. He was flying blind.

Almost blind. He had nav beacons along the coast and inland, and he knew the altitude of obstacles he'd be encountering on the far side of Weeks Bay. Still, this was not the way he liked to fly. He didn't know many pilots who preferred zero visibility to fifty miles blue and bright. At least no civilian pilots. Then again, he was not truly a civilian pilot. Hadn't been trained as one. And he was about to put those old skills to use.

"Whoa, where's he going?" the right-seater asked aloud. Their quarry had just made a right turn. A sharp right turn to — "He's cutting across! Across!"

Tango Alpha Seven's pilot pulled his aircraft up, giving the lunatic they were chasing plenty of room. He was still a good five hundred feet below them, but he was not taking any chances. Not with some fool who would fly across his front.

"He's off radar," the right-seater said. "He got behind us."

"Not for long," the pilot said, and began a tight turn to the right.

Five hundred feet above Weeks Bay, pulling as tight a turn as the Cessna 402 could at top speed, Mills was about to put his faith in Nico Trane's little "extra." Upgraded avionics and radios, superior night-vision gear—none of that would help him right now. All were part of the normal equipment complement that Mills had turned to the top flight system's mechanic for on all his planes. But now, considering the spot he was in, and Nico's assertion that his addition might come in handy, Mills was beginning to think that beyond being one hell of a grease monkey, Nico might also be a pretty fair psychic at that.

"Maybe we'll see about a pardon for you, Nico," Mills said, and pressed the first of four small release plungers the prescient mechanic had installed on the throttle hump. A *click* and a *whoosh* emanated from the extreme aft of the Cessna and, without seeing a thing, he could just imagine the thousands of thin Mylar strips clouding the air in his wake.

The right-seater saw it first. Actually, didn't see it first. The "it" being the Cessna 402 that had been clear on their radar screen just a few seconds before. Now the whole damn electronic picture was a dazzle of electronic noise.

"What the . . .?"

Tango Alpha Seven's pilot glanced at the screen. He

needed no more than that to see what had happened. He was pissed . . . and more than a little impressed. "Chaff."

"Chaff?" the right-seater asked, incredulous. Not that he needed explanation what chaff was. He had four years in the Air Force in his past, crewing on transports mostly, but he had not been so removed from potential combat situations that he wasn't aware of the effect thousands of thin foil-like strips cast into the air could have on radar. It was the effect he was seeing now. But . . .

. . . where the hell did this guy get chaff?

"Anything?" the pilot asked, less than hopeful in his query.

"Yeah," the right-seater answered, adjusting his controls frantically. "A whole lotta nothing."

Tango Alpha Seven's pilot shook his head and started bringing the Citation's nose up. There was no way he was going to stay on the tail of this guy, not when he couldn't see him, visually or electronically. "We're off him."

The right-seater looked to his pilot. "Let me work this."

"That's not a military set," the pilot reminded him. If it had been, they might have been able to defeat the unexpected countermeasures from the Cessna. But it wasn't. And there was no way they were gonna make it so. "We're off this guy, okay?"

The right-seater thumped the map strapped to his flight suit's leg and shook his head at the soup outside the windscreen. He made a little wish that their well-equipped quarry out there somewhere would fly himself into the side of a lonely old mountain someday. Or worse.

12

[THE DEAD AND THE DYING]

Unit 12, Redy Stor, Baton Rouge, Louisiana. The door of the long and narrow unit was up. It had been that way when the night manager did a drive-through of the facility at six that morning.

Special Agent Ariel Grace stood just outside the unit staring in. The light differential made seeing difficult. But she could see enough. Almost too much.

Jaworski came out of Unit 12, lifting the yellow tape to pass under. A forensic team from the local field office remained inside.

"Art," Jaworski commented to Ariel. He glanced back in at Lee Tran, suspended upside down from a ceiling beam, hands bonded to the concrete floor as if doing a handstand. A headless handstand. His gut was hollowed out and his severed head stuffed in there, facing out, and it seemed to Jaworski at least that the young and very dead fugitive was smiling at him. Some glue to the cheeks he thought likely.

"He has boxers on," Ariel said.

Jaworski knew where she was going. "No mutilation. That makes two now." Though boned and folded in a neat, naked package, Francis Gunther had retained his penis.

"These are different to him," Ariel said.

"We know that, Grace," Jaworski said with some shortness. He put a hand to his temple and rubbed. The early call, the hurry-up flight, the thought of another meeting with his doctors the next morning. The combination had given him a grade-A pounder. Either that or he now had a brain tumor, and wouldn't that be just his luck. "Ignore me. I'm mad at the world."

Ariel was herself right then, looking in at Lee Tran's grotesque acrobatic positioning. Mad at a little part of it, anyway. Whatever part had created the monster that was doing this.

"Has his attorney been found yet?" Ariel asked.

Jaworski brought his hand down and shook his head.

"Prints in there?" she asked further.

"Plenty." He had seen some himself, bright in blood. "Walls, floor, Tran."

"Why couldn't he just have gotten in a bar fight once," Ariel said wishfully. "Gotten busted, printed."

"He's a good citizen," Jaworski said. "That Gacy freak was a clown at kids' parties, for Christ's sake. Maybe ours is president of his lodge in his spare time."

Ariel looked hard at Michaelangelo's ghastly creation and doubted that. "I don't think he has spare time, sir. He works at this. He *thinks* about it. All the time."

Jaworski turned away from Unit 12. "Then we're even, 'cause I can't get this bastard out of my head either. Come on."

There was not much left for them to do in Baton Rouge. They'd come to confirm the obvious. To examine the scene. It had turned out like all the others. Plenty of evidence with connections to no one. Yet. That's what Jaworski told himself. Had told himself with every new death. And here he did the same. Maybe the forensic team would find something different. Maybe a witness would turn up. Maybe.

But he didn't think so.

"Damn," Ariel commented as they rounded the corner of the building and saw the main entrance to Redy Stor.

There had been a few reporters there when they'd arrived two hours before. Now there were dozens. Even a truck with a dish.

"Washington wanted to keep this quiet?" Jaworski said as he and Ariel neared the crush of print and electronic media. "Good luck."

Two police officers lifted the yellow tape at the entrance and let the agents pass into the pack of reporters.

"What's your name?" one reporter with a mike demanded.

"Is the victim Lee Tran?" another asked. "Sources tell us it's him? Is he dead?"

Jaworski and Ariel pressed their way through until a quick and determined reporter stepped fast in front of them and put her mike in their faces.

"I'm Stephanie Young, and we're live on YourNews. Could you tell us what's going on in there?"

They kept moving, hot lights hitting Jaworski now. Hot lights and thoughts of what it would look like to have two agents playing dumb on television. Not good. He thought he could say something.

"Nothing we can talk about right now," he said. Sweat was sprouting on his brow.

"Well, then, who are you, sir?"

The lights glared at him. Ariel was behind, following, keeping her mouth shut.

"What is your name, sir?" the reporter persisted.

The pack was around them now, moving with them. They wanted something. Jaworski wiped his brow.

"I'm Special Agent Bernard Jaworski, Federal Bureau of Investigation."

The reporter's free hand went suddenly to her ear. Someone from the station was talking to her. Her eyes brightened fast and she pressed the mike closer to his face.

"Are you the same Bernard Jaworski running the FBI's Task Force Ten?" she asked. "The one looking for Michaelangelo?"

Jaworski looked back to Ariel as they neared the street. His pale skin was flushing. His look told her the gig was up.

"Does Michaelangelo have something to do with this?" the reporter said.

Another chimed in, "Francis Gunther, the one in Minnesota, was Michaelangelo involved in that? Did he kill Gunther?"

"Is he going after people on the Most Wanted list?" another shouted.

Ariel and Jaworski got past the pack and to their car at the curb. Questions flew at them even after they were in and driving away, wondering if they'd done more harm than good by coming to Louisiana.

He was down. Safe. On the ground at the end of a little-used unmaintained strip in the south of Georgia. Three shots of chaff had taken care of the Customs plane. It would take more than three shots of something to fix Mills DeVane right then.

He leaned forward after rolling to a bumpy stop. Put his head to the console. Laced his fingers behind his neck. Squeezed hard. And harder. And harder still. Then exploded and sat straight and punched the padded cowling over the console. His fist thudded off of it, aching sharply. He tore the sunglasses from his face and tossed them aside, covering his eyes with his undamaged hand.

"Damn," he said with surprising softness. "Damn, damn, damn."

That had been too close. Too close. But for Nico's little extra he'd be in cuffs right now, his ordeal over, the operation a failure.

People might die because of him.

He shook his head and wished it done. Wished it over and done.

But wishes, he knew, could not overcome the impossible. It they could, he'd have a wife again. Would have her again a thousand times over.

The rap on his side window startled him. Looking in, kneeling on the wing, was Nita Berry. Gareth's Wagoneer was parked a few yards away with no sign of Gareth.

Mills came out of the cockpit to the rear of the Cessna and opened the bifold aft door. He crouched in the opening as Nita slid off the wing and came to him.

"Hey, Millsy, you okay?"

He nodded weakly. "Not a good flight. Customs is getting better at what they do."

She frowned with concern and glanced up at the sky. The cloud cover was beginning to break. "How close did they get?"

"Close enough to get the tail number and too good of a look."

She knew what that meant. "We'll have to burn it."

Mills nodded. One flight—then gone. Gareth was going to love that. Speaking of Gareth . . .

"Where is he?" Mills asked Nita. He handed her one of the two bags from the plane and climbed out with the other one himself.

"He and Lionel are doing something," Nita said, and heaved the bag away from the Cessna. Mills did the same.

"What kind of something?"

Nita seemed not to want to answer. She jogged back to the Wagoneer and, after a few seconds, returned with a pair of road flares. She lit them both, holding one in each hand.

"Nita . . ."

"Gareth doesn't want you to know," she said, and tossed the flares inside the Cessna's open cabin. Acrid smoke began to billow out. Mills and Nita grabbed the bags of coke and walked fast toward the Wagoneer.

"What's he doing?" Mills pressed her, but she wouldn't say a thing. Not as they tossed the bags in the Wagoneer. Not as they drove off with the Cessna's fuel tanks cooking off in balls of orange-black flame.

Tommy Manchester had been on the job for one year exactly when the masked man jumped from a car and put a gun to his head. He thought of reaching for his own weapon, but the robber's forceful nudge convinced him otherwise. The next second it mattered not at all, as a second man took the revolver from his holster and tossed it to the ground.

"Open it up!" the second man, also masked, demanded as he and his partner dragged the unlucky armored-car guard to the front of the vehicle where his partner inside could see him. The driver's eyes bugged with fright at the sight of his coworker with a pistol to his head. That was the intent.

"Open it the fuck up! Now!" the second man shouted. He adjusted his aim and pressed Tommy Manchester's face to the bulletproof side window, just inches from the driver safe inside. "Open it up or I'll splatter his face all over this window! We'll see how you sleep with that!"

Tommy Manchester said nothing. He didn't have to. His eyes said all that was necessary, and his friend gave a quick nod to the demands. The door clicked open. People on the streets in front of the National Trust Bank of Augusta were scattering.

The first man yanked Tommy back from the door as the second man pulled it open and yanked the driver out, disarming him quickly. Both guards were forced to lie facedown on the warming asphalt while the second man hit the control to release the back door.

That was when the first man shot both guards in the

back. Their bodies jumped. People screamed. Tommy Manchester rolled to his side in a ball and groaned. The first man shot him again and he stopped making sounds.

"Come on," the second man said, and they went to the back of the armored truck. Each took what they could carry while still holding their pistols. They had time only for one trip. Sirens were rising. They went to the car they'd stopped abruptly beside the armored car and tossed their take in the backseat as they got in the front.

Pulling away, they almost ran over Tommy Manchester where he lay dying next to his already dead partner.

13

[UNSPOKEN ACTIONS]

Jaworski stood before his assembled task force on Friday the 22nd in Base Ten's bullpen work area. It had been his newest agent's suggestion that they brief the task force en masse. Focus them.

Assistant Director Kellerman had called soon after offering a similar viewpoint.

Interesting, Jaworski thought, wondering why Washington would open a back door into his investigation. He also wondered if that was why Grace had been sent to him in the first place.

Either thing might have upset him, but this day it would not. No, it would not.

"Task Force Seven has had several reports over the past week and a half that Robert Jack McCormack is in the New Jersey area," Jaworski told his team, most of whom leaned against desks or stood as they listened. Ariel sat in a chair a few feet from Jaworski. Every so often he'd look down her way. "Sightings have put him in Vineland and Camden. His family and the last public defender to represent him are under surveillance for the purpose of protection. We know how our freak is operating now, going after family and people with ties to the fugitives, so by choking off that avenue we might force little Mikey to make a stupid move. Maybe stupid enough that we can catch him." Jaworski shot a glance at Ariel. "Agent Grace and I will be taking two teams to New Jersey to back up Task Force Seven. Rudy Kingman runs that show, so we'll be technically supporting their ops. Unless our freak makes an appearance." He looked to several points over the room. "Dane, Thomas, Dominic, Zacks, Peck, Romero . . . you'll be coming with Grace and me. We leave in two hours. Get your stuff together, and the rest of you move on what you've been working on. Move on everything. I want to know what happened to Lee Tran's lawyer. I want to know how our freak found Deandra Waley. I want to know how he got Francis Gunther into that playground with no one noticing. I want to know why the clerk at the Redy Stor took an extra fifty bucks so Mikey wouldn't have to fill out any paperwork." Jaworski stopped for a breath. He was tired, but not spent. There was energy in reserve. None of the agents assembled could remember seeing *that* in a long while. "And the secret's out after my brilliant performance in Baton Rouge, so no need to hide the fact that our freak is on a very specific hunting expedition now. Some folks won't be too amenable to stopping him, so just remind them that if he should punch his card all the way to number one, he may just turn back to less *deserving* victims. Are we all clear on that?"

They all were.

"Those of you who are going to New Jersey, we meet out front in two." Jaworski surveyed the room for questions. There were none. "All right. Back to work. You all look bored when you're in here."

The briefing broke up, agents moving quickly to get back to tasks that had been interrupted or to get on tasks that had just come up. Jaworski left the bullpen and headed for his office.

Ariel caught him in the hall and asked for a minute.

"I'm going to have to catch up with you on Sunday," she told him.

Jaworski crossed his arms and nodded slowly at her. "Is that so? Something else on your plate. Something for Washington, maybe?"

She began to speak, then stopped, unsure of what to say. Jaworski made saying anything unnecessary, though, in short order.

"Never mind, Agent Grace. It appears to this veteran agent that questions should not be asked about your activities. Am I correct?"

She smiled at him. "Thank you, sir. I'm sorry about the away time."

"Agent Grace, you couldn't piss me off today if you tried."

She looked at him quizzically.

Jaworski chuckled breathily. "The whitecoats yesterday . . ." He shook his head. "They think they're beating it. The damn thing's almost gone."

She reached out and touched his arm. "Sir, that's . . ."

He nodded. "I know, isn't it?"

It was good to see someone beat it. It was *damn* good to see someone beat it, Ariel thought. Beat the hell out of it. Especially Jaworski.

Jaworski smiled wide and swallowed hard. "You better get your butt to wherever it's supposed to be, Grace."

"Right, sir," she said, and watched him go. There wasn't a spring in his step. Not yet, there wasn't. But she figured there soon would be.

It had been one of the great successes of a failed war.

By the thousands they had been stolen. Pilfered. Copied. Some had been bought with money. Some sex. Some with threats of revelation. Homosexuality. Extramarital dalliances. Drug use. Some had even been handed over willingly by those of an ideological bent conducive to their doing so. Some who had provided these services were dead now. Some in prison. Some living normal lives.

Pavel Yurievich Borotsin sometimes wondered if they felt guilt for what they had done. For what he had been part of making them do.

But that was the past. The cold war was over. One side had won, another had lost. His once beloved KGB was gone now, replaced by an entity of another name whose mission, whose power, would never approach, much less equal, what its predecessor had been able to achieve. He looked at the list before him and still he had to marvel at it.

Aubrey Acosta. That was the first name on the list. Thousands more followed it. The list ran several hundred single-spaced pages. And for every name there was a file. Duplicates of ones kept in a five-sided building in the American capital. One for every pilot in the American Air Force, some past, some present. Men who would have (*might still?*) fly missions against Mother Russia. Their histories, medical and otherwise. Susceptibilities. Strengths. Weaknesses.

Mills DeVane. That name was on the list. Pavel Yurievich had circled it. He circled it again and turned toward the window of his twelfth-story office, looking upon the city. There were buildings out there in the heart of Moscow where old documents were kept. Old and still-secret documents. Very special archives. Their existence could be embarrassing. Their access was restricted.

But there were two truths Pavel Yurievich had learned in his many years both in and out of government, particularly in matters of intelligence and security: Nothing was absolute and everything was negotiable.

And, very fortunately, his old friend Valentin Yevgenovich had plenty of "negotiables." Pavel knew he could deal with the absolute aspect of access. He still had friends in high places. And such a request as this, to peruse virtually useless files from the war-that-never-happened era, well, a slight bit of *negotiation* on that end might help matters immeasurably.

But time. Time was the issue here. Things would not

happen overnight, and Valentin had not said by when he needed the information. Soon, Pavel had offered without being asked. But what was "soon"?

Soon would have to be soon enough. He needed to make some calls. Reestablish some acquaintances. Get his people moving. Yes.

He put down the list and picked up the picture of the American.

"Mills DeVane," he said aloud, studying the face. Studying the eyes. What was the American saying? "The eyes are the window to the soul." Pavel chuckled. If only it were that easy.

14

[RENDEZVOUS]

If they'd been playing for money, Mills DeVane would have been cleaned out. Tapped. Broke. But as it was, the stakes were much lower in the room in which he sat, across the table from the man who'd given him the name he could not use. The payoff, though, was immeasurable. The winnings were time.

"You should bring chips sometime, Pop," Mills said, and gathered the cards into an unkempt pile after another hand lost.

"Why?" Arlo Donovan asked him. "So you can quantify how bad your old man beats you? Ha!"

Mills nodded. Nodded and smiled and straightened the cards into a deck again, neat and square.

"We should make wild cards just for you," Arlo ribbed his boy.

"Yeah, yeah." Mills shuffled and cut the deck and set about dealing another hand, was on the verge of spinning the first card off the top, when a knock came at the door of room 152 of the Family Way Inn.

His hands froze and his eyes tracked warily to the door. He could see the light from the parking lot being blocked intermittently through the peephole.

"I'll check," Arlo Donovan said, and got up. His son rose as well, putting the undealt deck on the table and looking back toward the bathroom. Was there a window in there? He hadn't checked. He had gotten lazy. Lazy just wanting to be with his father. With his pop.

"Pop, look first."

Arlo Donovan nodded and went to the door, putting his eye up to the peephole. He lingered there, and when he came away he put his hand on the latch and turned back to his son.

Mills took a step toward his father. Just one. "Pop . . ."

"There's someone you should talk to, son," Arlo Donovan said, twisting the latch open as his son's gaze flared.

"Pop . . ."

The lock clicked and Arlo turned the knob. The door swung slowly in with little assistance. Ariel Grace stood just outside.

Mills DeVane's stare went to her as he took a step back now, then to his father, and again on the stranger as she stepped inside. Arlo closed the door behind her.

"Pop, what the hell . . ."

"My name is Ariel Grace, Mr. DeVane."

He slowly nodded. "I recognize you."

"She's here to help you, son."

He looked to his father, then again to Ariel, his mind racing through a thousand different possibilities as to why this woman was here. How she had gotten here. How she had *known* to come here.

"Can I call you Mills?" Ariel asked him.

"Sure." He stepped farther away still, backing down the wall on the far side of the bed until the wall stopped him there. "How did you find me?"

Ariel gestured to his father, and Mills's gaze burned.

"How in the hell did you . . . ?" But there was only one possible answer to the question he deemed unnecessary to complete. The fire in his eyes doubled. "I swore to God that if . . . I told Jack Hale what would happen if he involved my . . ."

Arlo went to his boy and gripped him by both arms. "Son, *I* trusted her."

He shook his head at his father. "No, Pop, I told him. I made him promise. You were on the outside of this. He just brought you in!"

"I brought him in, Mills," Ariel told him. "I was the one."

"You, Jack, I don't care. It was for his safety. My peace of mind." Mills's eyes implored her to understand. "That's gone now. Gone."

"Son . . ."

"Pop," Mills said, and took his father's hands in his. "Pop. Knowing you were only connected to me in our way, that made all this bearable. But now . . ."

"Now, Mills, you have to listen to me," Ariel told him.

He turned sharply at her. "I don't know you, lady! I don't know you! Do you know how important knowing someone is to a man in my position? Do you? How important it is trusting someone?" He let go of his father and came toward her. She stood her ground. "I'll tell you who I trust. Me and my father. Jack Hale used to be on that list, but no more. Not after he and you or whoever involved my father outside of our way."

"Son, please."

"Listen to him," Ariel told Mills.

"Why?"

"Because —" Ariel began, but Arlo cut her off.

"Because a crazy man is gunning for you, son."

Mills turned back toward his father.

"For you," Arlo said again. "And the others."

Arlo had obviously seen the news. It seemed to Ariel that his son had not.

"What others?" Mills asked them both. "What are you talking about?"

"The man who's number ten on the Most Wanted list is picking the rest of you off one by one," Ariel explained.

She saw his hard gaze soften. "He's gotten nine and eight already. That doesn't leave many until you."

Mills did not look away from her for a long moment, and when he spoke next he was still looking at her. "Pop, you should go."

A hand settled on Mills's back.

"Pop, leave. Now. I'm asking you."

The hand came off. Mills heard a coat being taken off the back of a chair. Heard keys jingle as they were removed from a pocket. Felt his father move past him. And all the while he glared at her. At this woman.

At the door, Arlo Donovan stopped. "I want to see you again, son. Okay? Not too long?"

Mills nodded but did not look to his father, and when the door had closed behind Arlo Donovan, his son waited until he heard the familiar sound of his car's coughing start to say what he wanted to say. "How dare you do that."

"I wasn't saying anything he didn't already know," Ariel reminded him.

Mills shook his head. "That doesn't mean you should have. Do you know what this has been like for him?"

"No, I don't."

"You're damn right you don't," Mills told her. "He doesn't need it confirmed that his son may be in more danger than he already is. Do you know the burden he feels? Being the only person I can trust?"

"Take some of that burden away, then," Ariel suggested.

"It can't be."

"Trust me."

"I don't know you."

"What do you want to know?" Ariel asked him, and he turned away from her. He walked to the table where he and his father had played dozens of hands of poker that night and sat. His fingers fiddled with the cards.

"What the hell can I do to make you trust me?"

"It doesn't just happen that way," Mills told her. "Trust isn't just given. Not in the situation I'm in."

"You're in a hell of a more serious situation than you think. This maniac is good at what he does. He . . ." Damn, she hated doing this, but if he picked up a paper or turned on a TV, he would know. "He gets to people on the list through people who know them. Loved ones."

Mills flipped card after card past where his father had sat so they fell to the floor. "Thanks for connecting him to me with this brilliant rendezvous of yours."

"We can put him under protection," Ariel said.

Mills shook his head. "That would mark him real good."

"Then trust me. Let me help you. Keep you informed of what's going on. What Washington wants you to know."

"Washington." Mills chuckled derisively.

"All right," Ariel said, offering alternately, "what I want you to know."

He looked to her and put the cards down. "I don't know you."

"I'm Ariel, Teddy."

His stare narrowed down.

"You're not Mills DeVane," she told him, and he looked away. She thought his eyes had begun to glisten.

"I have to be Mills until this is over."

"Just don't forget who Teddy is. That's the son your father wants back."

A bulge rolled down his throat. "I want this over so bad."

She wanted to come closer, but she did not. He was right— he did not know her. And she did not know him.

"I just want it over."

"This man who might come after you, he . . ."

Mills looked to her when the words got stuck in her throat.

"You might need someone to protect you."

"I can't afford that," he told her.

"You may not have a choice."

"I don't understand," Mills said. "What kind of man are we talking about?"

"I wish I knew," Ariel answered, believing that fully, because knowing Michaelangelo, knowing what he was, how he had become the madness that he was, might make him that much easier to stop.

15

[MICKEY D]

He was brought into the world on December 4, 1960, by Doctor Welford Elias, who had come straight from the bar to Talbot Memorial Hospital in Amarillo. The good doctor had been with friends at the Lone Star, putting back beers and vodka shooters, and was more than slightly annoyed when the call came in on the pay phone near the rest room that Muriel Strange had gone into labor. Bag of waters busted wide open. No waiting on her. He tossed a final shot of Stoli back and made it to his car.

On the way to Talbot Memorial he'd taken off a parked car's mirror but did not stop. He never even knew it had happened.

At the hospital, he scrubbed and gowned up. Nurses sniffed the air covertly as he passed. He was on the bottle again. He'd been off the previous month. On the month before that. His wagon took short trips.

No one said anything to him. This was 1960. Doctors were gods. Nurses were skirts. If you didn't know that, the saying went, then you shouldn't wear the skirt.

In delivery room 3 the nurses had Muriel Strange on the table and prepped. Her legs were in the stirrups. She had been given an enema. Her husband was not in attendance. Nicky worked for the railroad and was likely somewhere between home and the stockyards up Chicago way right then. Doctor Elias slurred a hello and got in the catcher's position, nearly falling off the stool that had been placed there for him.

He berated a nurse for not locking the wheels down and turned his attention to Muriel Strange. With his thumbs he spread her labia. There was some blood. Not too much. He squinted and saw the baby beginning to crown.

It was six PM.

At six forty-five Baby Strange was born. A boy. Wailing and pink. Twenty inches. Six pounds, twelve. A healthy boy. Everything looked good. Elias thought he might get back to the Lone Star by seven-thirty. Maybe get in a game of darts. Maybe get a pinch of old Sylvia's ass. Yessiree Bob.

"Is my baby all right?" Muriel Strange asked as a nurse mopped her brow.

"Fine, Mithes Stange," Doctor Elias assured her as a nurse held the baby for him. "A pink and prethy boy."

Another nurse handed him some scissors. Shiny and sterile and sharp. It was time to cut the little fella loose. Let him get out there on his own. Cut the ties that bind. Elias spread the scissors open and reached for the cord. Saw it right there, pink and prethy. Went for it. Snipped it as a nurse screamed and Baby Strange began to wail.

A nurse had snatched the neatly severed penis from the floor where it fell, but microsurgery was not a discipline conceived much less understood in 1960. All that could be done was the medical equivalent of a patch job by a surgeon brought in on the quick once Doctor Welford Elias realized what he had done. The bleeding was controlled. Skin was rearranged, folded and snipped and stitched. The urethra was fed through and made usable as best it could. No infection developed, but the doctors told the parents there would be scarring. They were right.

Talbot Memorial fired Doctor Elias. Criminal charges were brought and there was a trial. The good doctor was convicted and sentenced to three years. He served two and moved to California when paroled. A month after arriving he was knifed in a bar fight and lingered for a month before succumbing.

Those who knew of him thought it justice.

A lawyer offered his services to the Strange family soon after their son's birth. Mickey, they were calling him. The lawyer told them they were due compensation for what had been done. Nicky Strange liked the sound of that. Muriel wondered if it would help Mickey. In the long run, it could, the lawyer told her. Nicky asked about the short run.

The case was brought to court. Evidence presented demonstrated that hospital employees knew of Doctor Elias's penchant for the bottle. The Stranges' lawyer referred to him as "the drunkard" in court; in 1960 one did not have "a problem." The jury was shown a picture of the damage done to Mickey. The picture was taken a day after birth. There was tremendous swelling. It made an impact.

Muriel Strange kept Mickey at home during the proceedings. Nicky Strange was in court every day. His employer asked when he was coming back. When the jury came back with a verdict against the hospital, Nicky told the railroad they could shove their job.

The damages awarded were unprecedented in 1960. Then again, what had happened was unprecedented. The jury gave little Mickey Strange one million dollars for pain, suffering, and, as they put it, "future needs." They gave Muriel and Nicky Strange fifty thousand dollars for emotional distress. Nicky whooped when he heard the amounts. He thought he'd won some lottery.

The judge decreed the child's award be held in trust until he was twenty-one, and assigned administration of the money to an attorney in Houston. The man had managed similar trusts over his career and was known to be particularly adept at financial matters.

Nicky and Muriel Strange received a check for fifty thousand dollars, less attorney's fees. The amount on the check stunned Nicky. Twenty thousand dollars. The lawyer had taken over half their money. Nicky complained, but compensation had been spelled out in the contract they'd signed. Nicky shouted at the lawyer, and the lawyer suggested he read documents before signing them. Muriel told him that twenty thousand was a lot of money. Her husband slapped her and took it to the bank.

Through most of these events, Mickey Strange lay in his crib and slept and dreamt the things that only babies dream. He seemed a happy child.

He seemed that way for nine more years.

His parents divorced that winter. His mother got custody. His father got visitation. In the spring Mickey started Little League.

He hadn't wanted to, but his mother said he should. It would give him something to do on weekends while she worked, she explained. She'd gotten a job at the Hoover Chemical plant and they'd rented an apartment.

Some of his friends had discovered his secret and in the incomparable cruelty of childhood had labeled him "Mickey Dickless."

Times were hard.

So was Little League.

He was not a natural athlete. He could run, but throwing was not his strong suit. Hitting was a disaster. Catching worse than both. He was put in right field when they let him play at all. When he'd muff an easy catch, some polite people along the first-base line would yell out, "Nice play, Mickey D." Impolite ones let the D be what it was.

One day just before summer, his father came to watch.

Visitations were usually Wednesday night. Visitations were usually his father taking him for a burger and leaving him in the car while he talked dirty talk with the waitresses inside. Sometimes he'd bring one out with him and make Mickey hop over to the backseat of his Dodge. He'd drive the boy home with the waitress nibbling on his ear. Sometimes her head would disappear for a while. Sometimes his dad had to pull over.

The day he came to the field to watch his boy play, however, there would be no burgers. After an unimpressive performance, Mickey walked to where his father was waiting on the third-base line. His head hung low. His father lifted his chin and handed him a baseball.

Mickey's face beamed at it.

"That there's a baseball signed by a bunch of baseball players," Nicky Strange said. His mouth was half full of tobacco. "Yankees, I think."

Mickey examined it. The writing all looked the same. He looked up to his dad. "Thanks."

"Your mom never gave you nothing like that, now, did she?"

Mickey shook his head. His mother had not. She had given him a watercolor set the previous week, but he hadn't opened it yet. He'd told someone on his team about it. They'd said that painting was for sissies.

"How about some catch?" Nicky Strange asked his son.

"Okay," Mickey said, and they walked toward the parking lot. Every now and then Nicky Strange looked nervously around.

Mickey had thought they were going home, to the lot out back of the apartment building where he and his mother lived. His father drove right past the pale yellow building.

"Where are we goin'?" Mickey asked.

Nicky Strange spit a messy wad of chaw out his open window and kept his eyes front and center. "Goin' to play some catch."

"Where?"

"Up here a piece."

Up there a piece was behind the old Danbrook Warehouse. Fire had torn through it a dozen years before, leaving it decaying and deserted.

Nicky Strange pulled into the mostly overgrown lot behind it and parked out of sight of the street. Mickey held the baseball he'd been given in his hand, turning it over and over, trying to read all the names that seemed so alike. His father looked over to him. Put his arm on the seat behind his boy. Smiled half a smile with the side of his mouth not weighted by chaw.

"I talked to a lawyer man, Mickey," Nicky said, and his son looked up. "He said that money you got for what the doctor did would go to your momma and me if anything happened to you."

Mickey's look became confused. "If what happened?"

"If you was to die," Nicky said. His half smile drained away. "Or disappear."

Still unsure of why his father was telling him this, ten-year-old Mickey Strange felt a hand slide down the back of his head. To his neck. Fingers slipped forward around his neck. Began to massage his neck. Firmly. Then hard. Then harder.

"Dad . . ."

Nicky Strange clamped his right hand down hard on his boy's neck, and brought his left to the front of Mickey's throat. Together they squeezed. Choked off the boy's breath. Made him flail his feet. Arms. Whole body. He started to turn red above the neck, his mouth gaping open for air. Air that was not coming.

"Die, boy, just —"

Engrossed by the execution of what he considered his plan of brilliance, Nicky Strange never heard the other car pull up behind the Danbrook Warehouse. Never heard its driver's door open and its trunk come up. Never heard the quick steps coming toward his side of the Dodge.

Only turned to look when his own door was opened. And couldn't believe his eyes when he realized that it was his ex, Muriel, swinging the tire iron at him.

Justifiable homicide was what the police called it. Muriel Strange had been driving home from the plant when she saw her ex-husband driving the opposite way with her son. She'd turned, tried to follow, but had gotten caught in traffic leaving the games. Driving down the highway, she could not see them. Driving past the Danbrook Warehouse, she remembered it was where Nicky had taken her to make out before they were married. He'd told her then it was so deserted you could kill someone there and no one would ever know.

Six days after he'd almost been killed by his father, Mickey Strange told his mother he did not want to play Little League anymore. He told her he did not want to be in right field. Did not want to be called Mickey Dickless.

She told him that was not his name. He was not even Mickey if he did not want to be. He could use his real name. His full name. Michael. Michael Angelo Strange.

He thought that sounded good.

She said he did not have to play Little League, but she would still have to work. He would have to occupy himself at home. She asked him if he'd used the paints she'd given him yet. He said that he hadn't, but that he would.

She smiled at him right then and said that maybe he could be the next Michelangelo. He asked who that was and his mother explained.

Near thirty years later, Mickey Strange sat alone in the room where he was never alone and thought of his mother. Thought of that day. That week. That time. His father had tried to kill him, and she had saved him. People at Little League games jeered him. Kids at school maligned him with nicknames.

Those, he thought now to himself as he stared at the

walls, were not such bad times. Yes, they had been relatively good.

Not as good as now, of course, but could any slice of time throughout history be as good as these times? These days of his success. His creating. His making. His art. The process.

No times could. None.

He only wished his mother were here to see how far he had come, but . . .

He turned his head aside and closed his eyes. Closed his eyes like the walls. He did not want to remember. He did not.

But the memories wanted him.

16

[MOTHER MAY I]

He took fast showers in junior high.

In high school he did not date. He asked a girl named Suzy out once, and she refused him. But he was not lonely. No. He had his art.

He took classes. Learned. Absorbed. Painting. Drawing. Watercolor. Pen and ink. Charcoal. Oils. Acrylics. Sculpture. Clay. Marble. Exposed himself to all mediums. Practiced. Made a name for himself. Teachers told him he was talented.

He entered his art in contests but rarely won.

He worked harder. Perfected. Executed more perfectly. Studied. Entered more. Lost as much.

One judge commented that he had an eye for color. One said his drawings were "stark." One thought he might be able to sell some of his work at the swap meet.

In eleventh grade he stopped submitting his work.

His senior year he applied to a prestigious art school, but his portfolio was deemed inadequate. One person on the review committee thought some of his work amateurish and suggested further study. Two other applications were similarly rejected.

His mother told him not to give up. She praised him. Praised his work, though to her sister she confided that some of it seemed very dark. Very dark indeed. She wondered if what his father had done had affected his . . . outlook.

One day a substitute in his twelfth-grade art history class was calling roll alphabetically and called out Strange Michael Angelo. The class howled.

When he enrolled at a nearby community college in September, he did so as Mickey Strange.

He knew he was going to be rich. Not just well-off, but rich.

He received regular reports from a law firm in Houston once he turned eighteen. The man who had originally been assigned his trust had died some years back, but as a judge long ago had known, the lawyer knew his financial stuff. The law firm administering the trust by the time he was in college had little to do but sit back and watch the investments their predecessor had made grow.

Mickey Strange had turned into a millionaire. By the time he was nineteen he was that ten times over.

He would never have to work. He could paint. Study. And most of all, he could take care of his mother. In just two short years he could make her life easy.

He never got that chance.

She'd been coming home from work at the Hoover plant. A shift supervisor now, she was doing well. Working hard but doing well. She had never remarried but did date. It happened on a Friday night. She stopped off at a bar called Hoots. Had a beer. Talked a bit. Danced a bit. And never saw the man watching her from a dark corner booth. Never recognized him when, as she walked to her car in the lot next to the bar, he came up from behind and dragged her to his van.

The police found her nude body two days later in a culvert outside of town. Raped repeatedly. Beaten. Strangled.

Strangled.

Mickey stood among few others at her funeral, staring at the box that carried her down into the earth, thinking that she had been *strangled*.

Hands squeezed around her neck.

Her breath choked off.

By a man who had raped her. Who *had* put himself in her. A man who was never caught.

Never caught.

Mickey lived in the apartment for a full year after his mother died. Drove to school every day there was school. Took a job at the local hospital to pay the bills. Swept the floors there. Had keys to every space. Had access to many things.

Things he took.

He did not know why right then, but there was a vague knowledge on his part that he should begin to *prepare*. For what he did not know. But something. Something important. Something coming.

So many things he took that he bought an old foot-locker at an Army surplus store in which to keep them. Some items had expiration dates. He did not mind them. One thing had been delivered to the hospital by mistake. It had been destined for a veterinarian whose brother was an MD. Mickey took that as well.

He was never caught. If he had been he would have gone to jail. Would have been fingerprinted. Would have been known. He knew that was not acceptable. Knew not why that was so, but accepted it. Believed it.

After a while he stopped his taking and simply worked. Worked and went to school. Went to school and learned in the spring of his twentieth year what art was. Truly was.

He was not devoid of sexual feelings. Desires. Wants. If it had been possible he would have had a noticeable erection when the model took her clothes off. The class was doing a study in pencil of the human female form. Mickey was in the second row. He wished he'd been in the last.

Class lasted an hour. The teacher thanked the model. Several male students made clumsy approaches to her afterward. Mickey packed up his things and left for the night.

In the parking lot he saw her. The model. She recognized him. He had not been one of those to hit on her and so she said hello. He said hello back. She thought him shy, cute shy, and asked if she could see his drawing of her.

He wanted to reach out and put his hand to her breast, her left breast, because that had been the one he had full view of during class, but he did not. Would not.

She said she really would like to see what he had done and he agreed, setting his portfolio on the hood of his dead mother's car and taking out his sketch. She admired it in the dirty light of the streetlamps. She said it was good. Very good.

He was inches from her. He could feel the air around her leap at him as she breathed. As her chest heaved beneath the sweater that covered her. That hid her from him.

He asked her her name. She told him. He asked her why she modeled. She said for money. She was transferring to Texas A&M in the fall. He said that was terrific. She said tuition was expensive. That she had to make a lot more money. That she was trying to get some off-campus modeling jobs.

His heartbeat paused.

The world froze.

She smiled.

Would he be interested in hiring her for any private modeling? For oils or sculpture?

His heart began to beat again. To drum again. Loud in his ears now, as if the muscle had relocated behind his eyes.

Would he?

Sculpting, he told her. He had wanted to do a nude. She said she'd be willing and asked where. He suggested his place and she thought for a moment.

Say no, he remembered one part of himself begging her. *Say no.*

She said yes and told him her price. Was it too much? It was not.

They set a time and she shook his hand. The feel of her skin electrified him.

Three nights later she came. He'd cleared the living room of his dead mother's apartment of furniture. Closed the drapes. Unplugged the phone. Put a sheet on the carpet.

She put her purse down by the door. He asked her if she wanted something to drink. She asked for water. He poured it and made small talk. How was the drive over? She didn't have a car. She'd hitchhiked to the market up the street. Did she have to be done by a certain time? No, the evening was his. Did she mind posing on the floor? She looked to the clean sheet and said that would be fine.

Seven. He remembered. It was seven o'clock when they started. He brought out his clay and the pedestal on which he would work it. She kicked off her shoes. She took off her top. She was wearing no bra. His heart quickened. She took off her jeans.

She laid herself on the sheet and asked if she had it right. He asked if he could position her. She nodded, and he knelt next to her. Touched her. Put his hands on her. One beneath her back. One beneath her shoulder. Lifted her. Tipped her away from him. Put her back to him. She asked about her arms. He laid one along the long curve of her side. Made the other one a pillow for her head.

Moved one of her legs forward. Took his time positioning it. Let his hand linger, then slide slowly up the back of her thigh to her buttocks. Squeezed her there. She started to react, to roll back toward him, but he put the needle fast into the small roll of flesh he'd pinched. Plunged the syringe. She screamed. He put his hand over her mouth. She fought. He climbed atop her and held her down until she stilled.

When her movement stopped, he stood. She was awake. She was breathing. She could not move. Her eyes lolled this way and that.

He saw a tear upon her cheek. He wiped it away, but another came.

Her eyes rolled away from him.

He took in the sight of her. The magnificence of her form. Her form stripped bare.

He was more than aroused. He was inspired.

He went to the kitchen. Came back with a knife. Stood over her. Bent down to her. Put the knife to her throat.

He had not known what he would do to her beyond making her still.

He knew now.

He would make her still life.

She never moved. As he cut her she never moved. She seemed almost accepting as the blood spilled from her. Her eyes slowly closed. Her chest stopped its rise, its fall. Her skin grew pale. He sat beside her. And he saw it.

Color. Life. Death. All in one. A new trinity.

It was good. This creation was good.

Some hours later he wrapped the girl and her things in the sheet. Wrapped that in more bedding. After midnight he carried her out and put her in the trunk of his dead mother's car. Back inside he scrubbed the carpet. The stain would not come out. He cut out the marked area and put it with the girl. He drove her far out past the Hoover Chemical plant and rolled her into a crevice off the road.

When he got home after sunup, he sat on the bare spot in the living room and waited for the police to come get him.

He slept and did not go to work and waited another day, but still the police did not come get him.

Two days passed. Three days. His supervisor called and asked if he was all right. Mickey said he was. He was not sure he was.

Four days. Five days. His job said they would need a doctor's note when he came back. Mickey quit on the phone.

Six days. He sat on the bare spot every waking hour. Put his hand to the bare wood where the girl's life had pooled under the carpet. It was not sticky. He had cleaned it well.

Seven days. No police. He hadn't watched the news. Hadn't read the paper. Didn't know if she'd been found. Didn't know if she was even known to be missing.

Eight days. And now he stood over the spot. Looking down. Remembering. Wondering. Why was he not in trouble?

Why?

Why had they not come for him? Hadn't he done wrong?

He looked at the spot. He remembered. The confluence. Life. Death. Color.

What he had made.

What he had created. Of her.

For six more days he sat alone in his dead mother's apartment. On the seventh he packed up and paid to have the carpet replaced. He was gone on the eighth.

He drove north from Texas and never looked back. He worked odd jobs in towns along the way until his twenty-first birthday. On that day he contacted the law firm of Grant, Mullavey, and Scanton in Houston, Texas, and told them of his whereabouts. They requested proof of his identity and he mailed it along. A week later he received a check for more than eleven million dollars. He was set. He would never have to work again. He had all the time in the world to decide what he wanted to do.

For the next seventeen years he did just that, the madness in him smoldering, flaring on occasion to consume another, to *provide* another, as he expanded his creative repertoire. Learned it. Perfected it. Practiced it. Here and there. In personal ways. Art for him. For his satisfaction.

Until the day another understanding came to him. An understanding of progress. Of evolution. The next step his art must take.

Yes. He had been selfish with his greatness for too long. Far too long.

It was time to share.

And did they appreciate it? Michaelangelo asked himself in the room where he was not alone. Mickey Strange might think yes. That any notoriety was good notoriety. That to be spoken of was enough.

But it was not.

Mickey Strange thought himself mad, and at times Michaelangelo could feel his lesser half still toying with the idea of guilt. But lesser that part of him was now. Greater was what he was now. What he was doing. His process.

Greater was what he was giving the world. Proof of his superiority. His master status.

They had challenged him, and he was responding. Much like he had responded with his creations before. With men. How great they could be without that which made them men. How he could make them greater through art.

How he could cleanse them of that thing through art.

He smiled to himself and reached into his underwear.

He closed his eyes. He would leave in an hour. If there were more time he might take a whore into his company. Might blindfold her this time. But there was not time. He had only himself. That would have to do.

He had no doubt that it would.

What the heck is everyone so pissed off at this Michael-angelo guy for?" "Racy" Rob Logget asked a good portion of the northeast through the power of his microphone. He sat close to it, his lips almost touching it at times, his electronic lover, as he had been known to call it on the air. "I mean, this guy is doing us a favor."

Beyond the glass that separated the booth from the producer, Leigh Taday shook her head at her bad boy and held up one finger. In the booth, Racy Rob pressed the button on his phone for line one. "All right, caller, go ahead. Give me a piece."

"Am I on?"

"You're on something," Racy Rob chided the dumb shit. Where did these doorknobs come from? he wondered. "Yes, you're on WMBZ. It's Monday, the twenty-fifth of October. This is earth. Earth calling caller. Are you there? Hello?"

"Yeah, yeah, Rob. I'm here."

Racy Rob rolled his eyes at his producer. "Okay, what's your name? My screen's screwed up here."

"Jimmy."

"Okay, Jimmy, what do you think about Michaelangelo and his community-service project?"

"Hell, I think we should turn him loose on the drug dealers."

"Yeah, Jimmy, but then how would you maintain that even temperament of yours?" Racy Rob clicked line one off and looked seriously over the mike as if he were a giant gazing upon a good chunk of the United States. "Okay, folks, come on. I mean, since this story broke we've had all kinds of bleeding hearts bemoaning Michaelangelo's lack of humanity. *'He killed a woman. He killed an innocent lawyer.'* They seem to forget that that *woman* was keeping her fugitive son in underwear and good cooking. And the lawyer . . . Well, if you can't get a medal for killing a lawyer, then I don't know. Come on. We owe Michaelangelo a big thanks for scraping some of society's scum off the planet."

Leigh Taday pressed her mike button. "Some thinking people might point out to you, Rob, that he killed people before this 'community service project,' as you call it. People who weren't criminals."

"So he's making amends," Racy Rob told his producer and a million or so others. "All I'm saying is let him finish what he started here and then give him the chair. So, America, come on. What do you think? We'll be back in a minute after we make a little money."

Music rose, and a jingle rolled, and a hundred miles from the studios of WMBZ a car pulled to the side of the road. Its driver got out and walked to a pair of phone booths sitting unused beneath the yellow glow of a streetlamp. He put in some coins and dialed.

"WMBZ, the *Racy Rob Show,*" the call screener said for about the thousandth time that night.

"Yes, I'd like to talk to Rob. I have an opinion about his topic tonight."

The screener checked the queue on his computer screen. "Okay, we're on a commercial break right now. You'd be like sixth in line after that. Maybe fifteen minutes on hold. Can you wait?"

"Will you be coming back on to update the wait?"

The call screener shook his head. "Uh, no. You'll have to commit to the wait." Rob was right sometimes. Half the country was a bunch of doorknobs. "Can you commit to fifteen minutes on hold?"

"I certainly can."

"All right, then, what's your name?"

"I'm Mike."

They were split in two. Jaworski, Sam Dane, Jenny Thomas, and Anthony Dominic were with part of Rudy Kingman's Task Force Seven patrolling the streets of Camden, New Jersey, in rentals that looked not a thing like Bureau cars. That was the plan. Ariel and Les Zacks, Joe Peck, and Tom Romero prowled the streets of Vineland with another four agents from the task force assigned to nab Robert Jack McCormack. They had no plan, other than to be ready if one of the police's local informants came through. Or if they just happened to get lucky with a citizen spotting the fugitive.

The truth be told, though, they really did not want to catch Robert Jack McCormack that Monday night. They simply wanted to be near him. He was their bait. The difficult part was not having a line attached to him. That would make it harder to reel him in if Michaelangelo decided to bite.

And that would make Robert Jack McCormack about as useful as a bucket of chum.

The wait was sixteen minutes, not fifteen, and when Leigh Taday came on the line she thanked the caller for waiting and told him the next voice he heard would be Racy Rob's.

A half a minute later Mike's wait was over.

"All right, caller, you're on the air with Racy Rob. Thanks to the complexity of modern electronics I don't know your name."

"Hello, Rob. My name is Michaelangelo."

Racy Rob chuckled and made a spinning motion at his temple. Leigh Taday threw up her hands beyond the glass.

"Okay, buddy, cute. You got an opinion, or should I cut you off?"

"I do have an opinion."

"Okay, then let's hear it. What do you think about public enemy number ten?"

There was a pause. "That's just the kind of talk that got me started on this crusade."

Racy Rob hit the kill switch on his mike and spoke to his producer over the intercom. "I'm gonna have some fun with this nut." And back on the air: "Really. So, tell me, Michaelangelo . . . or do you prefer Mike?"

"You don't understand my art, do you?"

"No. You know I don't. What is it? Finger painting with your own feces?"

A longer pause now. "You can ridicule me if you please, but that will not change the fact of who I am and what I am doing."

"Right," Racy Rob said, patronizing the loony for the million-plus listeners tuned in, two of whom were in a plain-looking Chevrolet Lumina on the streets of Vineland, New Jersey.

"King Five, you copy?"

Ariel picked up the handheld from where it lay on the floor between her feet on the passenger side. "King Five here."

"You got your radio on, Ariel?" Les Zacks asked from King Three, the designation of the unit he and Joe Peck comprised that evening.

"I'm responding, ain't I, Les?" she radioed back.

"Other radio," Les told her from a few miles away. "AM twelve sixty. There's some fruit on a talker claiming to be Michaelangelo."

Ariel looked left to Tom Romero and sniffed a laugh. "This oughta be good."

She punched on the radio and dialed in the station and shook her head at the stunts some people would play.

"Okay, *Michaelangelo,* just what is it you're doing? Besides the obvious."

"What obvious?"

Racy Rob scratched his ear. "Killing, buddy boy. Erasing human garbage heaps number eight and nine."

"You truly don't understand."

"Clue me in here, baby, before commercial, okay?"

"I'm righting a wrong. I'm sharing my greatness."

"Okay . . ."

"It's not easy for you to understand. I might need to convince you."

"You got a note from your momma or something, Mikey?"

Fuming silence, then: "I'd like you to speak to someone."

The sound of tape ripping away from skin scratched the airwaves. Racy Rob looked up to his producer. All the humor had drained from his face.

"Say hello," the voice of the caller said, seeming distant, away from the phone.

"Hello," a small and terrified voice said. A different voice.

"Tell them your name," Michaelangelo instructed.

"My name's Bobby . . . Bobby Jack."

Ariel sat ramrod straight in her seat. "Stop here! Stop!"

Romero brought the rental to a dead stop in the middle of the deserted streets, its brake lights glowing bright.

Ariel was bringing the handheld to her face when it came to life.

"King Five. King Five. That's him! That's him!"

Ariel keyed her radio. "Unit calling identify."

"This is King One, Task Force Seven. Agent Mintzer. That's McCormack! That's his voice!"

"Jesus Christ," Ariel muttered after letting the key up. She thought fast and keyed the radio again. "Get a hold of that station. Tell them to keep him on the air. Keep him talking. And get a trace going. Fast!"

"Copy, King Five. King One out."

Romero looked to her from behind the wheel. "What do we do?"

"Wait," she said, and turned the car radio up.

Racy Rob's head cocked a bit at the mike. "You're who?"

"Your full name," the instruction came, as if from behind the man now on the phone.

"Robert Jack McCormack," the caller said.

In the booth, Leigh Taday was drawing a finger across her throat, signaling to Racy Rob that she was going to cut this off. He shook his head vociferously back at her and moved the mike close to his face. As close as it had ever been.

"You're saying you're number seven."

"Man, help me. . . ."

There was a loud slap, and a whimper, and then directions given that were only a mumble coming over the air. "Art is . . ."

The statement degenerated into a roiling cry. During that, Leigh Taday killed Racy Rob's mike. He looked up and she was holding a phone to her face. She said to him over the intercom, "It's the FBI. They want us to keep him talking."

"No problem here," Racy Rob told her. He was dreaming of astronomical ratings. "Now make my mike hot again."

"Art is . . . suffering," Bobby Jack told the audience.

"What do you mean, Bobby?"

There was some commotion, sounds of movement,

then the principal was back on the line. "He can't explain that. He must experience it."

"What does that mean?"

"I'll demonstrate."

A quick second later, Bobby Jack was on the phone. "Oh, man, help me, please. . . ."

"Tell them what I'm doing," Michaelangelo said from behind.

"Oh, man . . ."

"Describe it."

"Please . . . Please . . . PleAAAAAAAAA-AAHHH-HHHHHHHHH!!!!!"

Racy Rob jumped instinctively back from the mike. The sound, the scream did not emanate from it, but it was his connection to what was happening.

"I'm gonna cut this off," Leigh Taday told the FBI agent still on the phone with her. "We can't have this on the air."

"If you cut this off you may be condemning more people to die," Les Zacks told her. "We've got a trace going. It won't be long."

"It's too fucking long already!" she yelled at him. "What's he doing to that guy?"

Racy Rob was wondering the same thing. He came close to the mike again with the cries of Robert Jack McCormack ringing in his ears. "Hey. Hey. What's going on?"

"Tell him," Michaelangelo ordered, and the phone scraped against Robert Jack McCormack's wet cheek.

"Oh, man, he cut my fucking finger off. Oh, man."

In the booth, Leigh Taday missed the delay and "fucking" went out to the northeast United States. She didn't consider it terribly troubling compared to what she was being practically forced to leave on the air.

"He cut it off with AAAAAAAAAAAAAHHHHH-HHH-HH!!!"

This time Racy Rob shuddered where he sat. Leigh

Taday screamed again at Les Zacks. Her phone lines were lighting up like a Christmas tree. One of the callers, she was certain, would be the station manager wanting to know if she'd gone as insane as her caller.

"Christ! God! Help me!"

"Got it!" the call came over the radio. "King Five, we've got it! Carlls Corner. A half mile outside town. A phone booth on the north side of Route 56."

"Got it." Ariel looked to Romero. "You know how to get there?"

He'd familiarized himself with maps of the area that morning, and had driven the roads since arriving late Friday, so all Tom Romero did in response to his passenger's question was put his foot to the gas and get them moving. Fast.

Racy Rob Logget was beginning to sweat. His stomach was churning. This was not what he had wanted. It was only a radio show, for Christ's sake. Only a topic meant to get people talking. Calling. Thinking.

Jesus, all he'd wanted was ratings. He didn't think the guy would do *this*.

"You still there?" Racy Rob asked the dead air. It had been silent for ten seconds. An eternity on the radio.

Sounds. Shuffling. Wet noises. And then, "I'm still here."

Racy Rob swallowed. "Where's Bobby Jack?"

A crunch and a snap assaulted the airwaves. "From life comes death. From life I make death, and from death I make art."

"Is . . . is Bobby Jack alive, Michaelangelo? Is he still alive?"

"You wanted to crucify him for his sins, didn't you?"

"I was trying to get people . . . I was just trying to start a conversation."

Crunch. Snap. No cry. No scream. Just one voice.

"You succeeded."

Racy Rob put his lips almost to the mike. "Is he dead?"

"You must appreciate what I do. The sacrifices I make. I should not be degraded."

"Is he dead?"

Sirens began to rise, small sounds far off over the phone.

"Is he dead?"

"You will respect what I do. You will honor it."

Racy Rob looked up to Leigh Taday as the sirens grew loud now over the airwaves. Her eyes were saucers, round and shocked at what was transpiring.

"Is he suffering?" Racy Rob asked, the sirens wailing now in his headphones.

"That is the process," Michaelangelo said. "The way of my art."

There now. There now. The sirens were on top of him now. They had to be. Racy Rob took the mike in hand and pulled it and the arm that suspended it with him as he turned in his chair. "Well, you sick fuck, I hope you suffer. I hope that after they put the cuffs on you they beat you with their sticks and stomp you with their boots. What do you think of that? Huh? Are they about to whale on you, Mikey? Huh?"

"I don't believe so."

Racy Rob's face went slack. It wasn't the only one.

Two New Jersey State Police cruisers had led the way from Vineland, and others were converging from Millville and Bridgeton. They and three FBI units screeched to a stop at the pair of phone booths on Route 56. Ariel Grace had the passenger door open even before the car had stopped and she hit the pavement running, drawing her weapon as she did.

The only problem was, there was no one to point it at.

"Where is he?" one of the state police officers asked as he and six others converged on the booths.

Ariel Grace moved slowly toward the booths. Les Zacks and Joe Peck skirted the side of the road with one of the state police officers and checked the area behind the booths. It was clear.

"This is crazy," Zacks said, keeping his weapon ready.

But Ariel knew it was not. Behind, not completely drowned out by the sirens still wailing, she could hear the conversation still playing out on the radio. Michaelangelo and Racy Rob Logget were still on the air. And in front of her, made very apparent as she reached the phone booths, was the way Michaelangelo had made that possible.

"I don't believe this," Tom Romero said, coming up to join her and seeing the handset from one booth taped to the handset from another, mouthpiece to earpiece and earpiece to mouthpiece. Michaelangelo was talking to Racy Rob, all right, but he was doing it from somewhere else.

Ariel went to the phones and ripped them apart. She put one to her ear and heard Racy Rob asking what was happening. She dropped that one and snugged the other to her face. On the other end she heard a breathy chuckle.

"Hello," she said.

"I suppose you'll try to trace the call I made to the phone you're holding before I connected it to the one you're not."

"You're on a cell phone," Ariel said. "In other words, don't bother."

"It would be a waste of your time."

"We have ways of locating cellular calls," she told him, but she could imagine his head shaking at her.

"I'll be finished here before that would bear any fruit. I might leave the phone so you can put it to your cheeks and feel where I've been."

The sirens were cut off. Ariel still turned into the confines of the booth as though she were having the most intimate of conversations. "When does this all end?"

"Art never ends."

"Why is this art?"

"Explaining myself seems to do no good."

"I don't see how it's art, Michaelangelo. It's murder. It's slaughter."

"Each creation is carefully planned."

She nodded doubtfully. "Doris May? Deandra Waley? Did you plan their 'creation'?"

"Purpose, dear lady, whoever you are. I, as you put it, *slaughter* only for a purpose. To further my art."

"Right. Doris May was a big obstacle to you."

"I had a question for Doris. She couldn't answer. She went to pieces."

Ariel sniffed a humorless laugh. "You can't keep this up."

No answer came.

"Hello."

Ariel heard a car start. Heard a car drive away.

"Damnit," she swore, and let the phone drop from her hand. She looked at it as it swung at the end of its cord and realized his offer concerning the cell phone was needless. He'd held this phone to his face. Breathed upon it.

She rubbed her cheek softly and walked away.

18

[RUNNING TO SAFETY]

It was right there, six pages in, taking up almost the whole page, and Desmond Grace could not take his eyes off of it.

He heard something out in the hall and looked away from the Wednesday edition of the *Star*. Looked away and picked up the pistol lying next to him on the old couch. He pointed it at the door as the sounds grew louder, louder, louder, and then passed as a wave of giggles. Children running in the halls of the old tenement in Harlem. That was all it was. All it was.

Desmond Grace set the gun down again, his hand shaking as he did. He closed it in a fist, which he put to his mouth. It trembled there as he looked again to the tabloid folded open to the page that was scaring the shit out of him.

A photographer had gotten there first. That was obvious. There was no sheet on the guy. No nothing. The cops would have never let a shutterbug take that picture. It was almost as if the guy, the maniac, *wanted* people to see what he had done.

What he had done.

Desmond Grace's heart raced as he studied the picture. The picture of some unlucky bastard named Robert Jack McCormack sitting on a bus bench, his fingers snipped off and somehow stuck around his head, protruding like a crown of thorns. Like Jesus, Grace thought. Like the sweet Jesus his mother had taught him about.

He unfolded the fist at his mouth and looked at his own fingers, wondering what the maniac would do with them if he found him. That, though, was not his only worry.

"Oh, momma," he said aloud in the dark and run-down room he had paid some hooker a grand for. Just to sleep in. For a few nights. Until he could figure this out. Figure out how to stay away from this guy. How to stay safe. And how to keep his momma safe.

God, if the maniac went after her like he did that first guy's momma . . . it would be for nothing. She didn't know where he was. She hadn't even talked to him in six months, since that last time he called her and asked for help, and she told him he should turn himself in and pray for forgiveness.

He wondered if praying to Jesus would do any good now and laughed tearily at the co-opted image of Christ tucked inside the *Star*.

But the laughter did not last. Could not last as long as that maniac out there would come looking for him. Sure, there was a little time. He wasn't next on the list. But what if his turn did come? What would happen to him?

What might happen to his momma?

He couldn't stand the thought of that. He could not.

The gun resting next to him drew his attention. His protector. It could also be his savior from this nightmare. A pull of the trigger, a flash. Maybe he wouldn't even hear the sound. Feel the bullet. Maybe it would be that easy. Except he did not want to die. He did not. Especially by his own hand. The truth be told, he was afraid to die that way. Much more afraid than if he was to go down while pulling a job. That might not be right, but his momma had told him when he was young that God sent those who threw away his greatest gift straight to hell for eternity and beyond.

It wasn't that he believed so much in hell. It was that he knew what his momma would think of him if he were to take his own life, and he could not stand that. However tempting it might be.

But what other choice did he have? he wondered, just as another gaggle of children ran laughing outside the door. He did not pick up the gun this time, but when they had passed he was still looking at the door.

Then he looked at the gun.

Then again at the door, where his gaze lingered, another choice presenting itself, one he would never have considered just the day before. But it was not yesterday. It was today. And a dead man made into Jesus was looking up at him in black and white.

He did not want to end up as a picture in a supermarket rag, and so Desmond Grace tucked his pistol into his waistband and headed for the door.

19

[SURRENDER]

Late Wednesday afternoon Ariel Grace was back in Damascus with Jaworski in his office, discussing how Robert Jack McCormack had been found. They were not alone in being unable to come up with an explanation.

"So aside from being a totally insane freak, our boy is a psychic." Jaworski leaned his back to the wall by the door and shook his head. His face seemed fuller. His color better. His mood, though, had not changed. "Is that about what we're thinking now?"

"Does it matter how he found him?" Ariel asked him. She was sitting in jeans and sweatshirt, her weapon exposed on her hip. She had planned to look again at two of Michaelangelo's earlier victims based upon something he'd said on the phone, but Jaworski had intercepted her and called her in. "If we beat our heads doing that, we might miss something important."

"I think it is important how this freak finds people that we can't. This time without apparently going through anyone else."

"I don't," Ariel disagreed.

Jaworski was about to drive his side of the argument home further when Les Zacks opened his door after a quick knock. "You might want to come see this."

Ariel and Jaworski followed Zacks out to the bullpen, where a TV was running. They joined three other agents who were gathered around it. The scene was the steps of the Federal District Courthouse in Manhattan. A man in a suit was talking. Mikes were ganged before him. His teeth were yellow, but he smiled.

"What is it?" Ariel asked.

Jenny Thomas was the one who answered. "Michaelangelo just got outmaneuvered. Number two just turned himself in."

Son of a bitch, Ariel thought, and looked back to the TV.

"Mr. Rhodes! Mr. Rhodes!"

The shouts came from a dozen different places among the crowd of reporters, leaving it to Aaron Rhodes to pick one. He flashed his sickly grin at a cute reporter he had seen on one of the local stations. "Carol, yes, go ahead."

"Aren't you afraid for yourself now, Mr. Rhodes, since Judge Fredericks has appointed you to represent Desmond Grace?"

Appointed, Aaron Rhodes thought to himself, glad that he was already smiling. Hell, he'd practically begged Calvin Fredericks to give him Desmond Grace when word got out that he'd turned himself in. Luckily old Cal owed him a favor or two, otherwise this juicy one might have gone to some overworked public defender, and what did a PD need media coverage for? It would have been a waste. "Carol, my client is in federal custody. Michaelangelo couldn't use me to get him out if he wanted to." He chuckled now for effect. "Plus, I have a few spaces to wait, so why would I be worried?"

More questions flew at him, but Aaron Rhodes waved them off. He had places to go, interviews to give. This had been a good start. He was certain that just oodles of people had seen his face and now knew who he was.

He was right about that. Right about that in spades.

20

[LIVING TRUST]

They had hardly said a word through eight hands, but that didn't mean they weren't glad to be together. They were always glad to be together. It was simply that the same thoughts were weighing on each of them. Thoughts of what was happening. What danger might be spinning this way.

Arlo worried for his son, and knew his son worried for him. Especially now.

"They'll get him," Arlo said for the sake of doing so as he gauged the pair of jacks in his hand. "They've got plenty of time to get him. He can't just keep going boom boom boom."

"We don't have to talk about it, Pop," Mills told him.

"You don't want to talk about it?"

Mills shook his head and rearranged his hand. It was still crap in any order. "I don't think it matters. I just . . ."

Arlo put his hand down on the table, faceup. He was conceding this hand to move to other matters. "What is it, son? What's on your mind?"

Mills chuckled, still holding his hand. It was something to focus on. "Pop, let's not get into stuff that nothing can be done about."

Arlo watched as his son picked the cards. Watched him slowly and precisely tear the corner from one, as if marking it for a big score, though he knew, he could tell, that he was doing so absently. Absorbed by something. Something that wasn't fear. Something that seemed to be eating at him, almost as if he were guilty about something.

"Son," Arlo said, and reached across the table to tap his boy on the back of his hand. "What is it that's got you?"

Mills shook his head, mostly to himself. It was not a reply, a refusal, to his father's question.

"What, son?"

Finally Mills looked up to his father. "Last week, Pop, do you remember hearing about a robbery in Augusta?"

"Yeah. An armored car at a bank, wasn't it?"

Mills nodded. "Two guards were killed. Executed."

"Yeah?"

The day he'd flown in and Gareth hadn't been there. And Lionel hadn't been there. Just Nita. He'd wondered where they'd been. . . .

"The guy I'm working for did it," Mills told him.

"Son . . . are you sure?"

"Yeah. I asked him about it. He gave me some cash this week to outfit the new plane, and the bills were all new. All in sequence. It wasn't drug money, Pop. I've seen enough of that. He was gone the day the robbery went down. It was putting two and two together."

"He admitted it?"

Mills nodded solemnly. "I know the stuff I fly in for him hurts people. Some of it gets through."

"But they stop more because of you."

"Maybe," Mills allowed. "But this thing that he did, it's blood money, Pop. People were killed for it."

"You have no control over what he does."

"But if this had been stopped two weeks ago, three weeks ago, those guards would be alive."

"There's more to this, son," Arlo reminded him. Though he knew not what the "more" was, what the bigger picture beyond hurting the drug dealers was, he was aware that there was a bigger prize. His boy had never told him that in so many words, but this very moment was confirmation of his belief. If there was not a bigger fish out there he would not be agonizing about going on. He would end it and see that the people he had worked for were punished. Put away. That's what his boy would do.

"That doesn't make it easier," Mills said. "It doesn't make what I do . . ."

He stopped himself there. If he hadn't, he didn't know what he would say. What he might do. Call it off. End it. Shut Gareth and his crew down. Maybe the good guys would be able to get to Costain and the fat Russian. Maybe.

Or maybe the things they were selling to Gareth that he was going to sell to some group somewhere would get to their final destination anyway. What did the Bureau think they were? SAMs. Well, wouldn't that be lovely? What if they were just cases and cases of grenades? Better? Or machine guns? Would that be okay? Could he stop now if that was the merchandise Gareth was buying with his blood money?

No. No, it would not be all right. He could not stop.

Mills looked to his father. To the soulful, worried eyes that had been that way for two years now. He wanted the worry to be gone.

"Pop, it's okay. I'm just— "

"You know what I think?" Arlo said. "I think you should tell the lady when you see her next." He saw his son's gaze dip. "You are going to see her again, aren't you?"

"I told her how and where to find me if she needed to."

Arlo smiled. "So you decided to trust her. I'm glad you did."

"Why?"

"Because you need someone besides me on your side."

Mills nodded and tore the corner off another card.

"You don't agree?" Arlo asked his son.

"I do, it's just . . ."

"It's what?" Arlo asked.

"I haven't had to trust anyone but you for a long time, and . . ."

"What?"

"I don't want to trust too much."

"Why would that be a problem, son?"

The third corner of the card came off. "She seems like she'd be an easy person to put your faith in."

Melancholy. That was the word Arlo thought of when looking at his boy right then. It was a big word, but his son seemed more than sad right then. Yes, more.

And that was something he should not be feeling, Arlo knew. He considered it his job for the past couple years to keep his boy's spirits up, and letting him go on like this was an exercise in futility. So enough of it. On to better thoughts. Better things. Happy plans.

"Son, how about we forget the damn papers?" Arlo said, and Mills looked up, confused. "Let's make a regular thing, okay?"

"You know I can't make plans, Pop. I could be flying down to who knows where on a moment's notice."

"So? If you don't make it, I'll leave. I'll hang around awhile just like we always planned. Okay? We can meet right here. Next Friday. Every Friday until you're done." Mills doubted his father with a look, but did not quash his desire outright. "If you think we should change the place, the time, we decide the week before. Move things around if you want. Just so we have something planned. Something to look forward to."

Mills considered it in silence.

"What do you say, son?"

After a moment Mills smiled at his father. The man who had known him better than he knew himself for a long time now. Smiled and said, "I guess I'll see you next Friday."

21

[DEAD LETTER]

Every piece of inmate mail arriving at the Metropolitan Detention Center at 100 Twenty-ninth Street in Brooklyn, New York, was subject to opening and inspection by MDC staff. The only exception were communications between lawyers and their clients. Simple fluoroscoping sufficed then, and would not violate the sanctity of attorney-client privilege.

A single letter bearing the preprinted name and address of Aaron Rhodes, Attorney-at-Law, arrived by U.S. Mail Saturday morning, the thirtieth of October, and was treated in this manner. It was thin and light, and examination by electronic means revealed that no objects of metal construction were contained therein. Not a staple, not a paper clip. If there had been, the attorney would have been contacted and requested to come to the MDC to remove said objects personally.

As it was, though, this was not necessary, and the letter bearing the destination Desmond Grace, Inmate, was forwarded forthwith to Cell 17 in the protective-custody ward.

There had been publicity concerning this inmate. He arrived with some notoriety already attached. Certain segments of any prison population were known to prey upon those of a higher profile. MDC Brooklyn was no exception, and for this reason Desmond Grace was tucked quietly away in his cell when a guard came early Saturday morning and tapped twice on the solid door, then slid the letter from his attorney through the food slot.

Desmond Grace got up from his bunk where he'd been reading a comic book and retrieved the letter from the floor where it had fallen. Returning to his bunk and sitting with his back against the wall, he opened the letter wondering what his attorney would be sending him this soon. Reading it, tears began to stream slowly down his face, and anyone passing Cell 17 in the next few minutes might have heard soft weeping.

After that they would have heard nothing at all.

22

[WRITINGS]

He was not under suicide watch and required no special handling other than the isolation of a PC cell, so unless Desmond Grace made a fuss or asked for something he was to be left alone like any other inmate. It was not a surprise, then, when the guard bringing his lunch just after noon found him clothed from the waist down and slumped on the toilet, his T-shirt shoved in his mouth, and blood everywhere.

Ariel and Jaworski arrived just past three that afternoon and stood with Warden Nat Hayes outside Cell 17, looking through its open door.

"We're on lockdown," Hayes told them, then considered the scene inside the cell and shook his head. "Not that it's likely he had help."

Ariel stepped gingerly inside, minding the puddled blood on the concrete floor. Jaworski stayed out.

"What wounds did the doctor notice?" Jaworski asked the warden.

"Before he backed away? His finger, the way it is." And the way it was, his right index finger, was missing the last inch of itself. "It's a pretty ragged wound. The doc says it looks like he gnawed it off."

"Did you find it?" Ariel asked from inside Cell 17.

"No. We didn't tear the place apart, though."

"Where'd all the blood come from?" Jaworski asked. "He didn't bleed to death from the finger wound."

Hayes bent and pointed low toward Desmond Grace's neck where it was obscured by the T-shirt hanging from his mouth. "Carotid. If you look at the nails on his good hand, they're all packed with flesh underneath."

"Like he clawed through his skin," Jaworski said.

"Right." Hayes now pointed to the wall above Desmond Grace's bunk. "We might not have even called you if it weren't for what he wrote on the wall."

Ariel looked up from Desmond Grace's lifeless form and read what had been written on the wall. Written in blood, likely by Desmond Grace using the tip of his severed finger as a stylus.

art is

"'Art is,'" Hayes read aloud. "I don't know what it means, but considering this guy's very recent connection to Michaelangelo, we thought you should take a look."

Jaworski nodded and leaned in, not wanting to crowd the space where Ariel was having a careful look-see.

"It's obvious the guy committed suicide, but it's a damn strange way," Hayes commented.

"Nobody heard a thing, right?" Jaworski checked.

"Not a thing," Hayes confirmed. His lieutenant had briefed them on the way up from his office, but seeing, he figured, was a bit different from hearing. Or believing. "The way it looks to me is he used his shirt to gag off his own screams. I mean, this could not have been painless."

Ariel squatted down next to where Desmond Grace sat on the toilet, his body slumped back but his head lolled forward, and examined what she could see very carefully. The hand whose finger had been mutilated lay palm up on his lap, blood pooled in the natural cup it formed. A fly had landed near its edge like some animal come to a watering hole. Ariel shooed it away with a wave. Then waved the scent away as well. Desmond Grace's bowels had released their contents sometime earlier. There would be plenty more flies soon if the coroner didn't get him out of there.

She continued looking, bending somewhat awkwardly over a large pool of blood at Desmond Grace's feet to see where his other hand was. It was dangling next to him, the nails and fingers bloody, just as Warden Hayes had said. Her nose twitched severely. The odor this close to him was strong. A little too strong. She leaned back and started to rise out of her crouch but . . .

"Wait a minute." She stopped halfway up, then bent forward at the waist, putting her face very close to the dead man. Very close so she could look down into the darkness between and below his slightly parted legs. "Flashlight. Anyone have a flashlight?"

A guard had a small one and passed it in. Ariel reached back and took it and twisted the lens to a narrow beam, shining that down into the dim recesses of the toilet bowl. "There's something in there."

"In where?" Jaworski asked. "The toilet?"

She looked back to him, nodding. "It looks like sheets of paper."

Jaworski turned to Hayes. "Get the coroner's people in here now. I want him off that toilet."

Bryan Marks had had a long trip. A long, long trip. He'd turned a lot of miles that day and still had more to go, but as he got closer to his folks' home in Watertown, as he rolled through the increasingly familiar landscape between Binghamton and Syracuse, he started to get hit with a major case of the nods.

Christ, he thought, blinking fast and more often as he rolled up I-81. It was only three damn thirty. Still light out, though that was fading fast. Sure, he'd started off at four that morning and had only stopped for gas and a couple burgers—plus the one bathroom break that coincided with neither gas nor food (the forty-four-ounce soda he'd picked up at the minimart while filling up had been the culprit there). Sure, Roanoke was seven hundred miles and eleven-plus hours behind him. And, yes, sure, he could have left yesterday and not tried to compress the annual trip to his parents' monstrous Halloween party into a twelve-hour dash from Virginia. But Shelbee had wanted to *be with him* last night, and, God, if *being with* Shelbee wasn't as close to heaven as a man could get without dying first. And, well, she had left about midnight, and though he had fallen asleep pretty quickly thereafter, that meant he'd gotten about three, three and a half hours of sleep. And . . .

. . . and man, he was just about ready to close his eyes and drive off into a phone pole somewhere. What a gift that would be for moms and pops.

"Fuck it," he said to the windshield of his suddenly very unwieldy Paseo and signaled toward the exit that would let him off near Whitney Point.

Whitney Point. Hmm. Didn't he have a high school buddy that moved there? Got married and moved there. Worked as an accountant, he thought. What was the guy's name? Mark Wills. The teachers used to call them the comedy team of Marks and Mark. Jeez, how long had it been? Six. Seven years. Man. Too long. Too long for old buddies to be incommunicado.

"Stroke of luck," Bryan Marks said to himself as he glided down the off-ramp and turned toward the bright yellow sign of a roadside motel. Stroke of luck for sure. It would be perfect. He'd call his folks, tell them he'd be there first thing in the morning, then he'd catch a little shut-eye, maybe three, four hours, just to freshen up, then he'd take a shot at looking up his old buddy Mark Wills and see if maybe they couldn't get together for a few Saturday-night beers for old times' sake.

Yeah, Bryan Marks thought as he turned left into the

half-empty lot of the Super 9 Motel. That sounded like
a plan.

The coroner's people had Desmond Grace off the toilet
by four. They bagged his hands and placed him on a sheet
before wrapping him up and zipping him inside a body
bag. They wheeled him away on a gurney just as a Bureau
forensics team from Headquarters, Manhattan, arrived.

They noted two sheets of paper and an envelope
mostly floating in the blood/water mixture that had filled
the bowl. As they removed those and placed them on
plastic sheets laid out on the bunk, they saw that the missing tip of Desmond Grace's right index finger had been
hidden by the paper.

But Ariel was not interested by the found portion of
Desmond Grace's finger. It was the two sheets of paper
and the envelope that drew her attention. She took out her
notebook and jotted down what she could read of what
was now clearly a letter. A letter done on stationery bearing the same name as the one on the envelope: Aaron
Rhodes.

But the letter had been signed by someone else.

Ariel looked up at what had been written on the wall
above the bunk. No—correction—partially written on the
wall. What was intended to be written there was fully in
the letter, and it was the last things she jotted quickly
down before dashing past Jaworski, yelling at him to
check on Aaron Rhodes as she made her way for the
nearest phone.

Ariel found a phone in the guard station, but there were
correctional officers there, as would be expected. And they
had ears. She asked where the warden's office was, knowing he was still with Jaworski, and was shown there by a
second-year officer whom she kept telling to hurry up.

The warden's secretary let Ariel into the office and
closed the door for her. It was obvious this call the agent

needed to make was urgent and likely private. You could see that on her face plain as day.

Once alone, she picked up the phone and dialed the Atlanta field office from memory and was connected to Jack Hale's office. She was told he was in a meeting, and Ariel told his assistant right back to get him out of it, pronto.

He came on the line two minutes later.

"What is it?" He did not sound pleased.

"Agent Hale, it's Agent Grace."

"Ariel. What is it?"

"You heard about Desmond Grace?"

"He offed himself this afternoon, that's what the word from Bureau of Prisons is."

Ariel was shaking her head. "No. I'm going to read you a letter the coroner pulled out of the toilet in his cell about five minutes ago, along with a piece of his finger. The letter is on his attorney's stationery, but it came from Michaelangelo."

"What?!"

"Listen . . ." She flipped her notebook open and read it word for word.

Desmond Grace

Your mother Edina is a lovely woman. I drove past her house yesterday. The hydrangeas are wilting, it would appear, and the yard is a bit overgrown. She must be tired after a day at the sewing shop. Too tired for upkeep.

I can relieve her tiredness if you would like . . .

I think you do not wish that. If that is so, you simply must follow these instructions. Read them carefully and dispose of this letter. They provide toilets in your cells, do they not?

First, you will bite off the tip of your right index finger. The one you point and pick your nose with, I presume. This will hurt, so stuff something in your mouth to seal your screams in. A pair of dirty underwear, I would imag-

ine, would serve this purpose. Next, on the wall of your cell you will right in your own blood: Art Is Not Linear.

Ariel stopped there. "'Art is not linear.' Do you know what that means?"

Nearly a thousand miles to the south, Jack Hale was nodding. "It means he's going out of order."

"He could go after Mills anytime."

"Can you get to him?"

"It'll take a day or two to find him."

"Get to him, and stick to him. Have you got it?"

She did.

Back at Cell 17, Bernard Jaworski stepped inside the small, square room in which Desmond Grace had been made to die. Their freak had come here. Had killed through the mails. Had killed through intimidation. That made him different, Jaworski knew. That made him special.

If Jaworski didn't know that this was a man they were dealing with . . .

But it was a man. A very talented man. A very creative man. A very dangerous man. But a *man* nonetheless. A man who could be caught.

If only they could get a damn break.

The nap had done him wonders. Bryan Marks woke near eight in the evening feeling like he could go another couple hours with Shelbee, if she were here. Or even continue on and be at his parents' place tonight, ready to wake up and get to decorating for their annual Halloween bash, except that he had called them upon checking in and told them he'd be arriving bright and early—unless they wanted him to chance wrapping his car around a bridge abutment along the way. They didn't, of course, and told him to get some rest.

Well, he had done that. And now he wanted to get a little relaxed with some brewskis and an old friend. Except he still had to find that old friend. Mark Wills. So he went to the phone table next to the bed and opened the top drawer.

Wrong one. *Gideon Bible*. And a *Book of Mormon*. He wondered where the *Koran* and the *Torah* were.

Down to the lower part of the table, the cabinet, and voilà! There it was. The white pages. The guide of all guides—unless, of course, his old buddy was unlisted. Which was a distinct possibility. And would screw his very undefinite plans for the evening. Can you say, beer for one?

But, hell, maybe he'd get lucky. He opened the thick book of flimsy pages and flipped through to the Ws. Ran his finger down the columns. Got to the W-I-Ns . . . nope, too far. But . . .

His stare narrowed down at the mark on the page. A mark made next to and all about a name. One past where Mark Wills might be, though he wasn't looking for that anymore right then. This marked-up name was sparking a memory. He'd heard it. Somewhere. When was it? Where? Here? At home? Yes! He'd heard it when he was back at home. Visiting. There for his parents' fortieth wedding anniversary last Valentine's Day. He'd taken a week off work and came up and hung around the old homestead for a while. Right around the time there was all this news about some guy who'd been killed. *This* guy, Bryan was sure. Calvis Winkler.

The thought that struck Bryan Marks next came cold and hard and fast and sent a sudden chill washing over him. A chill that dove inward and coalesced as an icy rock low in his gut.

"Holy shit," he said to the lonely silence of the room, letting the thought come again. Was it possible? Was it? Could the man who killed Calvis Winkler have made this mark in this phone book?

Bryan Marks put down the white pages suddenly, not wanting to touch them. Not sure of what he should do. All thoughts of his friend, the friend whose name escaped him at the moment, had been swatted away.

For a long while he stared at the page. After a while more he decided to call his father and ask him if he thought he was being foolish.

His father thought not and looked up the number of the state police for him.

He wanted a whore.

The itch had come again. He really should stay focused. Focused like he had been just some minutes before, prior to the picture of the waifish nymph coming up on the computer screen. He had let himself wander. Had let himself troll for titillation. And he had found it.

He could be focused and satisfied. Yes he could.

Body. Mind. Separate.

He focused. Took his list in hand from where it lay next to the computer. The list he had taken from sweet Doris's place of work. The list that had denigrated him. Had altered the path of his work.

Focus. Four names had been crossed off. Four faces had large Xs drawn through them. Nine. Eight. Seven. Two.

Yes, two.

He could focus now. On the list. On his next creation.

Clarity now, and he thought of number two. His stroke of genius. Cleverness, more appropriately. Yes. They would think him clever for dispatching of Mr. Desmond Grace in the way that he did, but it so stretched the process that he felt unfulfilled. So much had been left to the creation itself that there was bound to be mediocrity in the process. If there was, he would know someday. And that, too, was a negative. Not knowing. Not being able to feel the creation as it slipped from life to death to always.

Unsatisfying, yes.

He wanted a whore now more than ever. He kept his hand where it was and focused on the list.

Who next? Who next? What jump would he make now? Back to six? On to one?

Not one, he knew. Not yet. Out of the country he was. More planning that would take. Number one would be a challenging creation.

He moved up the list. Number three. No. A similar proposition to number one. More difficult, even. A greater challenge for a still-greater creation.

Onward to number four.

Four. Attempted murder of a police officer. *Attempted.* A failure. He could do better this next time. Yes, he should do better.

To five.

A drug trafficker. A dangerous man. He had hurt a federal officer. How delightful.

What creations there were that could be made of him. What wonderful ways his screams would come during the process.

Number five.

He would look no further. He had chosen.

How precise these choosings were. How different from his previous, and certainly future, work. There was beauty in that which was random. Excitement. Challenges, even. But these choices. From a group. A fixed number. It was different. It was good. He wondered if it were the end he could envision to it.

But of course not. How could an end to creation be good?

He was energized now. The whore could wait. The tingle had left his nub. Beneath his shorts it was soft. Soft and unique. His alone.

He straightened in the chair in the darkened room. His favorite room. The room in which he was never alone. The room in which he had his computer.

His computer. So much could be done with computers now. So very, very much. They were like books. Books with infinite pages. And each and every thing that ever was, was in the book. Each and every person. Well, not *every* person, but those who mattered to him at the moment most certainly were. His computer had helped him how many times now. Three? Four?

And it would help him again. Help him with a man named Mills DeVane.

As he thought it, the last name gave him ideas.

She was sitting at a desk she had spent maybe an hour at since arriving in Damascus almost three weeks ago, and Jaworski was showing her photocopies of pages from the phone book.

"This was the first one," he explained, displaying the one a young man named Bryan Marks had stumbled quite accidentally on in a motel not terribly far from where their first victim had lived. "This came in last night. This morning forensics out of Albany established that there was a hole the size of a pen point obscured by the decoration around the name." He slid that copy aside and showed her another. "We canvassed as many motels as we could in the area since last night. We got another page, this from one in Rome. That's near Oneida, where Lew Bradford, victim number five, was found."

She looked. Another page from a phone book. The name of Lew Bradford all scrolled up nice, fancy swirls and lines adorning the area around it.

"A hole there, too," Jaworski said. "And in both phone books the hole had penetrated a few pages beyond the one with our victims' names."

Ariel knew where this was going, yet she could hardly

believe that this was how Michaelangelo had chosen his victims.

"Like he had flipped open to a page," Jaworski proposed, mimicking the action with a file folder on Ariel's desk, "and dropped a pen to see who'd be next."

"Who it marked was it," Ariel said, and Jaworski nodded.

"Dots," he said, thinking how appropriate his mantra seemed now.

"Major dots," Ariel agreed.

Jaworski closed the file on her desk and took the photocopies in hand. "We're going to have a list of all the motel guests around the times Calvis Winkler and Lew Bradford were killed near these places."

"Credit card slips?" Ariel asked doubtfully. "You think Michaelangelo would use a credit card? Leave a trail?"

"Our careful boy?" Jaworski shrugged. "We can hope, but it's not him that we need to find. We just need to find someone who saw him there. Someone who can give us a description. A license plate."

"There are gonna be a lot of cash transactions," she told him. "A lot of Mr. and Mrs. John Smiths."

"We only need one, Agent Grace. Just one."

Needle in a haystack, she thought, though that truly wasn't fair. It was simply that she wasn't into what Jaworski was presenting. Other things were occupying her mind right then.

"Rudy Kingman's people are helping out in New Jersey now that their boy is out of the picture," Jaworski explained. "They're going to check the motels around where Ricardo Lomanico disappeared. See if we can't find a phone book with his name done up."

"You could send some of our folks to Pennsylvania," Ariel suggested.

"Only two," Jaworski said. The rest would come from the Philadelphia field office to canvass motels in the Centre Hall vicinity looking for James Ondatter's fancified name in the book. He had plans for his own people. "We have two locations, and the credit card info from them should be coming in today, tomorrow. One of the places is a little hesitant. They don't want any of their guests to get, shall we say, embarrassed. Knock knock, Mrs. Jones, could we talk to your husband about his stay at the So-and-So Motel last February?"

"You going to go for warrants?"

"If I need to," Jaworski answered, and half sat on the edge of Ariel's desk. "What I need you to do is take the lead on the Super Nine in Whitney Point. They're the ones cooperating. Get the info from them and take four or five people and start knocking on doors."

Ariel glanced briefly away from her boss. Her boss who had shown trust in her and was demonstrating that further now. "Sir, I have to go do something. I'll be gone for a day or two."

Jaworski stared down at her for a moment from his partial perch on her desk. "I could really use you right now, Grace."

She didn't doubt that. But someone else needed her, too. Maybe more. "I'm sorry, sir."

Jaworski gave her a quick nod. "You'll explain this to me someday, Agent Grace, I hope."

"I hope so, too," Ariel told him.

Jaworski left her to her work, but when he passed by the bullpen just five minutes later she was long gone.

24

[PROTECTORS]

Mills DeVane had several places of residence, a necessity considering his status as a wanted man. An apartment in Atlanta, an old, worn two-bedroom house in Macon, and another apartment in Tallahassee. Nita Berry and Lionel Price dropped him a block from his Tallahassee place, pulling into a minimart parking lot on Springhill Road to let him out. He slid the van's side door shut and looked up. The sky billowed gray. The air smelled wet, but the ground was dry. There was going to be rain. Hard rain. Mills could feel it.

"You watch your back," Lionel told him through the open passenger window. He was speaking past Nita, who sat there dutifully with a pistol tucked between her thighs.

"He's nowhere near here," Mills assured them. He thought it a convincing example of bravado.

"Like he was nowhere near that guy in Jersey," Lionel said. He'd seen the picture in that supermarket rag, and it made him glad he was not Mills DeVane. It also made him wish he didn't know Mills DeVane.

"I'll be fine," Mills said, shrugging off their concern. Actually it was Gareth's concern. He had had them drive him home from Crutch Field after taking the new plane on a short hop down to Cali for a pickup. Down Monday, back Tuesday. Another lousy hundred pounds, but the flight was clean and sweet. No complications. And no Customs this time, thank God. But once on the ground his employer had Lionel and Nita hustle him off. Baby-sit him, if you will, and take him home. Make sure that he got there and didn't end up with his fingers cut off and glued around his head. Or worse.

Gareth had seemed particularly anxious, Mills had thought. He wondered if his employer's big score was no longer just close, but imminent. That was the vibe Gareth Dean Hoag was giving off.

Nita reached out the passenger window and put her hand to his cheek. "Be careful, baby."

He smiled appreciatively, though her touch revolted him. Their concern revolted him. "I will."

"Don't take any long trips," Lionel told Mills. "Gareth said he'll be in touch soon."

"Sure." Imminent, Mills was thinking again. Sooner than soon.

"Later days, Mills," Lionel said, then added, "and get a haircut." The big man behind the wheel shook his long red mane. "You're starting to look like me."

Mills stepped back from Lionel's dull blue van and watched it pull away. Two blocks up Springhill Road, it turned. Once it was out of sight Mills began to walk. Behind him he could hear planes taking off from Tallahassee Municipal, and farther off to the south the first pulses of thunder were beginning to growl. He ran a hand through the thickening mop atop his head and sped his pace. A block shy of where Lionel's van had disappeared, he turned.

He wished he hadn't.

A police car was coming up Dandywood Drive. His street. Coming at him. He continued to walk. Didn't dip his head. Avert his eyes. Stop and turn around. No, he walked on, just another citizen out for a stroll, maybe coming home from an early shift. Maybe coming home

from the unemployment office. It could have been anything. Anything that would not draw attention.

And it worked. Like a hundred times before that he had
been mere feet from an officer of the law, two in this
instance, and nothing had happened. The Tallahassee
Police Department unit just cruised on by and turned
north on Springhill Road.

But Mills did not see it turn. He did not look back.
Halfway up the block he made a fast turn up a driveway
and made his way to the back stairs of 4750 Dandywood
Drive.

It was a mid-seventies building, but looked like mid-
fifties. The blue paint was peeling, the grounds were
unkempt, and the stairwell that led up to the apartments
on the second floor seemed perpetually damp and populated by bugs that would skitter underfoot.

A fat black roach crunched beneath Mills's boot as he
mounted the stairs. He had his key out and let himself
into unit D.

The door had barely closed when he heard the voice.

"So this is how international drug smugglers live."

The first split second he'd been startled. Very quickly,
though, recognition calmed him, and he turned to see
Ariel Grace leaning against the half wall that separated
living room from kitchen.

"I imagined mansions and yachts," Ariel told him,
smiling.

Mills tossed his keys atop the small TV just inside the
door. "You buy mansions and yachts and all kinds of people get interested in you."

She nodded and flipped the wall switch to bring some
light to the situation. Heavy drapes held the day outside
at bay.

"You had no trouble finding the place, I imagine,"
Mills said. Twelve feet of ratty carpet separated them. He
closed a bit of the distance and sat in the recliner that had
come with the place. He ran his hand through his hair

and shook his head at her. "All I said was don't dress like a cop."

Ariel looked down at herself. Loose and shredded dungarees. Baggy shirt. Down vest. Old and floppy jungle hat from the 'Nam era. "What's wrong?"

He chuckled softly. "You look homeless."

"I've been living out of a suitcase for almost a month. I feel homeless."

She came and sat on the couch facing him. It creaked, and she was certain she heard fabric tear as her body settled into it. "I came through the park like you said."

"How long did you wait?"

"Yesterday. I left last night. Came back this morning."

He looked around. "You might have cleaned up a little."

She smiled. "Not in the job description."

"You're lucky, you know. I almost went to Atlanta."

"I would have gone there, then."

"We could have played tag for weeks."

"You may not have weeks," she told him direly.

"He's not going up the list anymore. I know. Hoag has his two right hands chauffeuring me now. Playing bodyguard." He picked at the arm of the recliner. "You know how that feels to have scum's scum as my protectors?"

"Now you have me, too."

He looked up at her. He shook his head.

"Special Agent Hale said yes."

"I don't care what Jack said. Having Hoag's people drop me home is one thing. You can't stay close enough to matter a damn without putting *me* at risk."

It hadn't been intended as a verbal slap, but to Ariel it sure felt like one. "You have to be protected."

"This thing is almost over." He stood and walked past her, rubbing at his head again, pulling at the strands gone wild. He should have gotten it cut weeks ago. It was friggin' driving him crazy now.

"If Michaelangelo shows up and you don't have protection, it *will* be over," Ariel said. She was following him now into the kitchen.

"I'm not goddamn defenseless, you know," he told her, but from the look in her eyes, eyes that had seen more of what the maniac was capable of than he had, she thought that not enough of a guarantee. "I've had —" He stopped suddenly and yanked at his hair. "Damnit! Damnit!"

"What?"

"I hate having hair like this!"

At first she thought he might be joking, but very soon she knew that he was not.

He stormed past her again and out of the kitchen, to the living room again, where he pointed at the dingy walls, the water-stained ceiling, the ratty carpet. "I hate living like this! I hate wearing these clothes! I hate getting chased by fucking Customs planes, by people that are on *my* side! I hate having to put in at Gurley, or Sugarpine, or Tangelo Flats, or any other piss-poor field that's just as likely to eat my ride as let me roll out safely! I hate eating what I eat, with people I have to —" He saw the way she was looking at him and stopped, scratching at his head. "I'm fucking tired, okay. I'm just fucking tired of my hair. That's all. It's just bugging the shit out of me."

"I understand," she told him, staying back, letting the steam that he'd vented dissipate for a minute.

"I just . . ."

She nodded. "Do you have a scissors?"

He looked to her. "You saying you can cut hair?"

"I'm saying I'll cut yours."

His fingers combed through the mop once more. "Have you cut hair before?"

"It's been a while," she told him. "But I don't think I can make it look any worse than it does."

A thin smile flashed from him, then it was gone. "Scissors are in the bathroom."

She glanced down the hall. "Sit down in the kitchen. At the table."

He listened to the blades slice together. Felt the excess of his hair fall away, some onto the sheet she'd draped around him, though most tumbled to the floor and was gathering in brown mounds.

"It's thick," she said.

"It's been a while."

She snipped. Moving up the back of his head, up from the nape of his neck, her fingers sliding beneath his hair and lifting it for each cut. When she'd started his neck was like stone, his shoulders flat and square. He'd calmed, she thought. There was a slouch to him. A relaxation.

"You've done this before," Mills observed.

"For my dad when I was in high school."

"How did he look?"

She laughed and gave his head a gentle shove. When it bounced back to her she started running her hands over his scalp to check for long spots. His head seemed to loll under her touch.

It settled back and came to rest against her breasts.

Her hands skimmed above his scalp now, palms hovering so that the ends of the hair she'd just shorn brushed her skin. His head leaned back more. She could see his face, his eyes. They were closed. He might have been asleep, lost in a dream, and she might have thought that if not for the tear rolling slowly down his cheek.

"Are you thinking about her?"

His eyes opened, but he did not look at Ariel. "He told you?"

"That she died."

Mills's head tipped a bit forward, his gaze cast at the threadbare carpet just beyond the kitchen's bubbling linoleum.

"How did she die?" Ariel asked, clipping still, but

slowly, wielding the shears with care, finger-combing his hair tenderly.

"Stupidly," Mills answered, a breathy something spurting from him. Not a chuckle. Not a cry. Maybe a remnant of some disbelieving gasp loosed long ago. "In an airplane, of all places."

A few strands gone and a few strands more, Ariel letting things be for a moment before going on. "On an airplane?"

He might have nodded had the blades of the shears not been upon him. Had the comfort of her touch not been upon him. "Turbulence."

She stopped. "What do you mean?"

"We're flying back from a vacation," he explained, a wisp of smile flashing, one she could not see. "From Hawaii. The big island. Have you ever been?"

She shook her head and tentatively began to clip again, catching what stragglers she had missed. "No."

His smile widened, as if a warm breeze were washing over him right then and there, spent waves lapping at his feet and fingers meshed with his. "It's a beautiful place. We swam, we walked. We drove this jeep we rented through canyons that were so green and alive that . . ."

Ariel could not see it, but the mask of joy that memory had dredged from within him drizzled away in the silence that trailed off his incomplete recollection.

"What happened?" Ariel asked. Prodded, really, wondering if this might be something he needed. To recount it. To release it. "You said something about turbulence."

A few breaths hissed quietly in and out before he replied. "Clear-air turbulence. Unstable air that's just there. A pilot sees nothing, knows nothing, until it hits. Until it tosses his plane around like a toy. His plane and everything in it like dice in a cup."

"You were thrown around," Ariel said, and felt the slight shake the back of his head gave to her supposition.

"Not me," he said softly, maybe shamefully. "I'm a pilot. I know better than to have my seat belt off when I'm a passenger."

"She wasn't wearing hers?"

"She was coming back from asking the stew for a soda," he said. Ariel heard him sniff deeply. "A soda for me."

Damn . . .

"I was thirsty, and she had the aisle seat. She's walking back with my soda when the plane hits bad air. It drops, and she's launched into the overheads." He quieted briefly. "It was instant. That's what the doctors told me. They say that like a broken neck is just the finest damn way to check out, but how do they know? How can they know?"

"I'm sorry," she said, and set the scissors on the counter to her right. With both hands now she caressed the sides of his head, his ears, his cheeks, his neck.

"I wish all the sorrys added up could bring her back," he said solemnly. "But . . ."

Her fingertips drew soft, feathery lines upon his neck. "What made you think of her now?"

He could have said that it just happens. That images of his dead wife, recollections of her look, her way, her scent, came to him from out of nowhere at the strangest points in time. Any of those reasonings would have, could have explained the surfacing of her bittersweet memory, but none would have been true to this moment. To this reason.

"You're the only woman to touch me since . . . her."

"I'm cutting your hair," she said, smiling sweetly. Her hands were on his shoulders. She didn't think they should be there, but let them stay. Let them move.

"Is that what you're doing?" He closed his eyes again. One of his hands came up and touched hers where it was upon his shoulder.

She breathed slow and deep through her nose, places in her trembling. This shouldn't be happening. It shouldn't. She thought that very strongly as his hand slid up her forearm, under the sleeve of her shirt, his fingers gliding so softly upon her skin.

"Say stop," Mills told her, his eyes shut tight, closing out all but the feel of her touch upon him, his touch upon her.

She said nothing. Her own eyes were open. Her chest was beginning to heave against the back of his head.

His hand progressed, up the wide sleeve, over her elbow, his other hand on her now as well, diving up the other sleeve, to the soft skin of her biceps, gripping her there, pulling her, pulling her down. Down to him. He opened his eyes. She closed hers. Their faces nearing.

"Say stop," he said again, and she said nothing.

So near now they were, so close, that the jolt of the phone ringing almost thrust them together. Mills shed the sheet draping him and jumped up from the chair, letting go his hold on her as he dashed past to the living room.

Ariel let her breath settle, let her thoughts settle, and came to the spot where she'd first waited for him. She watched him, saw him run a hand over his head, rub it approvingly as he hung up the phone.

He looked back to her. "I, uh . . . I've gotta make a call. Hold on."

He dialed from memory and waited through three rings. "Yeah. Mills. Teddy wants a meet?"

She let him conduct his "business," standing back as he slipped into Mills DeVane's skin again. He'd almost been in Teddy Donovan's there a minute ago, and she didn't know how to feel about that. Whether it was right or wrong. But she thought so very surely that for him it was a good thing, even in an abbreviated format. Which maybe was the best way it could be. The only way it should be.

"Did he say why?" Mills asked, listening as the person

on the other end spoke. "How much?" Again he listened. "That's all? Where's he want it to go?" He nodded to himself. "Okay, so it's short, right? 'Cause I can't be flying down to fucking Chile for him. I got things lined up." A pause. "So that's what he told you? He called you and told you this? That he just needs it run to Arizona? You're sure?"

Ariel admired his technique. His immersion in the persona. How it stuck to him like a second skin. And she could understand now why he wanted to shed it so badly. It was too easy to be Mills DeVane. He was too good at it. If he didn't get away from it, from the life that was not his, some of it might stick to him like scabs. Ones that if you picked at them, they'd leave scars.

He wanted to get out without scars, she could see now. And she wondered if he was going to be able to do that.

"Okay," Mills said into the phone and looked at his watch. "I'll be there."

When he hung up she asked, "Be where?"

"One of my regulars has a quickie for me."

Ariel stepped toward him, suspicious. "Did you talk to him?"

"No, but the go-between we use did. It's okay. I do this kind of thing all the time."

"Right," she said. "I have to go with you."

He shook his head. "Not on something like this. Your face has been on TV. If one of my customers sees you anywhere near me and I don't have cuffs on and a gun at my head, I'm a dead man."

"I'm supposed to protect you."

"I can't be protected everywhere and still do what I'm supposed to do."

He took his house keys from on top of the TV and grabbed the jacket she'd taken from him as she set about cutting his hair. He ran a hand over his head yet again and smiled at her. A smile that lingered.

"Thanks."

"I wish you'd let me come with you."

"No. Go stay somewhere decent. I won't be back until tomorrow."

He reached out and touched her arm. She folded them across her chest. There was something she wanted to say, but was it right?

"Be careful," she told him.

"Always am," Mills assured her, and then he was gone.

She went to the window and pulled back the drapes just a hair to watch him jog up the driveway and across the street toward a car parked at the curb. She noted its color and make and then let herself out the back, bounding down the rickety metal stairs and nearly hurdling the back fence to the park behind his apartment building. Across its narrow depth she ran to Shellmark Avenue. To her rental car parked across the street. She was in it and had it moving fast, making a quick U-turn and heading toward Springhill Road. Almost there, she saw the car that Mills had been going for cross in front of her, heading north. She slowed, and waited, and then got into traffic a few hundred yards behind him, following him covertly as he drove north out of the city.

She was not the only one.

Ariel parked a block away, stopping when she saw Mills pulling into a lot behind a decrepit old building in Bainbridge, Georgia. Old letters atop the structure said Marsden Ho el. A somewhat newer sign near the entrance said Burke's Gym.

She waited, slouching down behind the wheel where she'd stopped near a gas station, and saw him come around front from the lot a minute later. He looked carefully around, though not obviously, and entered the building. She looked at her watch to note the time.

And in that split second she missed another entrance into the building.

It was one of Teddy Meeks's favorite places to meet, and Mills could not for the life of him understand why. Coming up the stairs from the second to the third floor now, the smell of a dozen-plus men sweating was hitting him like a pungent breeze. He wiped his nose and continued on up.

He never met Teddy in the gym. Too many ears. Too many eyes. Their place was the old office on the back side of the building, far enough from earshot but close enough that you could hear the speed bags thumping and old crusty coaches telling their charges that they hit like little girls. Maybe it was the atmosphere that Teddy liked.

Because if it was the smell, then Mills was pretty sure Teddy must have been sampling his own merchandise and blown whatever sense he'd had in his prominent nose.

Past the sound of pugilistic hopes and dreams, Mills walked to the door at the end of the hall. A light glowed inside through the frosted-glass pane set into it. He knocked and opened it up and stepped inside and felt the large hand clamp over his mouth from behind.

"You must be Mills DeVane," Michaelangelo said, the syringe of napoxcypherin coming out of his coat pocket. He popped the plastic guard off the needle as his creation-to-be struggled, forcing them both into the hallway. "You'll be relaxed in a moment."

Mills twisted against the incredibly strong hold the man—the maniac?—had on him, but he could not break free. Could do nothing but watch as a syringe came into view from the right and started down toward his neck.

Only the three fast gunshots and the wood splintering upon them both from bullets hitting the doorjamb saved Mills. The syringe dropped and Mills rolled farther into the hall, coming to his side to see Lionel and Nita advancing toward him with guns drawn. He looked quickly back and saw the maniac disappearing down a long corridor that ended at the back stairwell.

A big hand grabbed him and lifted him up.

"Told you not to take any trips," Lionel said, and started dragging him back toward the front of the building with Nita covering their rear.

Even from a block away the gunshots rang sharp in the thick air. Ariel sat straight behind the wheel and looked down the street to the Marsden Hotel. She saw men in shorts, some with their hands taped, spilling out of the building, and within a few seconds she saw Mills being dragged out the front entrance by a man with red hair and a woman openly wielding a gun.

She recognized them from what she'd read on Mills's operation. They worked for Hoag. But why . . . ?

They were protecting him. They had followed him. As she had. But what was the shooting? What was the . . . ?

"Oh shit," she said in a surprisingly quiet voice, starting the car as she saw the large man trot out of the back lot and head up the street away from her. He wore dark clothing. A baseball hat. He was lean but powerful. She had stared at his picture for hours. Even from a block away she knew it was he.

She dropped the rental into gear and stomped the accelerator to the floor.

As she sped up the street she saw a van come at her and pass. The big man with red hair was at the wheel. The woman was next to him. Lionel Price and Nita Berry. Mills would be with them. In a strange way she thought he would be safe, and half watched in her rearview mirror as the van sped toward Highway 27 and made the turn to head south.

She, though, was not following. She had a target in mind. Straight ahead. Running up the sidewalk of the quiet southern town where rain was beginning to fall. Where a storm was blowing in.

She raced up the street and cut across the lanes to the opposite side, bringing the rental to a screeching stop angled at the curb. She flung her door open with her knee and had her weapon out. She pointed it at him. He was thirty feet away. His face was a shadow. He was pitch from head to toe.

"FREEZE!"

People on the street who'd run this way from the commotion at the gym now scattered across the main drag through Bainbridge. Getting away from the lady in the rain pointing a gun at the big man standing under the awning of Fred's Barber Shop.

"FBI! STOP!"

Michaelangelo did. Someone screamed. Ariel's gaze ticked that way. He took advantage of her lapse.

When she saw him fully again he had a gun pointed at her.

She dropped and rolled as he fired. The windows of her rental shattered and sprayed her with tiny blocks of glass, some that cut her as she turned over and over through it, trying to make it to cover. More shots hit the street around her, chipping asphalt up to nick her face. That pissed her off and kicked her into survival mode, her roll stopping, her body going flat against the street and her weapon in both hands pointed right at—

He was not there. She hopped up, keeping her weapon in front, at the ready, and advanced toward where he had been. Through the barbershop window she saw a dark blur disappear deep inside and followed, moving in measured steps, a few at a time, covering the path she would take. Behind her she could hear screams, and sirens, but in front of her she heard nothing. Saw nothing.

Cautiously she advanced. Past the three barber chairs, an older man cowering beneath one, covering his head. Into a short hallway, unisex bathroom on one side, a little flip-around sign on its door the signal as to who was inside. Skirt or Pants the choices there.

Ariel paused and kicked it open and saw the flashes before she could fire.

Three, four, five, bright and loud. Stunning her. Hitting her. Throwing her back against the wall. Sending her sliding to the ground, pain all about her chest, her hand empty, her weapon dropped. Gone.

She groaned and curled into a ball and saw a shadow pass over her as it moved fast out the back of the store.

It had gone badly.

Whoever had shot at him in the hall as he was about to sedate his next creation had not been expected. So very obviously not expected. And he might want to know who they were someday so he might make bolas with their eyeballs.

But to think of them now was not what was needed. What was needed was to overcome his failure. Yes, he had failed. Why was a question he would ponder, he was sure, but not now.

It was time to move on. Time for the next step. A better step.

And he already had that planned. Already had it laid out. Printed out for perusal, all the information he would need. It was not the preferred avenue that he would take, as it might take time. More time than he wanted. But it was the best plan, considering . . .

A strange fellow indeed, this DeVane. No family that might be persuaded to offer direction to him, though now he suspected that the loved ones of his intended creations would be watched. Protected. So that would not do. Nor would a lawyer be of help, as there was no record of one recently representing the fugitive. Alas, though, the same story would apply to them, particularly after his visit upon Mr. Rhodes. He hadn't thought the man's intestines strong enough to suspend him from that tree, but they had not broken. Funny.

No, family or friend—or fellow partners in crime, it would now seem—would not be able to help him. But there seemed to be someone who might. Someone who would not be able to point him directly to his creation, but who would be able to tell him *about* him. That might be enough.

But might or not, he was going to find Mills DeVane. And he was going to do something special for him. To him. With him.

Oh yes.

The doctors were letting her go. Twenty-four hours and about a mile of bandages around her bruised chest later, Ariel Grace was sprung.

She hadn't wanted to go to the hospital at all, but passing out and all when the ambulance arrived had made that point moot. Five hits she'd taken. All five in the Kevlar vest beneath her homeless attire, as Mills had nearly called it.

One of the doctors had asked her if she was Irish.

Bureau people from Atlanta and Tallahassee had rushed to the hospital on hearing that a fellow agent was down, and she'd had to do some quick thinking and fancy talking to explain what she was doing there without compromising Mills. A song and dance about a lead one of her confidential informants from her Task Force Five days had given her, bringing her here, and darned if the old junkie hadn't been right. A stroke of luck. A pile of hogwash. Take your pick.

Jaworski had called, and she'd told him she was fine. He was glad to hear she had gotten close to the "freak." He wanted him now more than ever for putting one of his people in the hospital. He sounded good on the phone and told her to hurry back. More motel leads were due in soon. She said she'd be there as soon as she could.

Whenever that might be.

She got a definite answer to that when she passed through the hospital's main entrance en route to the Bureau car and driver waiting for her. He was standing outside the vehicle with a cell phone in his hand.

"Special Agent Hale wants you to call him, Agent Grace," the young agent said, handing her the phone.

She took it and wandered a bit away from him, to a planter with cigarette butts piled around its base. As she dialed, her arms were tucked close to her body, an almost automatic reflex to the trauma she'd suffered. That and maybe the painkillers wearing off. They'd offered her more, but she'd refused. Sooner or later she'd have to get back behind the wheel of a car to find Mills.

Or so she thought.

"Hale here."

"It's Agent Grace, sir."

"Jesus, Ariel, how are you?"

"Sore."

"How bad?"

"I think I'm an A-cup now." She made the mistake of trying to laugh at her own humor. A spike of pain in her ribs put a quick stop to that. "Jack, I need a car. Mills is gonna be—"

"Mills isn't going to be anywhere for you to find," Hale told her.

Dread made her mouth go suddenly dry. "Why? Is he—"

"He's probably been dragged off for safekeeping by Hoag. But besides that, you're too known a commodity now. Especially now. A lucky news crew on your tail . . ."

She understood. He was right. But that didn't make leaving Mills out there on his own any easier.

"Meeks is dead, isn't he?" Ariel asked.

"He's a predictable lunatic, your boy," Hale said. "We should have known to have Mills's known associates watched. He's got no family for Michaelangelo to go after."

"*DeVane* has no family," Ariel reminded Jack Hale.

"You know what I mean, Ariel."

She wasn't sure that mattered to him, though. "If I'm not on Mills anymore . . ."

Hale had that direction all thought out. It was direct and pure in its simplicity. "Find him, Ariel. Find him and stop him."

Gareth's little spread outside of Gainesville was no mansion, but it was a far cry from what Mills had been used to. He was, however, going to be able to get accustomed to it. For a day or so.

"You are not getting out of my sight, number five," Gareth Dean Hoag told Mills DeVane as they sat in the living room of his house in the pines and shared a beer. "Not now. Not after I almost lost you."

Lionel and Nita had saved his ass, and in any other life, any other twisted universe, he might have felt indebted to them. But here he did not. "I was lucky."

"You were lucky I had people looking out for you."

Mills nodded and drew long on the bottle that was cold in his hands. "He almost got me."

"You, some FBI agent."

Mills did not react to that. He knew it was Ariel. Knew she'd been hit. Knew that her vest had saved her. The TV news had told him that. But she had been there following him. Obviously ignoring what he'd said. Putting her life on the line for him.

And he felt sick about it.

Gareth sipped fast at his beer and flashed a foamy smile suddenly at Mills. "Guess what, number five?"

"What?"

"Friday is the day. *The* day."

Again, Mills tried not to react. Tried not to look at the phone next to Gareth, the phone he could not chance using while he was here. Tried not to look out the window to Lionel, standing guard out front. He would not be able to sneak out to make contact. No.

"Friday, number five," Gareth repeated. "What do you think about that?"

"It's about time," was all Mills could say, knowing now that he was on his own. That he would have to play it by ear, and play every move right. Either that or all that he'd done would have been for naught.

27

[MULTIPLES OF ONE]

Mikhail Ivanovich Luketsin was confused.

For an hour now he had stared at the two photographs and for an hour now he could not make himself understand what he was seeing. He was only hoping Mr. Borotsin might be able to explain it when he got there.

Pavel Yurievich Borotsin arrived just as his young associate was swallowing three aspirin. Locally produced. He'd have to remember to get the lad some from Europe or America.

"Mikhail Ivanovich, there is a problem?" Pavel asked as he entered the office space his workers usually filled. This late hour, though, only one remained. The one he'd charged with a very important project. A very quiet project.

"I am sorry to have called you at home, sir, but . . ."

Pavel slipped out of his two coats and laid them over the back of a chair. "What? What is it?"

The young man hesitated, then showed him, laying the two photographs that had troubled him side by side on his desk. "This."

Pavel tipped his head back and looked down through his bifocals. "Earlier and later photos of the same man. What?"

Mikhail shook his head. "These are not of the same man."

"What?"

"This one," Mikhail said, touching the photo on the left, "is the man you asked me to check on. I went through the files Pyotr acquired for us."

Acquired for a very tidy sum, Pavel thought, though that was an expense, and it would be Valentin Yevgenovich who would ultimately be paying for the access. "Yes . . ."

"This is Mills DeVane," Mikhail said, tapping the photo now.

"And this is Mills DeVane," Pavel said, pointing to the other photo. "No?"

"No. I stumbled upon this one by accident. The last name is similar. Donovan."

"Donovan," Pavel repeated. "I don't understand."

"His name is Theodore Donovan."

"But he is almost identical to DeVane," Pavel said, looking at the eyes. The striking eyes.

And his gaze flared. The eyes. He bent forward and studied them. Both. Mills DeVane and Theodore Donovan. And from a pile on the young man's desk he took the photo Valentin had supplied him. He laid it between them.

"I had to put that one away," Mikhail told his superior. "Seeing three of them was driving me crazy."

Pavel stared at the three sets of eyes, two Mills DeVanes and one Theodore Donovan, and thought he might go a little crazy seeing this.

He was certain his friend Valentin was going to as well.

He had too much energy. Way too much energy. And wasn't that just the hap-hap-happiest fucking problem in the world to have, Special Agent Bernard Jaworski thought as he paced back and forth in his office.

CLEAN.

That's what the whitecoat had said. That's what two whitecoats had said. Not cured. No. No one was ever cured. They were CLEAN.

The MRI last night was CLEAN.

They couldn't find the tumor. It was gone. It had vanished. And he was feeling like a sixteen-year-old with a hundred years ahead of him.

Jesus H. Fucking Christ, he was CLEAN!

He swung his fist at the vacant air in front of him just at the right moment. A second later and he would have clocked Tom Romero coming through the door with a file for him.

"Sir," Romero said, holding the file out toward his boss. Holding it and smiling a big and fat smile.

"What?" Jaworski asked, then realized he was not stationary. He was bouncing up and down on his toes as if he had pogo sticks for legs. He stilled fast and made the gruffest face he could manage. It wasn't very convincing.

"Nothing, sir," Romero said as he started to back out. "Those are the Super 9 records you wanted."

"Right. Good. Thank you."

Romero was still splitting that grin when he closed the door.

Jaworski opened the folder and paged through the records. There were more than he'd expected. Then again, the Super 9 was right off an interstate. Weary travelers would be common. Less hanky-panky and more likely to use their credit cards. Or there might have been a plethora of people in the area of Whitney Corners who just didn't give a damn about their affairs being known someday. Or they were just plain stupid.

He closed the file and dropped it on his desk.

He stared at it for a moment and picked it up again, opening it to the several pages of contacts his people would have to make. His people in the field. Connecting the dots. Having all the fun.

"Like hell," Jaworski said aloud to himself, grabbing his coat from the rack by the door and folding the first page of contacts to a pocket-size square. He was the damn boss, after all, and if he was feeling like he wanted to do a little legwork, well, he damn well could.

It was either that or he was going to have to run some laps to burn off the energy flooding him. The life energy.

How good it felt to think that, Jaworski thought as he left his office with a very definite spring in his step.

28

[EYES]

She returned to Base Ten in Damascus, New York, late Thursday afternoon, and immediately asked where Jaworski was.

"Probably out getting shitfaced," Agent Anthony Dominic told her, and when her face said she didn't understand, he explained. "I think he got more good news."

"That's great," she said, truly feeling that, but her mind was moving in another direction right then. One that had started some days before, but had only picked up steam on the flight from down south. "Tony, you know where Tom is?"

"Romeo Romero? He was out, but now he's not."

"Funny. His desk, I presume?"

"Don't presume," Dominic said as he moved away from her, "You make a PRES out of U and ME."

Every place needed a joker, she figured. But right then she needed someone to bounce ideas off of, and she found that someone coming into the bullpen from a bathroom break. She corralled him, grabbed some files from her desk, and dragged him into the conference room that had rarely been used.

When she dropped her files on the table a dust cloud erupted.

"Would it break the Bureau to hire a cleaning service?" Romero asked, waving the dingy mist away from his face.

"Never mind that," Ariel said, and slid chairs out for both of them. He took the hint and sat next to her.

"Okay, what can I be of assistance with?"

Ariel opened one of the files and grimaced. She'd sat down a bit too fast. Combined with her refusal of painkillers still, she had a good hurt going between her neck and navel.

"You okay?" Romero asked.

"Fine," she said, a little too breathily to be convincing. She sucked up the pain and got herself going. "Here are the files on Doris May and Susan Rollins."

"The two female victims," Romero said, starting the process. Bouncing. Throwing things out. Back. Around. "He didn't send letters on them."

"They were different," Ariel said. "Not part of his plan."

Romero shrugged. "We don't know his plan, but, considering what he did with the men, I suppose you could say he had some sort of plan."

"A random plan," Ariel tossed out.

"Because of the phone books," Romero expanded. "Did you know they found more holes in some of the books, like he'd dropped the pen other places, but when it came up next to a woman's name he didn't doodle it all up?"

"Men were his plan," Ariel said. "For whatever reason, and we may never know that, he was planning to do his thing to men."

"So why Doris May and Susan Rollins?"

"We know Doris May," Ariel told him. "He was angry. He had seen himself tenth on the list. None of us can know exactly what was going on there, but my guess is that he was berating her about it. Wanting her to tell him about it. Explain it."

"What could she explain?" Romero asked.

Ariel shook her head. "Nothing to his satisfaction. So he kills her. Okay?"

"All right. Let's say that's the way that went down. That was·his reason. Next . . ."

"Susan Rollins," Ariel said. "Why her?"

"You got me."

"But there has to be a reason," Ariel said. "He told me himself."

Romero's brow folded at her. "What?"

"That night on the pay phone, he said he only kills for a purpose."

"He also says his murder is art, Ariel—"

"He *believes* it is. He also believes what he told me. So let's take it as gospel and see what we get from it."

"Okay," Romero obliged. "Go."

"What do we know about her?"

"She was killed in proximity with James Ondatter."

"A *planned* victim," Ariel said.

"Okay. So?"

"So what made Michaelangelo kill Susan Rollins? And before Ondatter by, what, a day?"

"Two," Romero corrected her.

"Why?"

He shook his head.

"If he killed her for a purpose two days ahead of a planned victim," Ariel said, "what are the possible reasons? Any of them?"

Romero thought for a moment. "She was an obstacle to getting Ondatter."

"No evidence to back that up," Ariel told him. "No relation between them at all. What else?"

Romero rubbed his head. It reminded her of Mills, but she forced that memory down and stayed on track. "Jeez, Ariel, I don't know."

"Me either," she said, and spread the contents of Susan Rollins's file on the table. "What else do we know about her?"

"Well . . . he restrained her."

"Right. Taped her up. Hands and feet."

"And mouth," Romero reminded her.

"Right. He couldn't have her screaming."

"And the eyes."

"Ri—" The eyes. Ariel's own gaze twisted on that bit of fact. "Why would he do that?"

"Tape her eyes?"

"Yeah," Ariel said, checking the file. Michaelangelo had removed the tape once his victim was deceased, to better shock his audience, no doubt, but traces of the adhesive were found near her eyes and mouth and wads of used tape were found in the wastebasket. "Why would he do that? He doesn't care if his victims see him. They won't be able to identify him. They're going to be dead."

"Maybe he didn't want her to see what he was going to do," Romero suggested. "Go into fits, you know?"

"He'd drug her, then," Ariel countered. "Like the men."

Romero nodded agreement. "You got me, then, Ariel."

"I got me, too," Ariel thought. Why? Why would he tape her eyes? There was no logical reason. None. She was going to be dead. She would never be able to identify him.

The hair on Ariel's neck stood suddenly. "Christ, Tom."

"What?"

"His purpose."

"What?" Romero repeated.

Ariel looked to him. "I think he killed her because he knew her. Because she knew him. Because she knew him and *saw* him."

Romero's face lit up now. "She wasn't from Centre Hall. She was from New Jersey. He might be from there. From near where she lived. From the circles she hung in."

Ariel nodded. "And the tape. That explains it."

Romero had read enough bulletins and texts out of the Investigative Support Unit to know what she was talking about. "He was embarrassed. He couldn't stand to have her looking at him."

"Right," Ariel said. "Do you know what this means? If we're right?"

"It means we have to know every tiny thing we can about Susan Rollins," Romero answered.

"And now."

The day was done in Tenerife. Valentin Yevgenovich Gryoko sat at a table in a bar overlooking the airport and snickered as he sipped his cognac.

Across the table from him, Yves Costain was not similarly inclined toward levity.

"It appears we were right about the American," Gryoko said.

Costain nodded slowly, soberly, and drew long on his cigarette. "A man with two government-sanctioned identities is not a man who would work against that government."

Gryoko nodded and watched a jet take off into the dark waters over the Atlantic. "We will need to take care of him."

Costain could not disagree. "But he is their pilot . . ."

"There are more pilots than planes in the world," Gryoko reminded him. "We can bring them another."

Costain considered this and nodded very slowly. He asked the bartender for a phone and called an associate of his in Spain, asking the former member of Spain's *Libre* squadron if he'd be interested in doing a favor for him. A very profitable favor.

He stepped from the terminal with his suitcase in hand and raised his hand for a taxi. One presented itself and drove him away from Hartsfield International Airport.

"Hotel, buddy, or are we going home?" the cabbie asked.

"Are there any decent motels downtown?" Mickey Strange asked. He was not Michaelangelo. Not yet.

"Sure, yeah. You want something cheap, or something dirt cheap?"

"Something cheap would be fine."

The cabbie nodded. "Cheap I know well. We'll fix you up fine, buddy. Leave it to old Freddy."

"One more question, Freddy. . . ?"

"Yeah?"

"Would you be able to direct me to a whore?"

Freddy laughed and looked in the rearview. His passenger was not laughing. He was, however, holding up a hundred-dollar bill. "Action, buddy? That's what you want?"

Mickey Strange passed the bill through the cage to Freddy's waiting hand.

"Yeah. Old Freddy can score you some action."

In the back seat, Michaelangelo smiled.

29

[GONERS]

They rolled the plane out of the barn on Gareth Dean Hoag's property north of Gainesville, where Mills had left it three days earlier. A beaut of a Piper Navajo Chieftain, long and lean and powerful as all get up. Stripped out and tricked up inside courtesy of Nico Trane, and ready this Friday morning to carry Mills DeVane on a trip across the water to Clarion Key.

"What do you want me to tell him?" Mills asked Gareth as they loaded six duffels of cash into the Piper.

"Who?"

"Costain."

"I'll do the talking to Costain," Gareth said, and Mills tried not to act surprised. Unsuccessfully.

Gareth threw the last duffel into the stripped-out rear of the Piper and looked at Mills. "You didn't think you'd be taking this one alone, did you?"

"I've taken the others."

Gareth put his hands to Mills's shoulders, facing him. "Yeah, but this time you'll be bringing something back. Something beeeeautiful."

Mills nodded as Gareth took his hands away. "Hey, I'll be happy for the company." He walked around the plane, giving it a quick visual, thinking. Without Gareth along, it would have been a cakewalk. Pay Costain, pick up the goods, and fly them to some Air Force base after alerting Jack Hale through the FAA. No problem.

But now . . .

"Gareth. . . ."

"Whatcha need number five?" Gareth asked, his arms around Nita Berry now, hands in the back pockets of her jeans as they stood near the right wingtip.

"How heavy is this stuff we're bringing back?"

Gareth's look settled on Mills, suspicion edging it. "Why?"

Mills stomped the soft earth. "This is one big plane, Gareth, and if we're carrying a heavy load . . ."

He hadn't thought of that. Hadn't thought of that at all. "You got any suggestions?"

"Crutch Field," Mills said, hoping Gareth would go for it. He was thinking five, ten steps ahead now, hoping that all of them would line up. Otherwise this thing was going to get nasty. Real nasty. "Where else?"

Gareth considered it for a moment.

"We can meet you there," Nita told him, and Gareth nodded.

"Crutch Field it is, number five."

Step one, Mills thought. Just a shitload more to go.

He checked the small bag he always brought with him. The tan satchel that his wife had given him more than thirty years ago. Beaten up, sure, but it did its job and, well, Arlo Donovan was a sentimental man. Always had been. Always would be.

Especially when it came to his son.

So he checked the bag twice. Cards. A couple magazines, picked up at the newsstand so there'd be no labels, just in case his boy took one with him. And, this time, just for kicks, Arlo was bringing a good number of chips. Red, white, and blue ones, just to keep track one time and see who could really whoop the other in five-card.

He zipped up the satchel and got his coat. The car was gassed up, and he thought he had the oil leak fixed up pretty good. Just a little bit of driving, a little bit of waiting, and he'd have a little while with his boy.

His boy Teddy.

Mills brought the Piper in low from the west, his usual procedure, and from a half-mile distance could see the plane that had brought Costain in its place a few dozen yards off the end of Clarion Key's single runway. A quarter-mile out he could see shapes standing near the plane. As they touched down he was able to count three.

The hard pack of the strip rumbled as the Piper slowed and rolled toward the date palms at the end of the runway. Costain waved as Mills turned its left side to them and stopped. The fat Russian was his usual self—stone. And the third man, he stood with hands behind his back to the side like some ever-ready servant awaiting an errand.

"Who's the mystery man?" Gareth asked. Mills knew who he meant.

"Never seen him."

Gareth nodded and grunted.

Mills cut the engines and shut down his system and moved back through the stripped-out back of the Piper, stepping over the duffels to get to the aft cargo door. He popped it open to the warm Carribean breeze and stepped out, Gareth on his heels.

"Mills, my friend!" Costain called out to him from a few yards away.

"Yves," Mills shouted back, and started toward him. Costain moved toward him as well, arms outstretched, anticipating an embrace. The fat Russian was moving as well, stepping to one side, out from behind Costain.

Costain smiled big. Bigger than usual, Mills thought. But then, this was a big day for him. For them all.

The first shot rang out loud behind Mills's right ear,

close enough that he flinched in pain at the retort, seeing from the corner of his suddenly restricted vision the fat Russian double over, a small dark spot exploding on his chest.

And a second shot, and right in front of Mills, Costain dropped awkwardly to his knees, his eyes open and blood jetting from a hole in his forehead as he fell face-first into the hard pack.

Mills made himself look behind now, and he saw Gareth with a pistol out, stepping over him, trotting quick to catch the third man, who was running fast toward the date palms. Gareth raised his pistol and fired, and the man dropped like a rag doll.

Mills looked up at Gareth as he came back his way. His employer passed, going to the fat Russian and delivering a coup de grâce to the back of his wide head.

"Gareth . . . Jesus . . ."

Hoag looked back at Mills and, squatting next to the Russian, reached behind him and pulled something from the sand beneath his girth. "Glad I came, number five?"

The pistol was small, but then how big did it have to be to kill a man, Mills thought? To kill *him?*

"You didn't see it," Gareth said. "Be damn glad that I did."

Mills got to his knees and looked around. "He has bodyguards."

Gareth, too, gave the area a scan. "I'll deal with them if that comes. Now . . ." He stood and extended his hand to Mills. ". . . we've got a package to move."

Mills accepted Gareth's helping hand and went with him to Costain's plane. The cargo door was already open. Gareth looked inside. When he turned back to Mills he was smiling. "Have a look, number five."

Mills did as Gareth went back to the Piper and retrieved a small knapsack he had brought. In the back of Costain's plane there was a box. A case, really. Four feet long, a foot and a half high, and about that much in width. Made of a dull metal, it bore several markings. Some numbers, some characters in Cyrillic. The fat Russian had come through.

But come through with what?

Gareth returned to Costain's plane and moved Mills aside, removing something from his knapsack. A small instrument with a probe at one end and a readout on its face. Gareth switched it on, and it began to hum.

When he moved it near the box it began to click. Click quickly.

He looked back to Mills, beaming. "Jackpot, number five."

Mills felt himself go cold throughout. Go icy.

This wasn't a case of shoulder-fired surface-to-air missiles. Not unless they made those with plutonium now.

"All right, number five, let's get this thing moved over."

Mills glanced at the gun in Gareth's waistband. He could go for it. And he might get it.

But if he did not . . .

If he did not, no one would know what Gareth Dean Hoag had bought from Yves Costain and the fat Russian. And no one would know to stop him. He would be dead, and Gareth, who had flown just enough in his earlier drug-running days to be able to maneuver from Clarion Key to the mainland, would deliver his merchandise to whoever had bought it from him.

Game, set, match. Lights out.

The gun. There. Close. But not close enough. He had to bide his time. Wait for the best chance. Because it might be his only chance.

All night they had pored over information about Susan Rollins as it came in from every conceivable source that could be roused. Employment records, medical records,

school records. Her family had helped with items from
her present and her past, giving them to an agent who
showed up at their door around midnight and flew them
in a Bureau jet to Oneida, getting them finally to Damascus near two in the morning.

It was noon now. Noon Friday. And neither Ariel nor
Tom Romero felt any closer to identifying a connection
between Susan Rollins and Michaelangelo than they had
more than a dozen hours before. They were beat. Beat and
beginning to wonder if there was any connection at all.
Maybe he had just killed her. Because. No reason. Just
because. He was a madman, wasn't he? Didn't that entitle
him to do irrational things?

Maybe, Ariel thought, but she wasn't ready to concede
yet.

"What are you looking at?" she asked a bleary-eyed
Romero, who was paging through a book retrieved from
the box Susan Rollins's husband had sent them.

"High school yearbook," Romero said. "Junior year.
Calvert High School in the great state of Texas."

Ariel nodded tiredly and took a similar book from the
box. Susan Rollins's yearbook from her senior year at the
same high school. She flipped it open and paged through
absently. Not looking, really, because what was there to
see? A picture of their killer? Really? Well, what was his
name, and what did he look like? Supposing she had gone
to high school with their Michaelangelo, about all this
book looked like it would do was provide them with
about five hundred, six hundred suspects. Yes, this was a
real productive shot in the dark.

But she needed a break. They both did. They'd been
going nonstop for more than twenty-four hours. And so
she allowed herself these idle few minutes, flipping
through the yearbook, gazing at the photos of touch-
downs made and pie-throwing contests in the quad. All
the faces and all the fancy artwork.

Her back slowly straightened. A wet bulge rolled down her throat. She reached with a single finger and traced it along the decorative scrollwork that adorned this page. That had adorned several pages. Vines and branches and coils that could have been snakes if you looked at them just so. She looked at these. Turned the page. Saw the adornment. Turned the page. Saw still more. Traced this work as well, traced it all the way down to the bottom of the page where a mark had been put. Where credit had been taken. Where a name was applied.

M. Strange.

"Look up the last name 'Strange,' " Ariel told Romero, her fingers already flipping fast toward the senior photos.

"Why?"

"M. Strange, just do it!"

There was no more tiredness. A wave of energy had just washed over her, through her, and her fingers worked so quickly through the yearbook that they felt disconnected from her. Disconnected but working in concert.

She found her page long before Romero found his, and when she saw on that page what she thought, what she hoped, might be there, she reached fast to him and gripped his arm so tight he protested and yanked it away.

"Look," she said to him, directing him to a photo on a page facing that which held Susan Rollins's senior picture.

When Tom Romero saw it, and in particular the name that was beneath it, his face went white. "Holy shit."

Ariel could not have agreed more. "Michael Angelo Strange."

They looked at each other, but it was Ariel who spoke. "Let's get Jaworski."

They ran to his office with Susan Rollins's senior yearbook in hand and didn't bother knocking before practically bursting in to find the space empty. He wasn't there.

"Where is he?"

Romero stepped past Ariel, seeing the folder he'd brought to his boss the day before still out on his desk. Out on his perpetually neat desk. Romero opened it. None of the information inside had been distributed. Nothing but . . .

"What is it, Tom?"

He picked up the file and showed it to Ariel. "The top contact sheet is missing. The others I put together when it came in are here."

A spike of dread shot through Ariel. "What did you put the contact sheets together from?"

Romero moved through the file to photocopies of credit card receipts and bank information on those to whom the cards had been issued. "These."

Ariel grabbed them and looked through them as fast as she could, passing the one she wanted by reflex before going back fast to it. The dread exploded within her. "Christ. He's on here."

"Who?" Romero asked, looking.

"Michael Strange," Ariel said, reading the charge slip from the Super 9 and the bank information. She looked to Romero. "And he just lives up the road."

"No . . ." Romero said, voicing the worry for both of them.

"We have to get there now!" Ariel said, dropping all but the information on one Michael Strange as she and Romero bolted out of Jaworski's empty office.

Lionel and Nita were waiting for the Piper when it landed at Crutch Field. Mills cut the engines and gave another look at Gareth's gun as his employer went aft out of the plane to take Nita in his arms.

"We got it, baby, we got it!" he shouted, picking her up and spinning her around. "We fucking got it."

Mills came out of the Piper behind him. He might have chanced a radio call right then, but Lionel was looking right at him through the side window and, beyond that, this was where he had envisioned making one of his moves. To do that, though, he would have to leave the Piper and the very dangerous thing that was strapped down in its aft compartment.

"Can you believe it, baby? We're gonna be fucking rich! Fucking richer than rich!" Gareth kissed her, and she kissed him back. "Oh man, we did it!"

Mills stepped from the Piper and walked past Lionel.

"Hey," Lionel said to him. "Where are you going?"

"To take a piss, Lionel," Mills said somewhat gruffly. "I just about had it scared out of me on that fucking island."

"What are you talking about?"

"Ask Gareth," Mills said, and walked as normally as he could toward Nico's office in the hangar. The bathroom was in back, and to get to it he had to pass the mechanic's desk, which was what he had planned, because as he did he very quickly and quietly snatched the small black cordless from it.

30

[HALE, HALE]

The phone rang at Jack Hale's house just as he walked in the door. He shed his coat and dropped his briefcase and scooted into the den to snatch up the call.

"Hello."

"Jack, where the fuck have you been? I called the office, I called your car phone. . . ."

Hale's gaze narrowed down as he loosened his tie. "Who is this?"

"It's Mills, goddamnit, and I don't have much time."

"Mills . . ."

"It's going down, Jack. It's going down now."

Hale sat quickly at the desk in his den and took a pen in hand. "I'm listening. Tell me where you are."

"I'm in a fucking bathroom right now, and I've got about fifty seconds before I've got to get out of here, but here doesn't matter. I'm not going to be here in about three minutes. Hoag's got his merchandise and he's having me fly it to his buyer. He told me on the flight from Clarion Key."

"Where's his buyer?"

"North Dakota. That's all I know. I figure he'll tell me on the way."

"He's going with you?"

"He went to the Key with me."

Hale scribbled some notes. "Are you armed?"

"No, but he sure as hell is. Three bodies on Clarion Key attest to that just fine." A fast breath hissed over the phone. "Jack, listen, what Gareth bought . . . it's not fucking SAMs. It's nuclear."

"Nuclear." The word came as a faint, disbelieving gasp.

"Something nuclear. He had a Geiger with him out there, and he checked it. It was hot."

Hale's pen was working the notepad fast and furious. "What kind of something? A bomb? Raw material? What?"

"It had a number and some Russian characters. I remember the numbers."

Hale turned halfway in his chair toward his computer. He hit a key and it woke up from its sleep mode, the screen coming to colorful life.

"Jack . . ."

"Hang on just a sec, Mills," Hale said, and logged on to the Bureau computer. He entered his password and navigated as fast as he could to the database covering operations against WMD, or weapons of mass destruction.

"Jack, I'm gonna get my fucking head blown off here. . . ."

"A second. A second." He was in the database now. "What's the number?"

Mills gave it to him, and Hale entered a search for it. A response came back in seconds. "You picked yourself up a Russian Tactical Destruction Device. A backpack nuke intended to be used by engineering teams to blow high-priority targets behind—" Hale stopped his recitation of what was on the screen and gave Mills the basics. "Three-, five-, and twenty-minute fuses. Default is three."

"Jack, listen, I don't *care* what it is. I care about getting it away from Hoag. Now listen. I have a plan."

Hale turned back to his desk and took pen in hand again, flipping the page on his notepad to a clean sheet.

"I'm going to have to deal with Gareth in-flight. I don't know how, but I'll have to. Once I do that, I'm going to put down at a field called Sugarpine. It's south of Atlanta in Pike County."

"Sugarpine, got it."

"It's a deserted strip, shit for a runway, but I've put in there before without cracking up. I can do it again."

"What about something maintained?"

"I don't want to fly this thing over any big cities, okay? Sugarpine's in the sticks."

"All right. I understand."

"Have an EOD team there. Someone who knows how to deal with this."

"Air Force and Army both have people," Hale assured him.

"Just get them there. And Jack . . ."

"What?"

"I want you to get in touch with my father. We're supposed to get together tonight. I don't want him worrying if this thing hits the news, or —"

Hale understood. "Where is he?"

Mills told him, and Jack Hale put it to paper.

"I've gotta go, Jack."

"You want me to wish you good luck?" Jack Hale asked as he was making his last notation. His answer was silence as the connection clicked off.

The Bureau Tactical Teams choppered in from Albany and stormed the house at 1251 West Lemontree in Cole Point, New York, less than twenty minutes from Damascus. They went in fast from multiple points, hoping surprise would give them an advantage.

In the end it was they who were surprised. Several of them came out looking shaken after clearing the property of any threats.

"Back room," the tactical team leader told Ariel Grace where she had waited across the street. Tom Romero stood at her side with a half dozen other agents from Task Force Ten. "Your boy is one sick fuck."

Ariel and Tom moved across the street and into the house, leaving the rest of the team to wait until they did a preliminary walk-through. They didn't need evidence trampled at this stage.

The front room was average, small and sparsely decorated, with just a couch and a chair and a television. A fan/light combination hung from the ceiling. The room looked normal. The room looked unused.

Kitchen, on the right, dining room connected. The table in the dining room gleamed. No dust. No water spots. Someone was neat. The kitchen was small. A single plate sat on the counter next to the sink, a fork resting on it. Next to a toaster sat a wood block with slots holding knives. Dozens of knives.

Down a hallway now, with bathroom on the right. Clean. Sparkling. Across from it a bedroom. Neat. Bed made. No clothes strewn about.

He's a tidy boy, isn't he, Ariel thought as she continued down the hall. A door was at its end. It was fully open. A light was on inside. A red glow filtered out.

Ariel neared with Tom close behind. She had the urge to take her weapon out, but she was safe here. There was no threat here. Was there?

And through the door she stepped, into a room with a table at its center and a chair at the table and a computer on the table and dozens of faces in relief staring out from three of the four walls.

"Oh my God," Tom Romero said softly as they progressed more fully into the place where madness did live and breathe and thrive.

His own gallery, Ariel thought as she walked to one of the walls, put her hand near to one of the faces bulging out, its surface red and skimmed with something that had peeled away in places. Plaster, she thought. Yes. She backed away.

Not a gallery, she corrected herself. No. This was his trophy room. From a time when he hunted differently than he did now.

"Ariel," Romero said from across the room. "Look."

She went to where her colleague stood near a low bookcase beneath a draped and shaded window on the far wall of the room. The only wall devoid of faces.

"What?" she asked, squatting and looking to where he was pointing, finding the answer to her own question on the spine of a tall, thin book. "Same year, same school as Susan Rollins."

"You were right," Romero said.

"*We* were," Ariel corrected him as she eased the yearbook from its place among atlases and art books and medical tomes. She rested it on her knee and turned its stiff front cover back, slowly turning the pages, reading some of the things Michael Angelo Strange's classmates had penned for posterity.

> Hey there Mickey D
> All I can say is YOU'VE GOT BALLS. Truly, isn't that all anyone can say about you? Isn't that all you can say about yourself?
> Good luck with the dicks . . . I mean chicks.
> Greg
> Penis Have you found your yearbook yet???

Another page, and she read:

> To the great Michael Angelo!!!
> How's it hangin'? (Ha Ha Ha)
> What do you call a guy with no arms, no legs, who hangs on the wall? Art! (Ha Ha Ha)
> Another riddle—what do you call a guy with no 'you know what'? Mickey Dickless. Or, just look in the mirror. (HA HA HA)

Judy wants to write something now.

Later, your freakiness.

Walter (I got a BIG OLD ONE) Brandon

Past more of these entries Ariel turned, Romero looking down from above, reading as she did.

"Nice friends," he commented.

"I doubt they were that to him," Ariel observed, paging farther on until she came to the senior pictures. Three pages into that, she stopped. Stopped and let her finger trace to the beaming photo of a young man named Jason LeValle. Let her finger play over the X that had been put upon it. She came slowly up, standing and looking to the walls.

Romero had seen what she had, a young man crossed out. Maybe . . . "Do you think?"

"I'm sure we'll find out."

She looked away from the walls of faces and closed the yearbook, tucking it beneath her arm as her gaze settled on the table at room's center and the chair in which the madman had most certainly sat. She studied the arrangement. The computer. The printer. The half-empty glass of water placed precisely on a coaster so as not to mar the table—or the papers resting very near.

Ariel went there, standing next to where the monster had sat. Standing close to the table. Close to the papers, all facedown. She began to turn them over. One by one by one, her eyes flaring with each new sheaf, with each glance at things that had been printed. Articles. Clippings. Pictures.

Pictures that she recognized.

"Oh my God," she said softly, in the way a quiet scream might sound if there were such a thing.

Romero came up behind her and got his own fill of what she was seeing. "Shit."

One more word escaped Ariel before she turned away

from the table, away from the chair, away from the papers the monster had availed himself of. One solitary word. A name.

"Jack . . ."

He needed his phone book. The Army Explosive Ordnance Disposal teams were at Bragg, weren't they? Or were their Air Force counterparts at Andrews? NEST was at Nellis, and somewhere else, right?

Jeez, Jack, get ahold of yourself, Hale told himself as he stood and turned to get his government directory from the bookcase and stepped right into a shadow with form.

Michaelangelo clamped his hand over Jack Hale's mouth and took his weapon from his hip holster before the man could arm himself. He squeezed tight on the man's jaw and drew him close, terrified eyes swimming now, and said, "I thought I might require your assistance for a while."

She didn't make it out the door.

That had been her intention. Her driving *need* right then. To get to her car and to a phone and in contact with Jack Hale to warn him. But something short-circuited the immediacy of that plan. A can of paint.

Red paint.

She caught sight of it sitting against the wall near the door. The door fully open, concealing that which was behind it. The adrenaline that might have fired her legs out of the room and to a phone ebbed right then, and she stepped that way. There was a brush in the can. He had been working. Recently. And he had not been tidy. Had not put his brushes away. He had been rushed. Rushed like with Doris May. Rushed like with Deandra Waley. And Aaron Rhodes. She reached the door and gripped its edge and swung it slowly away from the wall and saw Special Agent Bernard Jaworski's dead face plastered freshly there, a wash of red over agony gaping.

She shook her head and took one step back, bumping lightly into Tom Romero, who was saying something behind her, *Dear God*s and *Oh no*s prevalent among his mourning words. For a moment, a very brief moment, she took in the sight of familiar death before her. Took it in and let it stoke the fire that already burned within. The fire of hate for the monster. A fire that now raged indescribably.

Yes, for just that brief slice of time she let what Michaelangelo the madman had done fill the reservoir of enmity toward him to overflowing. And then she put it away. Put hate away before it could become grief. Because there was no time for grief. The monster had moved on.

For the moment she would have to as well.

She swung the door back and pushed off of her contact with Romero and sprinted down the narrow hall of the tidy house, bursting through the storm door so hard it flew off its hinges.

Jack Hale lay on the ground, bleeding from the gash across his neck. With every useless breath, a spray of blood leapt from the wound.

Michaelangelo stood over him and picked the man's notes up from the desk as the phone rang on and on and on. He skimmed them, and he smiled. He had stood in the shadows and listened. Listened to the FBI agent talk to the fifth most wanted man in America. How interesting. How puzzling.

Or so it had been, until he'd held the pages in his hand. And now he understood. Now he had ideas.

He looked down at Jack Hale as the last of the life spurted from him in a wet mess and said, "I'm afraid I won't be able to do much with you."

And with that he bent down and pressed Jack Hale's pen through his left eye and into his newly dead brain.

She was at her Bureau ride, cell phone to her ear, waiting through endless rings. Tom Romero had come out of the house finally and informed the other agents with them of what they'd found. What they'd feared they would find.

Les Zacks shook his head at the ground, his tears spattering the sidewalk across from 1251 West Lemontree. Jenny Thomas let hers roll down her cheeks, her puddling eyes daggers of rage. Sam Dane, Tony Dominic, and Joe Peck stood with their brethren, eager eyes on Ariel. They were attack dogs right then. Ready for someone to say sic 'em. And for whatever reasons, that person seemed to be Ariel.

Fifteen rings, twenty rings, and finally she clicked off, dialing another number from memory as she looked to Romero. "Call Oneida Airport and get a charter. I'm going to Atlanta."

"You?" Tom Romero reacted, the others' narrowing looks joining his in not understanding, though theirs were of a more complete nature.

"Look, the way I see it either Jack Hale isn't home, which means the call I'm making now to the Atlanta Field Office will put enough people on him to keep our boy off of him, or . . . or he's already dead."

"What the hell would Michaelangelo want with the Atlanta ASAC?" Joe Peck asked.

"It doesn't matter what he wants with him," Ariel said, sidestepping the minefield that question could expose. "It matters *that* he wants him, for whatever reason." Her call went through, finally. "Yes, this is Agent Ariel Grace, Task Force Ten, get me the SAC immediately. This is an emergency." Hold music hummed in her ear and she said, "You all need to tear this place apart. Tear this guy's life apart. Find out everything you can that will help us. If we all run down to Atlanta chasing a maybe, we're wasting our resources."

"There's plenty of dots here," Tom Romero said, and Ariel's heart sank as she nodded.

But there was still no time to grieve—SAC Atlanta was talking into her ear a second later.

Mills DeVane slipped the handset back into its cradle and turned toward the door, moving only one foot in its direction when Lionel stepped in from outside and blocked his path.

"The phone," the big man said, and Mills felt his blood go to ice. It was all over.

"What?" Mills DeVane said, letting loose the only word his suddenly stumbling brain could muster. Another second and he might have managed "Don't kill me." Another two and he would have slugged Lionel. What did a dead man have to lose, he figured.

Only, it appeared he was not that just yet. At least the pager Lionel Price held up in front of him made him allow that possibility.

"Where's the phone? I gotta return a page."

His brain in gear once again—in gear with the engine that was his heart still racing along near the adrenaline redline—Mills gave no affirmative answer. Hell, he didn't want Lionel to know that he *knew* where the phone was. "I don't know, check Nico's desk."

And with that Mills slipped past the big man and outside. The sun was low in the west beyond a thickening haze of gray. Light weather, he could tell, looking to the sky for his weather report. He doubted that Gareth would let him call a flight service station for an update.

"You got a horse's bladder, number five?" Gareth asked as Mills joined them at the Piper once again. He was still in high spirits. Still holding Nita as if she were some prize he'd won at the fair. The kind you threw away after your next trip down the midway.

"I was throwing my fucking guts up, Gareth," Mills lied, dragging his sleeve across his mouth for effect. "I ain't never been so scared in my life out there."

"Hey," Gareth said. "You're alive. Alive and rich."

"That was too close, Gareth. Too damn close."

Gareth let go of Nita and came to Mills now. "But now it's over, number five. Over. Just one more little hop and you can —"

The smile drained instantly from Gareth Dean Hoag's face as he looked past his pilot. Mills turned halfway around and saw a similarly glum look on Lionel's face as he approached.

"What is it?" Gareth asked.

"They won't be ready for us," Lionel told his employer.

Gareth pushed past Mills and stepped close to the big man, Lionel's red hair starting to dance in the rising but gentle breeze. "What do you mean they won't be ready?"

"They're going to be delayed," Lionel explained. "That's all they said."

"Delayed?" Gareth repeated, his face contorted as if speaking some alien word with indecipherable meaning. "Delayed why?"

"They didn't say."

Gareth's hands came to his hips, and he shot both Mills and Nita a disbelieving glance before looking back to Lionel. "I'm bringing these people the toy of their dreams and they can't make it on time?"

Lionel shrugged.

Nita shook her head and sneered in sympathy with her man.

Mills tried not to react at all. Instead he let this new wrench have its way into the works while he tried to figure how it would affect what he'd worked out with Jack Hale. Minimally, he thought. He hoped.

"Well, did they happen to say just when they might be

ready to take delivery?" Gareth asked with dripping and dangerous sarcasm, enough so that Mills was surprised to see Lionel Price hint at a meek side for the first time in his presence.

"They said they'd be about four hours late."

"Four hours," Gareth repeated, nodding and crossing his arms. He turned back to Mills and Nita. "Four hours. Wonderful."

"What are we going to do?" Mills asked.

"Do?" Gareth sniffed sharply. "We're going to waste four hours sitting here watching our cargo, that's what we're going to do. Unless, number five, you can tell me this aircraft is capable of circling over North Dakota for four hours while we wait for the 'Sorry We're Late Militia' to show themselves. Can you tell me that?"

Mills shook his head.

"I didn't think so," Gareth said, and stomped off toward the hangar, yelling back toward them, "Nita, get some damn burgers or something while I take a leak."

Once he was inside, Nita looked to Mills first. "You want cheese or onions or what?"

"I'm not hungry," he said, and went to the Piper and sat by himself beneath the left wing.

The charter was a Gulfstream Executive, one that under ordinary circumstances Ariel Grace would never be able to justify as an "acceptable and necessary expense." But these were no ordinary circumstances. The call that reached her on the Gulfstream's satellite phone was but one more confirmation of that:

"Atlanta PD found him," the Atlanta SAC told her. He was in his own car, hurrying to the scene of his number two's murder. "They were the closest to his house."

"Right," Ariel said, staring down at the closed high school yearbook on her lap.

"His throat was cut."

Ariel didn't need to hear that. Didn't want to hear any more than that. "Right."

"Our people have only been on the scene a few minutes. Forensics will run his house through the sieve."

Ariel wondered if that would do any good. She wondered that and other things. What did Michaelangelo know now? Was Michael Angelo Strange able to get from Jack Hale the truth about Mills DeVane? Or, more properly, the lie that was Mills DeVane? And, if so, what did that mean?

"Agent Grace?"

"Yes, sir?"

"Atlanta PD did find one thing right away. Jack Hale's weapon and badge are missing."

She thought for a minute before asking the obvious. "What good is that going to do him?"

The knock came at the door a little later than Arlo Donovan had expected, but late was better than never, and he stood from the table where he'd laid out the cards and the chips and even a green felt cloth he'd found in his basement and went to the door. And though he was anxious to see his boy, he did as he had learned to do. He did not open right up. He used the peephole, just to be safe.

When he looked through the tiny lens he saw a bright shiny FBI badge filling the view.

"Just a minute," Arlo Donovan said, and opened the door to the darkness.

The Gulfstream landed in Atlanta after a two-hour flight. A waiting car from the Atlanta Field Office got her to Jack Hale's house twenty minutes after that. She didn't find what she was expecting.

The place was nearly deserted, considering. Considering that a ranking FBI Special Agent had been murdered there just hours before. Sure, there was a good contingent of Atlanta Police there—some of the same ones who'd

been on hand for the Proper Peach debacle she'd orches-
trated some weeks back. Only, it hadn't been that way at
all. Dozens of local cops, at least, were outside the two-
story Tudor, and a few inside hanging back from the
Bureau forensic teams that had arrived and were starting
their meticulous sweep of the crime scene.

But where were the rest of them? The Bureau troops?
There should have been a sea of dark-blue windbreakers
on scene, each with that distinctive F B I in gold on the
back. But there weren't. She didn't get it. Not until she
had cotton booties over her shoes and was shown by one
of the lab boys into Jack Hale's den, where he still lay
with his pen sticking from his eye. Standing over him an
agent she recognized from the Atlanta Field Office was
talking on a cell phone, getting information from Bell
South on calls made to or from the Hale residence.

"Yeah, okay. Got it. Got it. Just that one, right? And
none out after that? Okay. Got it." He clicked off and
looked to the new arrival. "Ariel, hi."

"Woodsy, hey," she said in greeting.

"Not a good day," Special Agent Dick Woodson said,
then punched in a number on his cell phone, pushing his
bifocals up on his nose once his finger was free. "Give
me a minute. I've gotta get this to the SAC."

"Where is he?" Ariel asked. "Where is *everybody?*"

"On the way to North Dakota, I'd say," Dick Woodson
answered, holding his hand up to staunch any more questions as the SAC came on the line. "Yes, sir, I just got the
phone traces. One call in from an airfield in the north of
Florida and . . ."

Ariel's ears perked mightily at that.

". . . no calls out after that. The call came in"—Woodson looked at the clock on the dead man's wall—"a little
over four hours ago."

As Woodson listened, Ariel motioned to him. "I need
to talk to him."

Woodson held up a single finger to hold her off.

"Right, sir, I'll make the call. Tallahassee's closest, I think. They could be there in twenty minutes, half an hour. Or I cou—"

The finger could hold her back no longer, and so Ariel reached fast toward Woodson's face and snatched the phone from him midsentence. He half-glared at her over his slipping bifocals as she took over the conversation. "Sir, Agent Grace here—"

"Grace, what happened to Woodsy?"

She glanced at the half-confused, half-peeved agent, then turned away. When her eyes fell upon Jack Hale's dead and abused form, she shifted her focus slightly again. "Sir, what's going on with DeVane?"

A breathy pause came her way from who knew how many miles away and how many feet up in some Bureau jet. "It's odd hearing someone talk about him. Someone who knows. Hell, I guess everyone will know by morning."

"The phone call from an airfield, sir. Was it? . . ."

"It must have been. We found a note on Jack Hale's desk, something to the effect of 'it's going down' and 'Hoag with him' and 'North Dakota.' " Another pause here, but there was no hint of relief in this brief interlude. "Also something about a nuke, Grace."

"As in nuclear?"

"Jack Hale's computer was logged on to a Bureau database dealing with weapons of mass destruction, apparently at the same time as this call was coming in. Apparently Hoag wasn't buying missiles. If only he had. . . ."

Ariel gave the room a look, her gaze settling upon Hale's dark computer screen, an orange light glowing at its base. A move of the mouse would power it up again, bring it to life, but what would that tell her? Something more about this nuke? That was Mills DeVane's mission. One he was apparently succeeding at, if all of what she was hearing and piecing together was true.

"Do you have any location on DeVane?" Ariel asked.

"The Air Force is putting an AWACS up in the path he'd likely take to North Dakota. We've got five hundred people converging on the area. A thousand in another hour. We'll have a good picture of things, Grace."

So they didn't know where he was. That wasn't comforting. Not to Ariel. Not in the least. She'd been within shouting distance of Mills not that many days ago—as the dull ache in her sides could attest to—and Michaelangelo had still gotten to him. Had nearly *gotten* him.

No, she wouldn't feel half comfortable until those thousand FBI agents the Atlanta SAC was promising were on Mills like a second skin. Not all the way relaxed until her bad boy was in cuffs.

Or in a body bag.

"Is there anything new there, Grace?" the SAC asked. "Anything that can help you?"

Ariel rubbed a hand over her head, her fingers wrapping around the tight tail her hair was pulled into at her collar. "I haven't had much of a look, sir."

"Well, look, and look good. DeVane is out of your man's sights now. Out of the picture. But he still needs to be stopped. The son of a bitch is going to get the chair if I have anything to say about it."

The connection hissed loudly and clicked off. Purposely or not, Ariel could not tell. She brought the phone away from her ear and looked at it for a long moment before handing it back to Woodson. "Sorry about that."

"It's okay," he assured her as he pocketed the phone. "You know about DeVane."

She nodded and stepped around Jack Hale's body to the desk. "I know."

"Won't be a secret much longer, I'd wager," Woodson said, shaking his head after a moment and taking his phone in hand again. "I guess I should call Tallahassee. Not that DeVane's still at that airfield, but I'm sure everywhere he's been in the recent past is going to have its share of Bureau feet trampling upon it."

Ariel nodded and nudged the mouse on Jack Hale's desk with her knuckle. Static crackled on the screen's surface and an image grew from the gray darkness. It was what she'd thought. What the SAC had explained should be there. Bureau tags at the top of the window, technical information about some Russian device. All things that probably should have scared the crap out of her, but which at this moment could not, because for the second time that day she was standing where the monster had stood, near the dead form of one she knew, and right then there was no room for fear because the fire that had been fanned from a smolder at 1251 West Lemontree as she stared at Jaworski's dead and painted face was now whipped to an inferno.

She wanted her madman in the worst way. In the I-shot-him-even-though-he-was-surrendering kind of way. In a way she hadn't known since that night in the lot of the Proper Peach Motel, when she'd wanted the lie that Mills DeVane was to her then so bad, so very, very bad.

Without warning she made a fist and thumped it hard on Hale's desk, and Woodson looked to her as he conversed with someone in Florida.

Smart, Ariel found herself thinking as she stared at the desk near where Jack Hale's notepad lay. A little pink sticky note was pasted to it with a notation that evidence had been removed. It bore the Atlanta SAC's initials. That was where Jack Hale had put his final words. Words made final by her very smart madman. Her madman that didn't make mistakes.

But . . .

Her eyes tracked off the small pad of paper.

But if he was so smart, why is he so dumb here?

She straightened where she stood, her fist unclenching, the rising throb in it forgotten for the moment. Overshadowed by an inconsistency. A glaring inconsistency.

Why would he leave Jack Hale's note?

DeVane was his prey. Number five on his punch card. He wanted him in a way maybe as powerful as Ariel's wish to put a bullet in his insane brain. So why leave that note that might lead him to DeVane? Why leave it for others to find? Others who might get to DeVane first.

Ariel's fast reasoning presented just two possibilities. One, Michaelangelo now knew just who Mills DeVane was, that he was not truly one who belonged on the Ten Most Wanted list, and for that reason he was no longer deserving of attention. Yes, that was possibility number one. And possibility number two . . .

Possibility number two was that he *wanted* that note to be found. He wanted half the FBI heading off for North Dakota. He wanted all of them, her included, to be as far away from here as possible because . . .

. . . because maybe Mills DeVane wasn't going to North Dakota.

Ariel came fast out of her introspective consideration of what she knew and turned to Woodson just as the phone was sliding back into his pocket. "Woodsy, I need to know everything that's been found here so far. And I'm not talking about fingerprints."

"Found?" Woodson sniffed a humorless laugh. "What you see is what you get. One body, one computer on, one notepad less a note." He glanced down at Jack Hale. "One pen."

Ariel shook her head, knowing that could not be it. There had to be something more here, she thought, one finger tapping absently on the desk. After a moment she picked the notepad up and asked Woodson, "Was there anything else in that note?"

He shook his head, knowing that the SAC had filled her in. "North Dakota, nuke, and Hoag. Isn't that more than enough to make a nightmare."

Again she shook her head, looking down at the pad. There had to be something else. Something else here.

Or not here, the thought came to her as she saw it. Or, more appropriately, saw remnants of it. "Woodsy, there are indentations on this pad."

He leaned close and tipped his head back to get a good gander through his bifocals. "There was a note on top of that page, Ariel."

She tipped the pad at different angles to Jack Hale's desk lamp, seeing faint, impressed lines in the thin paper, but was unable to make them out. After a futile few seconds she put the pad back on the desk and snatched a pencil from a Bureau mug next to the monitor that had gone dark again.

"That's evidence, Ariel!" Woodson protested when he saw her bend close to the desk and start rubbing soft strokes of graphite upon the top sheet of the pad, dusting it like one might a fingerprint, giving the high spots shading and leaving the low spots to stand out like pale shadows.

Pale shadows that were the true last words of Jack Hale. Words that Ariel could read with amazing clarity now. Words that wrapped her heart with a sudden, sick chill.

"Shit . . ."

"What is it?" Woodson asked, but his query came too late. Ariel was already moving away from him, stepping right over Jack Hale's body on her way to the door.

"Time," Gareth Dean Hoag said finally as the first hint of mist began to settle on Crutch Field's tarmac. "It's time you boys get going."

Mills crawled from under the Piper's wing where he'd sat for nearly four hours and stood just as Lionel stepped from the open passenger door of the Wagoneer.

Gareth smiled at them both from the open cabin door of the Piper. He came down the pair of steps, saying, "Chop chop, number five, we're sorry for the inconvenience, but your flight is now cleared for takeoff. Thank you for flying I'm Filthy Rich Airlines." He hopped onto the dampening tarmac just as Nita reached him from the Wagoneer. "Now go get my money."

Mills came toward him. "You're not going?"

"You have something against Lionel?"

Mills did, but shook his head. "I thought since you went with me to the Key you'd be making this last hop."

Gareth grabbed Nita and dragged her to him. "Nah. Me and my sweetness is gonna have some lovin' to celebrate. You can dig that, number five, can't you?"

Nita kissed him and pressed herself close. Obscenely close.

"Sure, Gareth. Sure."

Behind him Lionel nodded and smiled. The gun tucked in the small of his back already had the safety off.

"I can dig it."

"I knew that you could," Gareth said, and turned toward Nita, his tongue out of his mouth before their lips even met.

Mills jumped when Lionel put his hand on his back. "Ready, flyboy?"

"Ready as ever," Mills said, and went first into the Piper with Lionel right behind him.

Out front of Jack Hale's house Ariel trotted up to the agent who'd brought her from the airport. "How well do you know the city?"

The young agent, barely four weeks out of Quantico, shrugged nervously at the amped-up agent's question. "Not well."

Ariel turned fast and surveyed the scene, fixing on the nearest uniformed Atlanta PD officer. She covered the distance to him in a few fast breaths. "The Motel Niagra. Where is it?"

The officer, twenty years Ariel's senior at the least,

gave her a quick once-over. When he hesitated, she
tapped the shield clipped to her belt just to remind him
she was on the team.

"West of Centennial Park," the officer finally said.

"How far from here?" Ariel pressed. "In time."

"Twenty minutes in good traffic. Forty in bad."

Shit! He could have gotten there and been gone an
hour already, Ariel thought as she turned and stalked
away from the bearer of bad news. She could still go
there, of course, but what would she find? Nothing.
Likely just that.

"Damnit," she swore softly, her hand fisted around the
note, squeezing down on it hard. She hated this. Hated
chasing the monster. Hated following the trail of bodies
left in his wake. She needed to not do that anymore. She
needed to get ahead of him. But how?

She stopped halfway between the hardly helpful officer and the mostly helpless rookie who'd been given
gofer duty that night. Stopped and stood in the street and
released the note from her fist, opening it and reading
Jack Hale's last written words again. "Father." "Motel
Niagra." She blinked hard at what that surely meant, and
wondered what that which was penned beneath it meant.
"Sugarpine." "South of Atlanta." "Pike County."

All right. She tried to calm herself and think. Think.
She'd been in Atlanta. Assigned there in the not-so-
distant past. And though she didn't know every flophouse
in the area, Motel Niagra among them, she did know the
area, and there was no city, town, or burb south of the city
in Pike County named Sugarpine. That she knew.

But it felt nowhere close to good to know the negative.
She needed some affirmative knowledge. Just what the
hell did Sugarpine, capital "S," mean. Where was it?
What was—

—*hate*—

Yes.

—hate—

She'd heard of Sugarpine before.

—hate my hair—

It was coming.

—and . . .

Coming

—and . . .

"And you hate putting in at fields like Sugarpine," Ariel said softly, but aloud. "It's an airfield. An airfield."

She ran to the gofer agent. "Is there a map book in this car?"

He looked at her strangely and nodded. "In the pocket behind the seat."

She opened the back door and got it, then held out her hand to the young agent. "Give me the keys."

"I signed the car out."

The look she gave him in response was more convincing than any words could be, and he fished the keys from his pocket and dropped them in her open palm.

She was doing fifty by the time she blew the stop sign at the end of Jack Hale's block.

32

[UPSTAIRS, DOWNSTAIRS]

Five thousand feet over the south of Georgia, Mills DeVane was running about a million options through his head and none of them seemed very good at all. Not worth a damn, actually.

The big man sat next to him, belted into the right seat like a good passenger. Like any good passenger packing heat, that was. Mills could see no weapon, but it was certain there was one on the big man's person. Lionel Price without a gun was like rice without white. It just didn't work that way.

But the gun Mills knew his passenger had was just punctuation of the obvious. Lionel outweighed Mills by at least fifty pounds, and had six, maybe seven, inches on him. Forearms like lodgepoles. Biceps like pythons. Gun or not, it didn't seem likely Mills could take him in a physical confrontation. Not likely at all.

Gareth? Maybe. But then, Gareth would have been armed, as well. Armed and able and willing, as he'd proven on Clarion Key. So if Gareth had been the one to make this hop, this final flight, Mills wondered if the possibilities would have been any better.

Again, likely not. Maybe even less so than with Lionel. The brain factor made him think that. Take away the weapons and the big man had size, but Gareth had smarts. Not Phi Beta Kappa smarts, but an intuitive sense. The ability to know when something was not . . . copacetic. Lionel? He'd think you put "copacetic" on a cut.

But what was the point in running either *im*possibility over and over again in his head as he drew nearer and nearer the place where he would not be able to land? The place at which he *had* to land?

Had to land.

Damnit, Mills thought, his fingers flexing hard on the yoke. He *had* to get down there. Down to Sugarpine. Down to Jack Hale and hopefully a good many colleagues with guns would be waiting. But how?

Get down there! a voice inside him screamed. If only it had screamed the "how" as well. You couldn't just command a plane to get on the ground. This wasn't some in-flight emergency where getting down was the *only* thing a pilot could . . . could . . .

Mills's grip on the yoke eased. Relaxed as tension became possibility. Relaxed as he realized how lucky he was that it was Lionel Price sitting next to him and not Gareth Dean Hoag. Because Gareth, aside from some street smarts, had one other thing on Lionel—he was a pilot. A rusty, part-time flyboy at best, but that was enough. Enough that he would never have fallen for what Mills was about to do.

"Shit!"

Lionel instinctively grabbed for the armrests as Mills swore loudly and the Piper bucked hard to the right.

"Damn! Damn!"

Lionel's eyes bugged, doubling in size, and he looked frantically at the instrument panel, searching for what he did not know, then finally he locked his wide-eyed stare on Mills, who seemed to be fighting the yoke, his feet working the rudder pedal furiously beneath the console. "What is it, man?! What is it?!"

"Shut up!" Mills shouted, surprised not at all right then that the big man did just that, because if there was one truism that spanned time and nations, it was that no one, absolutely *no one,* wanted to die in a plane crash. And pestering the pilot in a moment of "obvious" trouble could not be considered a wise course of action for one who did not want to plow into wet Georgia earth at a hundred and ninety knots.

Of course, one man's "obvious" trouble was a more learned man's mere manipulation of a Piper Navajo Chieftain's control surfaces. Hell, what Mills was doing was little more than what some Hollywood stuntman might do behind the wheel of an out-of-control car, jerking the wheel back and forth in rapid swings to make the car *seem* and *look* and *feel* out of control. It was an illusion, the same kind of illusion Mills DeVane was employing, only he had more controls to work—rudder, elevators, ailerons—and therefore could generate a whole heck of a lot of motion. Particularly in the three dimensions he had to work with. A stunt driver could take his ride left and right and forward and maybe toss in some sway and body roll. Mills could do all that, and was, but was also taking the Piper through an unsteady series of up-and-down motions, as if it were riding some monstrous wave. That and the quarter and half rolls, both left and right, and that healthy fear of dying in a head-on with mother earth, and Lionel Price was, at the moment, being a very, very good boy, albeit one who seemed just about ready to wet himself.

"Fuck it! Fuck it!"

"What is it, damnit?!" Lionel pleaded, his fingers digging into the armrests' soft padding as the Piper took a severe nose-down attitude and picked up speed. "Mills! What the fuck . . . ?"

Mills feigned difficulty in pulling the Piper level for a long moment, then brought it back to a shaky semblance of level flight, with all the rolls and gyrations he was attaching to it.

"Goddamnit, man, what's going on?" Lionel demanded, the oddest shrill to his voice. An almost feminine whine so unbecoming him that Mills had to fight the urge to look his way and see if there were an equally uncharacteristic expression of sissylike fear upon his face.

"We've got a control problem," Mills said, using his calm but firm voice. His in-control voice. His I'm-the-pilot-and-we're-gonna-make-it voice. "Hydraulic, electronic . . . I don't know. But we've gotta set down."

"Shit man, set it the fuck down. Set it down."

Mills kept his shaky plane in a shallow, undulating descent, and shook his head at the windscreen. "Gareth is not going to be happy."

"Gareth?!" Lionel said loudly above the metallic creaking and popping that seemed to be coming from everywhere around him. "Fuck Gareth. He can bring us another fucking plane. Just land, man. Land."

"I'm gonna try."

Lionel pushed himself back hard against the seat as the Piper went into another steep dive, his eyes fixed forward on the gray-black collage of sky and earth coming up at him.

Ariel missed the turn and slammed on the brakes just past a sign telling her she had three miles to go to Concord. But she didn't want to go to Concord. She wanted, she needed, to turn right off the main road between Zebulon and Concord. A turn she was now seeing in her rearview through billows of tire smoke rising from the blacktop.

She looked back over her shoulder and dropped the Bureau car in reverse, stomping on the accelerator and flying backward east in the westbound lane of travel, which was thankfully devoid of any travelers at the late hour. Hell, she'd hardly passed a soul once she left the main highway coming south out of Atlanta. She had seen zero signs of life after Zebulon, save the rare spot of a house's light far off in the distance beyond the expansive fields of cotton, fields like those on either side of the single-lane road she was now throttling down, having gotten the car going forward again after a hard right. Wide, wide tracts of open land with clumps of trees and thickening brush showing themselves every now and then, getting thicker as she progressed down the rutted lane, encroaching on the road the farther she traveled.

She slowed and finally stopped, killing the headlights and turning the dome light on. She reached right, but the map book was not there. Not on the seat. Instead it was on the floor, having slid there with the madman's yearbook during her skidding stop. She undid her seat belt and retrieved the map book, leaving the yearbook she'd brought with her from 1251 West Lemontree. The yearbook she'd pored over on the lonely two-hour flight down to Atlanta. The yearbook that was her only glimpse at what the killer Michaelangelo had once been.

But that could not help her now. The map book could, and she flipped through the pages to get back to the one representing a small square of Pike County. A small square between Zebulon and Concord. A small square with a faint line representing a road. A road at the end of which was a short, thick line with the tag "Sugarpine Field" fixed to it. After a few seconds she found the page. She traced the tip of her finger along the faint line from main road to the airfield, then she looked out the windshield.

"Fuck," she muttered, wondering if this was the road. The right road. If it was, she couldn't just go blazing up there in the Bureau car she'd acquired from the rookie gofer. All that was likely to do was alert anyone at the end of the road that someone was coming.

If . . . If this was the right road.

Ariel put the map book aside and opened her door, stepping out into the damp chill hugging the earth that night. She could feel fog on its way.

But there was no fog yet. Just a gray cast to the lowering sky. She blinked at the mist settling from it and looked up the road with tangles of growth fencing it on either side. How could she be sure this was the road? That this wasn't a waste of time? She might not have time to . . .

Her uncertainty died right then and there. Not through any revelation. Not because of any signpost spotted near the single track through the fields. No, it retreated and certainty came as the hum of an airplane met her ears. A motoring drone rising, growing louder and nearer behind and above. She turned and looked and in the sinking shroud of clouds almost directly over her now she saw a brilliant, diffused glow as the lights of a descending aircraft came on.

She glanced quickly inside the Bureau car, at the phone in its cradle on the hump between the seats. She hadn't called for backup, for assistance, because of one simple factor. A factor that was a man. An aging man. Arlo Donovan, father of Teddy Donovan, a son missing in action, some might say. Yes, she hadn't brought anyone into this attempt of hers to get ahead of the madman because there was the very real likelihood that Arlo Donovan was with that very madman. And alive. He would have to be alive because what purpose would he serve dead?

Dead. What he could very well be if a hundred agents swarmed the area. Not that there were that many Bureau types east of North Dakota right then. There were local police, to be certain. State police. Any and all would have assisted her. But assisted her in what? Getting an old man killed. And killing the only link Mills . . . the only link Teddy Donovan had to who he really was.

No. That could not be the way. They'd thrown manpower at him for how long now? Too long, she knew. They hadn't been smart.

She needed to be that in spades right now. And she would have to be that, and more, on her own.

Ariel left the door of the Bureau car open and started up the road at a cautious trot, taking her weapon from her holster as the plane descended in the unseen distance ahead of her.

Sugarpine Field was no longer in regular use, and had not
been lit in the evening for some years now, and though he
would have preferred to use Nico Trane's night-vision
gear to set the Piper down with, the aerobatic song and
dance he was performing to keep Lionel Price convinced
he was on the edge of death made it a necessity that Mills
DeVane keep his eyes forward. Looking out of the aircraft, through the windscreen, and not at some shaky,
green-tinted, computer-enhanced version of what lay
ahead. And that meant one thing: lights.

He'd put those on at five hundred feet and a mile out,
bringing the Piper in slow, both hands tight on the artifi-
cially jerky yoke. It had been six months since he'd put in
here, and he had no idea what the runway conditions
were. At least there still was a runway, he could see as the
Piper descended finally below the soup.

"Hang on," Mills told his frightened passenger for
effect. It was a useless warning; Lionel price had never
held anything so tight as he was the armrests of the seat
he feared—almost *believed*—he was going to die in.

The Piper's xenon lights lit up the pitted and weed-
ravaged strip of concrete that had once been a pristine
runway. Mills eased the throttles back, slowing the plane
and taking his aerobatics down several notches. If there

was one place a pilot didn't want his rocking and rolling, it was when rubber was about to meet the road, because the road was hard and would chew up a plane in the blink of an eye.

"It's speed sensitive," Mills told his passenger as he kept focused on the approaching runway. "It's not as bad at lower speed."

"Good," Lionel said, liking the sound of "not as bad." The only thing he would have liked hearing better was "We're down."

"Here we go," Mills said, gripping the yoke tight with both hands now, for real, because he truly didn't know how bad Sugarpine's runway was. It wasn't great the last time he landed on it, and six months of weather could do a number on an already battered bed of concrete. "Hang on. . . ."

Again, no prompting was needed for Lionel, and when the Piper's wheels finally contacted the hard runway his grip that could not have been any tighter on the armrests intensified, and the fabric covering the fireproof padding ripped. He closed his eyes, briefly, expecting the crunch of metal to be what he next heard. But instead he heard the engines begin to spin down. To slow. And when he opened his eyes he saw the runway ahead level out as the nosewheel touched down, just a mild yelp from it, and he felt the Piper move on a straight, if somewhat bumpy course down the worn ribbon of concrete toward a pair of leaning old buildings at its end.

"Holy shit," Lionel swore with relief, his head dipping forward and his death grip on the armrests loosening. "Oh fucking Jesus."

Mills cut the throttle way back and steered the Piper toward the old abandoned hangar and service center at the north end of the runway. That would be where the troops would be. Maybe a sharpshooter or two with beads already on Mr. Lionel Price. Good. Good times two, Mills thought, and kept the front of the Piper pointed just that way as he brought it to a stop, leaving any rifle-man a clear shot.

The sensation of not moving. Of not flopping around in the air like he was strapped to the back of some drunk duck, was the most amazing relief to Lionel Price. But it was a relief that lasted but a few seconds after the Piper rolled to a stop.

"Oh shit," the big man said in a quivering voice, then hastily undid his seat belt and stepped past Mills, hunch-ing over and hurriedly moving toward the cabin door on the aft left of the aircraft. Mills looked back and watched as Lionel, steadying himself with one hand on the inner fuselage, released the latch and swung the door out, not even waiting for the steps to fold down. He hopped out, and a second later Mills could hear the big man chucking his lunch all over Sugarpine Field.

It was down, Ariel thought as she moved carefully up the lane, her weapon ready to her front. It had to be. The night had become silent. Gone was the whine of an aircraft, replaced by the chirps and clicks of bug and beast in the growth, thick on either side of the road. Quiet but for these night sounds. Sounds she could tune out, making the world around her quiet. So quiet it could unnerve one.

A split second later, though, the quiet was gone. Gone with a crack of man-made thunder.

Mills was looking forward out the windscreen when he heard it. The shot. A very *close* shot. And not the sharp crack of a long gun fired at a distance, but the sharp pop of a pistol very near. Just outside the cabin door of the Piper.

For a moment Mills froze, expecting lights to come on from everywhere. Expecting cars to pull out from behind the crumbling buildings. Expecting voices to rise, and commands to be given.

But there was none of that. None of that at all. There

was only silence and a whiff of spent gunpowder. And then . . .

. . . then there was a voice.

"We meet again, Mr. DeVane."

The skin all up and down Mills's spine tightened. He recognized the voice. Only once had he heard it, closer then than now, in his ear before. Now it came from several feet behind. From the open cabin door. He turned in his seat and looked back past his deadly cargo to a form of death itself leaning halfway into the Piper.

"Would you be so kind as to join me outside?" Michaelangelo said, and pointed Jack Hale's pistol at the man in the cockpit.

Mills stood slowly, knowing now that he was in as bad a position as he possibly could be.

About that he was soon to be proven wrong.

At the sound of the shot from ahead and to the right, Ariel bolted off the lane and into the brush, moving to cover by instinct. Once there among the brambles she paused, listening, but the retort of the shot had come from some distance off, she figured, and if there was more to be heard of softer value than that it would not be apparent from where she was crouched off the road. The shot had emanated from a hundred yards ahead. A hundred and fifty, maybe. A place she could not see. A place she needed to get to.

As she moved off through the thicket, she wondered if that shot meant she was too late.

Mills hopped down from the Piper to the runway much as Lionel Price had and heard something wet splash underfoot. He looked down and saw a dark pool beneath his feet, and followed it with his gaze until he saw its source—Lionel Price lying facedown in his own vomit beneath the Piper's left wing, a good flow of blood percolating from the back of his head and a gun showing in his back waistband where his denim jacket had ridden up.

"He won't be needing this," Michaelangelo said, bending to retrieve the late Lionel Price's weapon as he kept his own trained on his quarry.

Mills watched as the man snatched the gun up and tossed it off into the scrub at the side of the runway. He was tall. Not as tall as Lionel, but somehow he seemed larger, his presence a dark, animated blot. A silhouette that was itself.

"You know who I am."

Mills nodded. "I know who you are and I know what you are. Crazy."

Michaelangelo smiled, the expression a bright nothing upon his shadowed face. "Do you know how many feet of arteries and veins there are in the human body?"

"Tell me," Mills said, trying to sound cool and calm, though that was getting increasingly impossible as he realized that this thing being here with him meant one thing: Jack Hale wasn't coming. No one was coming. He was on his own.

"Shall I cut you open and see?"

The thought made Mills's stomach tighten, but he did not let that dread show. That was what the thing a few feet from him wanted. "If that's your plan, then go ahead and get it done with. Just know that I'll go down swinging."

Michaelangelo nodded pleasantly, acceptingly. "It was my plan, but then, plans change. Plans change with situations, and neither you nor I are in the same situation we were just this morning."

Now the madman had him wondering. Thinking. Trying to guess where he was going with this. From deveining to situations . . .

"You are not who you pretend to be," Michaelangelo said, switching the weapon from right hand to left so as to retrieve something from inside his long coat. When he produced the piece of paper and deftly unfolded it with his fingers, Mills knew what he was talking about. "You are not number five."

Mills stared at the bulletin. Ten men upon it. Ten faces. Or, more properly, ten likenesses. Ten likenesses, some with Xs through them. This was his scorecard. And what Mills knew he was getting at was that he had been bumped from the lineup.

"Am I right, Agent Donovan?"

Mills's gaze flared. Jesus! How much had Jack Hale told him?

"You are not a worthy member of an exclusive club, as we both know, but you are important. Important because of what you have on that plane."

Mills let it sink in for a moment, the thought of this thing and that thing, together, combined, madness and the madman, and he began to shake his head.

"Oh yes," Michaelangelo said. "Oh yes."

Mills understood. If the madman had simply wanted what he had on board, he could have had it already. All it would have taken was one more bullet. But he didn't just want it—he wanted it taken from here.

"No way," Mills said. "Not a chance."

Michaelangelo refolded the bulletin and slipped it back in his coat. "I think chance has nothing to do with it. It is a certainty that you will help me."

"Not on your life," Mills said, and watched the madman's hand come back out of the unseen pocket fisted around something.

"It is not my life you need to worry about," Michaelangelo said, and flipped something from his hand to the bloody ground at Mills's feet.

Mills looked down and saw in the diffused glow of the moon precisely what lay at his feet. A single poker chip.

Then another joined it. And another. And when Mills looked up again the madman was flipping chip after chip toward him.

"You maniac . . . if you . . ."

"Who has all the chips, Agent Donovan?" Michaelangelo asked. "And the cards as well?"

"Where is he?" Mills demanded, stepping bravely toward the madman. *"WHERE IS HE?!"*

Michaelangelo reached out, dropping the remaining chips and grabbing Mills roughly by the hair, putting the gun to his cheek for good measure. "Do you want to see him?"

"Damnit, where is he?" Mills pressed, bravery having nothing to do with his demeanor. Fear all of it. All but a small part that was becoming rage.

Michaelangelo pulled Mills's face close to his, into the shadow of it. "Let's go have a look, shall we?"

She caught sight of the tall tail of the aircraft over the brush and moved toward it at an angle, hearing voices as she did. Small voices. Too small to make out, to identify. But there were more than one. Two people were conversing. Two people were *alive*.

But which two.

Twenty yards farther on the thicket began to thin, to both front and sides. To the left she could make out the dark strip of clear earth that was the lane far beyond where she'd left her car. To the right was the plane, most of which she could see through breaks in the foliage.

And she could see more than the plane. Enough to make her heart leap and her fingers flex around the grip of her weapon.

Damn . . .

He had him! Michaelangelo had Mills!

She steadied herself in a crouch and brought her weapon up, trying for a solid aim. But how good was her aim at, what, thirty yards? With a pistol. A pistol just like the one Michaelangelo had planted against Mills's head. That she could see clearly. Could she hit her target and not her target's victim? Could she take him out with one shot? A head shot? Before he could squeeze off a round?

Could she?

She didn't know. She couldn't know.

Ariel lowered her weapon a bit. Lowered it and watched as Michaelangelo walked Mills toward a pair of decaying buildings—

"No," she whispered aloud, seeing what was there, parked on the far side of the buildings. Just the back of it she could see, but the back was enough. How many K cars were still on the road?

She thumped her knee with a fist and tried to think. Think how she could get ahead of Michaelangelo. How she could get ahead of him now when he had what he wanted.

But did he have what he wanted? she wondered, and her gaze tracked right toward the Piper parked on the runway.

Michaelangelo dragged Mills past the old hangar and service building, almost around the corner. But then almost was enough. From where Mills now stood he could see the car. The old Dodge. His pop's car.

"Damn you, if you . . ."

The madman's hand pressed down hard on Mills's head, forcing him to his knees. "Stay there."

Mills watched as Michaelangelo went to the back of the car, keeping his weapon on him, and drew a set of keys from his pocket. A second later the lid popped up and the madman reached inside. With a heave he pulled something out, hesitating briefly before coming around the car once again with Arlo Donovan in his grasp.

"Pop," Mills said from his enforced genuflection. His father was bound and gagged, hands tied before him and a strip of tape over his mouth. His eyes were wide. Wide with fear, Mills knew, and the rage inside him boiled.

"You know each other, I believe," Michaelangelo said.

Mills did not take his eyes off of his father as he said, "You don't know how lucky you are he's alive."

"I do, actually. Because I am certain now that you will

help me. That you will take me and your precious cargo where I choose to go." Michaelangelo paused just long enough to shift his aim from Mills to the side of Arlo's head. "I am correct, am I not?"

Still Mills looked only at his father, his teeth clenched as his head moved in a slow, deliberate nod.

The gun came away from Arlo's head and aimed once more at Mills. "Good."

Finally, Mills looked to the madman. "But let me tell you one thing. One very true thing. If one hair on his head is hurt, if he doesn't walk away from here alive after we're gone, so help me I'll fly you and me and that thing onboard into the ground. We'll crash and burn. Do you understand me?"

Michaelangelo chuckled. "We have a deal. Get up."

Mills did, facing his father now. "You'll be okay."

Arlo Donovan couldn't speak right then, but his eyes said all that needed to be said. *No. Don't do it. Don't go with him.* They were all things Mills wished desperately could become reality, but this was not a time for wishes. For him, at this moment, it was a time for sacrifice. True sacrifice.

If the madman was stupid enough to believe that he wasn't going to plow into a field somewhere regardless, then let him. At least his pop would be okay. His pop would be alive.

"Move," Michaelangelo said, and after a last look Mills turned away from his father and back toward the Piper, the madman following him close with the weapon pressed to his back.

Arlo Donovan took one step forward and watched. Watched as his boy walked off with the killer.

Just outside the cabin door Michaelangelo took Mills's collar in a fisted grip and pressed the gun hard against the back of his head, stopping him from entering. "Would you do me a favor?"

Mills's eyes angled back toward the madman. "What are you talking about?"

"Would you kindly ask your friend to step from inside the plane?"

Mills's brow bunched down with confusion. "What friend?"

"Your lady friend."

No lower did he think it could go, but Mills's heart sank to its foundation as he looked back to the Piper, back through its door to the darkened cabin within, and said as calmly as he could, "Ariel?"

Shit . . .

She was crouched in the small space just inside and aft of the door, hugging the fuselage and planning, *hoping,* for one quick head shot as Michaelangelo came through the opening. No *Freeze.* No *You're under arrest.* No warning. Just a squeeze on the trigger and put an end to him.

That had been the plan.

Shit . . .

But the plan was in the dumper.

How? How did he know?

"Did you think you could hide in the shadows, my dear lady? Did you?"

She listened to him talk to her from outside. Listened and wondered if he had somehow seen her as she sprinted from cover while his attention was on hauling Arlo from the trunk. Had he seen her then? Caught a glimpse?

Did it matter how?

"My dear, I live in the shadows. It is my world. You can't hide in *my* world *from* me."

What now? she asked herself. What the hell could she do now?

She knew. And she hated it.

Mills saw her first, crouching into the doorway just feet from him, her weapon held grip-first in surrender. She looked at him, her face calm but seething below, and then she looked above him to the man who could see in the shadows.

"Toss your weapon to the ground," Michaelangelo instructed her, and she complied. The pistol thunked metallically off the concrete and came to rest near Lionel Price's still body. "If you have any more weapons it would be prudent to —"

"I don't have a backup piece," she told him, sharing the truth that she wished were a lie.

"Good," Michaelangelo said. "But you do have something else, I hope."

Ariel chewed at the inside of her lip. "What?"

"Handcuffs . . ."

After a hesitation she reached slowly behind to her belt and came back with a gleaming pair of cuffs dangling from one finger.

"Good," Michaelangelo said. "I think we will be needing those. Now"—he gave Mills a shove toward the plane, and Mills turned back to look, with Ariel, at the madman with the gun pointed at them—"let's all take a trip."

34

[PILOT, PRINCESS, AND PRIZE]

At the point of a gun they'd boarded the Piper, and under the same threat Mills had taken his place in the left seat and started the plane's two engines. Behind him, in the Piper's stripped-out cabin, Ariel was left with the madman. And to his front . . .

. . . to his front, as the xenon landing lights blazed to life and bathed what was left of Sugarpine's runway in a hot, white glow, he saw his father—standing there next to his car in the partial shadow of the crumbling structures, hands bound but looking as though they were locked in prayer, his eyes squinting at the glare thrown his way. Squinting to watch, to witness, as his boy left him once more. For what was likely the last time.

And then Mills could lay eyes on his father no more. His gaze dropped to the instrument panel, to the gangs of lights and displays and dials come to life. It was hardly a preflight to be proud of, but for this trip it was all that was necessary.

But was that really true? he wondered, glancing over his shoulder to the stripped-out cabin behind. To Ariel, crouched low against the bare inner fuselage, her head barely at window level and her eyes set upon the madman who held a gun at her with one hand while running the other gently over the dull metal case that was strapped to the Piper's cabin floor. She was here. With him. With them. With it.

Could he still do it? Could he still just take them all up a few thousand feet and nose the Piper into the sweet Georgia earth? Could he do that to *her?*

Damnit, he swore silently, cursing her in thought. Cursing her for being there. For getting there. For somehow getting there. For being a complication.

He hated complications. Hated them.

But he didn't hate her. Couldn't hate her.

"How secure is this?"

The question caught Mills off guard, and he looked from Ariel to the madman who had posed it. "What?"

Michaelangelo tapped the dull metal case with a single, long finger. "How securely is this fastened down?"

Five straps anchored to ten metal hardpoints on the Piper's exposed metal floor—that thing wasn't going anywhere. Pilots hated things that weren't bolted down, and if not that, strapped down, because in any turbulence . . .

"Very," Mills answered, truncating his line of mental reasoning. Stopping a memory coming. Of happenstance. He didn't want to go there now. Didn't need to relive that now. Didn't need to revisit the image of his dead wife launched about the cabin of a jumbo jet and coming to rest as still and lifeless as a rag doll at his feet. No, he didn't need to think about that at all.

Not at all.

"Very good," Michaelangelo said, and swung one of the steel handles affixed to the case away from its silver-gray body. "Here, please."

He was looking now at Ariel. Ariel and the cuffs she held in her hand.

"One end here, the other on your wrist," Michaelangelo instructed, gesturing with Jack Hale's pistol. "Your right wrist."

He was smart, she saw. Up close and personal she saw. Making her cuff her strong hand. Her gun hand.

"Now, please," Michaelangelo prodded, and the pistol's aim settled on her face. "Right hand."

Ariel hooked her wrist up with an expert strike just above the joint, the cuff circling the narrowest part where arm met hand and latching itself with a solid set of clicks.

"Tight, please."

Her free hand squeezed down on the restraint, pushing a few clicks past where it had set, until it was almost painfully tight against her skin.

"And to the handle."

Again she followed his direction, and with a final loud snap she was anchored to the box marked with Cyrillic characters. She tried not to think about what was inside. There was enough to worry about without throwing that in as well.

"Very good," Michaelangelo said, then held his hand out to her, palm up. Waiting.

"What?" Ariel asked, but she knew. Knew because he was smart. Because he would not overlook that.

Michaelangelo's mouth approximated a smile, his teeth baring and rigid cheeks swelling. "Your keys, my dear."

Ariel slapped herself mentally for even *hoping* that he would overlook that one small, crucial detail, and fished her key ring from the pocket of her pants. She handed it over, but her captor was not yet satisfied.

"Turn your pockets out."

She sighed a breath and turned the one out from which she'd drawn the keys, exposing the linted innards of the white pouch.

"And the other . . ."

Awkwardly she reached across to her right front pocket, slipping her left hand in and hesitating through a single breath before tugging the material, exposing the inside and spilling the small pair of keys ringed together.

Michaelangelo's smile did not fade, but now Ariel thought that it never had been that. Never had been an expression of pleasure, of satisfaction. She wondered if maybe it had simply been an icy expression of low, coming anger.

"With the others, please," Michaelangelo told her, and Ariel picked up her spare set of handcuff keys—a spare set like all officers of the law carried just in case they were ever disarmed and had their own restraints employed against them—and dropped them in Michaelangelo's still-open palm. They joined her regular key ring with a clink and the hand began to close around them, long fingers folding over, flexing down, down. Down hard. Hard. Hard until it was a fist that Ariel barely saw as a flash when it snapped out in a fast arc and backhanded her across the face.

She reeled backward against the fuselage, her arm jerking painfully against its anchor and her free hand coming up to cover her face.

A few arm's lengths forward, Mills spun suddenly out of his seat and was ready to launch himself at the madman when the gun snapped fast his way, planting a precise bead upon his chest. His center of mass. Heart, lungs, other vitals right there. Right there at a distance that a blind man could not miss at.

"Sit down." Michaelangelo commanded Mills, but the order was not immediately heeded. "I can do worse to her, if you wish. . . ."

Mills half stood there in the space between pilot and passenger seats, his hot stare shifting between Ariel and the madman. "You fucking touch her again . . ."

Now Michaelangelo did smile, truly smile, that dim twist curling his thin lips and letting the cabin's faint light gleam off a few teeth. "So very brave, the pilot is, wanting to protect the princess."

Ariel's hand eased off her stinging face and she looked to Mills. "I'm okay."

Still, Mills stood his ground, and to that defiance Michaelangelo pocketed the keys he'd grudgingly been given and returned to the open with something else in hand. A knife that flipped open with a snap and a shine.

"I think the princess might look better with a crown," Michaelangelo threatened coyly. "Every princess needs a crown. And I do have experience. . . ."

Robert Jack McCormack, Mills recalled. The fugitive made messiah by the madman. No . . . made *dead*, first.

"A nine-point crown," Michaelangelo suggested. "Maybe leave her a finger to scratch with. Hmmm?"

Mills gave Ariel another look, and her eyes implored him to retreat. To back off. And that he could do. That he would do.

"Good," Michaelangelo said as Mills backed himself away to his place at the controls of the Piper once more. "The pilot is a bright man. The pilot knows his limits."

Mills belted himself into the seat and took the yoke in hand, if only to have something to hold. To grip. To bear tightly down upon. Because though he had retreated, he understood full well that there was a difference between that and surrender. He had backed down, but one more tactically inclined would consider it but a chance to regroup. To wait. To bide his time.

But for what? For what?

That he did not know. Not yet, at least.

"Take us away from here," Michaelangelo said from behind. "We have somewhere to go."

Arlo Donovan heard the plane's engines spin up, their throaty whine rising until it began to move, lurching forward at first but then settling into an easy roll. It came at him a bit, then swung hard to the right, the harsh lights sweeping off of him and letting him see for the briefest of moments his son through the pilot's side window. Their eyes did not meet. His boy was not looking his way.

Instead he was focused. Focused ahead on what he was doing. On what he would have to do.

The plane turned full around, the prop wash blasting dirt and debris at Arlo. He turned his head until the windy assault subsided, then looked back to see that his boy had the Piper lined up on the extreme left side of the runway, well clear of the body that lay near its long-disappeared centerline. He did not want to roll over the obstacle, though Arlo doubted it was because of any gruesome sensibilities. It was because any obstacle, especially something as large as a man, and that body in particular, could damage a plane, and his son was too good a pilot, too careful a pilot, to let that happen.

And in that Arlo Donovan found his only solace of the moment, for a few seconds later the Piper's engines came up to full speed and pushed the light airplane down the runway. It bounced a bit on the old surface as it gathered speed, moving faster and faster until the jittery glow it cast to its front smoothed out and tipped up, lighting the clouds from beneath until it rose into their misty depths and disappeared from view.

35

[HECATOMB]

They were a minute in the air when the madman slouched his way into the cockpit and planted himself in the passenger seat.

Mills glanced his way, then back to Ariel, who was sitting on the cabin floor, tethered to the Russian tac nuke that he had helped bring into the country. He thought suddenly that if any hint of foresight had been present in his genes, he would have ditched the plane, Gareth and all, in the deep water between Clarion Key and the good old U.S. of A. Let the sharks have at them. Let the Navy someday hoist up the thing Costain had sold for blood money. Let that all happen, as long as this would not have happened. Him, here, with her. And with the madman.

Mills looked back through the windscreen and out into the soup. "Do you just want me to fly?"

"That's your way of asking where I'm going," Michael-angelo observed. "You can fly west from here."

"West," Mills said, keeping the yoke back and power near full as the Piper climbed. He wanted to get above the clouds, above blind-flying conditions. Into clear air. To a place where he could see another plane coming. Away from obstacles. As far above innocents as he could possibly manage. "West is a big slice of air. You care to narrow it down?"

Michaelangelo stared straight ahead. Into the gray nothing outside. But memory tunneled through the veil, past the weather, and across the miles to where he wanted to go. Across time to where he had come from. To where he was going to return. "Texas," he said. "We're going to Texas."

Some feet to the rear, Ariel heard the destination given, and realization came to her with a stone-cold shudder. She understood. Where he was going. And what he was going to do.

Do with the thing she was lashed to.

An easy, sweeping turn brought the Piper to a westerly heading, and the miles ticked off behind them, the feet beneath them. Five thousand, ten thousand, fifteen thousand, and higher still. The clouds broke at twelve, and by seventeen five there were a million and one stars dotting the black heavens above, but Mills gave the display of nature's grand beauty only passing admiration. Powerful as it might be, it seemed frivolous in light of his present situation.

Correction, their situation.

"You okay back there?" he asked without looking, though Michaelangelo did consider him with a sideways glance.

"Yeah," Ariel replied without enthusiasm. There was little to be enthused about. Nothing had gone as she'd planned, or even hoped. She hadn't gotten a break. Neither of them had. Not one thing had gone their way. And why was that?

She knew.

Yes, he was still out front. In the lead. Being *chased*. They were reacting to him. He asks for her gun, she tosses it away. He wants handcuffs, she produces them. He asks for keys, she *gives* him keys. *Twice*. And all she'd gotten so far was a closed-fist bitch slap that still stung.

Reacting, she thought, angry at herself. Wishing she had spit in his face when he'd ordered her to turn her pockets out. He would have struck her, to be sure, maybe even done worse, but at least he would have been reacting to something *she* did.

They were still following his lead. And damn if that didn't burn.

"Spit in his fucking face," Ariel muttered softly, absently.

"What did you say?" Michaelangelo asked from the cockpit.

Ariel shook her head. She hadn't meant to say anything. "Nothing. Not a damn . . ."

She stopped suddenly, the pause coming abruptly but almost unnoticeably. Coming when she realized something. Something so simple that the barest breath of a chuckle slipped from her, not enough to be heard but enough to bolster her. To convince her. To remind her what had just happened when she'd intended nothing to happen. He had *reacted.* To something she'd said.

Yes. To something she said.

She wondered. Wondered if she could do so again. And if she could, would it do any good?

A shudder of turbulence that rocked the Piper a minute later made her think that it could. That it maybe just could.

"You really hate that place that much," Ariel said aloud and intentionally, several minutes later. Several minutes that had seen her gather all she could from memory, every piece, every scrap, hoarding them like stones to be used in some childish rock fight.

In a way, that was not far from the reality of her plan.

"Are you wasting air back there?" Michaelangelo asked with insulting disinterest.

"Me?" Ariel shook her head and hoped that Mills

would catch on. That he would catch on and act when the time was right. "I'm just trying to clear the air."

Michaelangelo's stare narrowed down, and he looked back to the cabin and his chained-up prisoner. "Your obliqueness is tiresome."

"Mills agrees with me," Ariel said, and noticed his head tick a bit her way. "Don't you?"

Michaelangelo's gaze shifted to the man at the controls.

"Don't you think we should clear the air, Mills?" Ariel asked. "Clear air is good for everybody, isn't it?"

"What is she droning on about?" Michaelangelo asked Mills.

"I don't know," he said, quite truthfully in fact. Yet he knew she wouldn't just be droning on. So what was all this about clearing the . . .

. . . *air.*

Mills looked back to her. His face was flat. Emotionless. Empty.

Clear air . . .

Ariel saw him look her way. At her. More important, she saw *how* he was looking at her. He was remembering. Connecting.

"Clear air," she said, pausing as he turned away from her, back to the instruments, the controls. To what lay ahead. "All I want to do is get a clear appreciation as to why you hate that place."

Michaelangelo ignored her and faced forward once more.

His deliberate disinterest lasted but a second, maybe two. Only until she spoke again. Spoke words of old.

"Why is it you feel that way about Calvert, Mickey D?"

Ariel swore she felt it before Michaelangelo turned back toward her, a chill rushing from him. Leaping at her.

"What did you say?"

She smiled, so very deliberately, so very childishly, as

one much younger might to announce without words that a secret was no more.

"Was Calvert really that bad of a place? Bad enough to want to blow up?" She shifted up a bit, onto her knees. "That is what you're planning now, isn't it? Now that your other gig is up?"

His fingers pressed down hard around the grip of Jack Hale's pistol. He glared at her. At her insolence. Her ignorance. "Art changes. Artists adapt."

"Right," she said, nodding with exaggeration. "Your little hunt up the Most Wanted list is over. . . ."

"For now," Michaelangelo said, rebutting her.

"No, for good, Mickey D," she countered.

"Don't call me that," he said, almost casually.

Ariel ignored his request. "Your house. Your name. Your picture. We have it all, Mickey D. Your little . . ."

"The name is Michaelangelo."

". . . game is up. I mean, how sad." She shook her head, ready to hit hard now. To hit hard with what she'd learned from his yearbook, and from a full hour of fast phone calls on the flight down from New York. Calls to places, to people, who had known him. Who had known of Michael Angelo Strange. People who told her things. Explained the most horrid of things. Things that now she would use. The biggest, sharpest rocks that she'd gathered for this fight. "First you start lopping off men's dicks, and that doesn't seem to fix your problem, does it. I mean, you didn't grow a new one, did you?"

Jack Hale's weapon came up in the death grip that held it. Slowly up from Michaelangelo's lap, moving and tracking an arc that passed over Mills and fell finally upon Ariel. "I think you should stop."

Mills glanced sharply at the madman's aim. "Don't even think about shooting that in here, at this altitude. If you missed, we —"

With a gun in hand it was no bitch slap. The more

proper term was pistol whip, and it was that which Mills suffered without warning, a strike so quick, so hard, that when he was able to recover and look back from where it had come the weapon was pointed at Ariel once more. Rock steady as if it had never come off its aim.

"Fly the plane," Michaelangelo instructed without looking to Mills, his full attention on the woman who was severely testing him. Quite nearly taunting him.

"I'm right, I gather," Ariel continued, matching his stare with her own full of mocking contention. "No new growth. But that makes sense. One thing doesn't work, you can't make yourself a man that way, so you've gotta do something else. Take a different approach. Say, taking out your own kind."

"I no longer think you should stop," Michaelangelo said. His arm stretched out, putting the barrel of Jack Hale's weapon that much closer to Ariel. "I am *certain* you should stop."

"Clearing the air, Mickey D, that's all I'm doing."

"My name is —"

"Your name," Ariel said, cutting the madman off, "is Mickey Dickless. Mickey *Dickless*."

He said nothing. Made no move for a moment. There was just the rush of breath in and out of his nose and the heave of his narrow, taut chest beneath the dark clothes he wore.

"I've got the name right, don't I?" Ariel asked, and she saw very clearly his index finger begin to twitch upon the trigger. He was reacting to *her*. "Mickey Dickless."

"I'm going to enjoy killing you."

"Don't pull that fucking trigger!" Mills shouted, and the madman snapped a look his way.

"Is the bruise swelling on your face not convincing enough? Shall I give you another?"

With one good eye and one slowly closing eye Mills matched the madman's stare. "I don't care what you do, but unless you want to experience emergency depressurization and kill everybody onboard—you, me, her—then you'd better save the fucking gunplay for when we get on the ground!"

"The name fits . . . Dickless," Ariel said, smirking obviously.

His finger shook, aching to bear down upon the trigger. But for the pilot's admonition it might have.

It would not have to, though. A gun was an easy, detached way of killing, but by no means the only way. Others were available to him. Other ways. Intimate ways. Blade. Cord. Hand.

Hand.

The most intimate of ways. He could see it, imagine it, choking the offending breath off. Stopping the flow of words of lies of . . .

. . . *truths* . . .

"Dickless," Ariel said again, and Michaelangelo exploded.

"SHUT UP!" he screamed, coming out of the seat and into the cabin, hands clamped suddenly over his ears as he crouched low in the restrictive space. "STOP CALLING ME THAT!"

"Dickless!" Ariel herself cried back, though not at a level that could approach the almost pained wail the madman had loosed. And pained it likely was. Pained she knew it was. From old, painful memories of terrible, terrible events. Things that had shaped a boy and twisted a man.

Yes, there was pain in him, but hurt could not erase evil, nor the evil he had done. Or the evil he was planning to do to a town that had mostly forgotten him, moved on.

"Dickless!" she shouted again, and despite the realities of what she had to do, it hurt now to call him that. It hurt to hurt him. But she had to. *"DICKLESS!"*

His hands came fast away from his ears, and he ripped the cap from his head where it touched the Piper's bare ceiling, revealing a face less shadowed. A chiseled, pulsing mask of hate aimed at Ariel. Right at Ariel.

Coming right at Ariel.

He moved a stooping step, still holding the gun, his free hand reaching out toward her now. She backed away as much as her tether would allow, increasing the distance, making him *have* to come to her. Wanting him to come to her. Beckoning him to come to her.

"Dickless," she said one final time, and the whites of his sunken eyes flared, hate becoming rage. Becoming desire. A desire to kill, and kill only for killing's sake. Not for art. No, now it would not be for art.

Another step and he was fully into the cabin, just the Piper's deadly cargo between them. Between Ariel and the long, sinewy fingers reaching out for her. Coming to her. Coming at her face.

"CLEAR AIR!" she shouted as loud as she could, and for only the briefest of instants there was a reaction to what she'd cried out on Michaelangelo's face. A flash of confusion among the hate. Just a dancing twinkle of wonder in his eye.

And then he was tossed hard against the left side of the fuselage as Mills tipped the Piper severely in a hard right half roll, his head and back slamming into the bare metal between the line of windows. Ariel, too, was thrown, her body flopping like a rag doll, feet impacting the crumpled form of the madman while her upper body stayed fixed to the tac nuke's case.

And then, as a bit of composure was trickling back into the madman's senses, a half roll snapped the Piper to the left and flung its aft passengers hard against the right side of the cabin, Michaelangelo nearly crushing Ariel as his weight came down upon her.

She gasped, and Mills pulled the Piper's nose up sharply, its speed dropping as it crossed through twenty-three thousand feet, stall speed approaching and all that wasn't tethered in backsliding aft. Most of Ariel's body moved that way, no choice in the matter for her, physics and a stout pair of handcuffs vying for supremacy right then. And she felt it. Felt like a tug-of-war was going on, and for sure her arm was going to be the loser. Her arm and those ribs that had suddenly come to painful life, adrenaline no longer enough to mute the hurt.

Michaelangelo, though, was completely at the mercy of the laws of motion, and he hit viciously against the aft bulkhead. In some aircraft of this make there would have been a very confining but usable toilet there, but Nico Trane had stripped this Piper to its bones, and all there was to meet Michaelangelo was a thick panel of aircraft aluminum that at the moment might as well have been a concrete slab. It felt the same, and knocked the wind right out of him.

But with a loud, animal-like gasp he sucked breath back in. Drew it deep and looked up and forced himself to his feet just as Mills cut power back and put the Piper into a steep dive, Ariel sliding forward. All that was not tied down sliding forward.

All but Michaelangelo.

In the narrow, short confines of the cabin, he planted his feet wide on the floor and, stooping, his strong shoulders and both hands pressed against the ceiling, wedged himself in place. Negating the effect of the man-made turbulence Mills was creating.

Except this last maneuver was not meant for him. This Michaelangelo realized when the Piper leveled out and Mills leaned partially out of the cockpit, twisting severely and reaching for something. Something on the cabin floor.

No!

By instinct Michaelangelo looked to each of his hands. Hands planted firmly upon the Piper's roof. Hands that held nothing. Hands that held no gun.

Mills got a finger on the weapon and scratched at it, pulling it toward him. Quarter inch, half inch, inch, until he had two fingers on it, and three, and four, and a thumb, and his whole hand now curled around the grip and even before he brought the weapon up he was looking. Looking aft. Aft at the madman, who was looking at . . .

Shit!

She was dazed, but then that was not an unlikely potentiality considering the beating she'd just been given in the guts of this angry metal bird. Dazed to the point that she was momentarily unaware of her surroundings. Unaware of the danger still present. The danger she was pulling herself toward as she dragged herself toward the point where her stinging arm was tethered.

And toward the madman.

Mills brought the gun up fast, but not fast enough. By the time it was pointed at where Michaelangelo had wedged himself, he was no longer there. He'd launched himself at Ariel and now had her in his grip. Had his hands around her throat as he held her body between himself and Mills. Between himself and the gun.

Mills put the gun on him there. Aimed at him there. But could not get a shot. Not a clear shot. Pieces of the madman ducked in and out behind Ariel as she fought against the fingers constricting her throat. Choking off her air from behind, thumbs pressing dangerously at the soft base of her skull. Her eyes bulged, her face a scarlet bubble seeming ready to explode, and in the moment before she was certain she was going to die she saw Mills, leaning back, gun in hand as he flew the Piper one handed, and she said something to him. Not in word, because that was impossible. Instead she mouthed it. Mouthed her plea. Her *permission.*

Take . . . the . . . shot. . . .

He saw her. Heard her. Wanted to do as she wished. But there was not enough of the cowering madman to shoot at. Just flashes of him. And if he fired and missed, just as he'd warned Michaelangelo, there could be . . .

It all came so fast. So quickly to him, the realization,

the decision, the sight of Ariel beginning to go limp and his own hand letting go the yoke just briefly to cinch his seat belt, his aim shifting, moving off of the jittering madman to a window on the right side of the aircraft, one almost opposite the cabin door on the right. Mills set his aim there and took hold of the yoke once more, hard hold of it, and squeezed the trigger just as Ariel's eyes began to flutter shut.

At twenty-three thousand two hundred feet above sea level, the difference in air pressure between the thin, cold atmosphere outside and the comfortably pressurized cabin of the Piper was considerable. Not what it would have been at thirty thousand feet, but then it didn't have to be. Mills knew that. Michaelangelo was about to learn that.

The bullet struck the thick window farthest back on the Piper's right side, punching a small hole that would not stay that way. In an incomprehensibly fast moment the vacuum created by the opening of a passage from thick air to thin widened the hole to include the whole window, the glass that had been there instantly pulverized by the negative pressure and sucked into the darkness beyond. The window frame, too, was compromised, welds and seams failing as the ring of metal tore free and pulled with it a strip of the outer fuselage that opened a narrow tear from inside to out. A hole that everything not tied down now rushed to. Now was sucked to.

He weighed upward of two hundred twenty pounds, and when the differential in pressure worked to equalize itself it yanked Michaelangelo off of Ariel Grace with a force so sharp that no man could resist it. Instantly Michael Angelo Strange became a projectile, and when his still-living body hit the tear in the fuselage it became a cork, and when the laws of physics overcame the resistance his body was providing, the tear in the fuselage splintered into hundreds of weblike tears. The tear became a hole. A hole edged with razor-sharp jags of metal that shredded the killer known as Michaelangelo into dozens of unrecognizable pieces as he was sucked finally into the night and scattered over Arkadelphia, Alabama.

Mills had sucked a last breath as he squeezed off the shot, and his eyes closed instinctively when what was inside the Piper began being sucked out, but when he opened his eyes and looked once again and saw the gun gone from his hand and the madman gone from his plane he might have breathed a sigh of relief. But for two things he might have done that.

There was little air to breathe, and Ariel, still tethered to the tac nuke's metal case, was hanging limply at the end of her binding, legs drawn toward the opening in the Piper's fuselage, flapping in the hurricane wind being whipped up in the now equalized pressure of the cabin.

He turned fast back to his instruments and reached for his oxygen mask, putting it on and putting the Piper into a steep dive. He could breathe now, but he knew that she could not. There was precious little air up here for a human being, which meant he had to get her down to an altitude where she could breathe.

If she was still breathing.

He turned on the radio and did something he had not done for so very long—put out a call to the authorities for help.

The controller responding to his Mayday directed him a few miles south and west to the nearest field, a near mile-long strip of asphalt in Walker County near the city of Jasper. He might have flown on to Birmingham, a big city with a bigger airport and bigger runways and cops and hospitals close by, but he needed to get down *now*. He didn't know how much longer his battered plane would fly. Didn't know how much damage had been done. And he didn't know how much time Ariel had. If she had any at all.

Bevill Field was a daylight airport, which meant the

runway lights should have been out. Mills could have fixed that with a few clicks of his mike on the specified frequency of 122.8, but that turned out not to be necessary. When he broke through the cloud cover at two thousand feet he saw a string of lights stretching out in the distance. And he saw a sight he thought more beautiful than that. He saw lights of red and blue, spinning in gangs up and down the sides of the approaching runway, and more lights coming on a road leading to Bevill Field. And when he lowered his gear and the wheels groaned down and locked in place, he thought that the most beautiful sound he'd ever heard.

Until, of course, the Piper touched down with a jolt and he heard Ariel wince with pain and ask groggily but aloud what the hell was going on.

"It's over," he said in answer as the Piper rolled down the runway toward the waiting lights, looking back to her as her head came up. "It's all over."

She put a hand to her bruised and aching head and smiled at him. Smiled and chuckled, even though it hurt. "Thank God."

EPILOGUE:
[FALL TO GRACE]

He testified for a week at each trial, his appearance a sensation to news media and lawyers alike. In the end two juries believed him and convicted Gareth Dean Hoag and Nita Berry of multiple crimes. The death penalty was an option, but that decision was yet to be made. If they needed to hear from him again, Teddy Donovan would come back.

But there were other trials to go, and on the fourth day of spring the year after he had almost been killed by the monster called Michaelangelo, Teddy Donovan left the Federal District Courthouse in Atlanta after a mild day on the stand telling of the illegal exploits of the Moreno brothers. He walked down the street and loosened his tie. Another southern summer was still officially months off, but it was sending out warnings already. Be ready, it said, it was going to be a hot one.

He bought a shaved ice from a vendor on Peachtree and kept on walking. Walking out in the open. Not caring if anyone was watching. Not caring if anyone recognized him, which people did on occasion after the news frenzy following what had happened. He could be out. Be who he was. Be Teddy Donovan.

Mills DeVane was gone. Gone that night in a plane over the Heartland.

Teddy. I'm Teddy, he reminded himself often. Teddy Donovan. And if he didn't, his father made sure to do so for him.

"Teddy!" someone called, and he looked back the way he'd come, expecting to see a reporter or a lawyer or someone telling him he'd left his wallet at the courthouse. But he did not see anyone like that. Instead he saw Ariel.

She jogged between cars on Peachtree and met him on the sidewalk.

"I missed you back at the courthouse," she said to him, smiling. It had been almost four months since they'd last seen each other in the Piper as the night tried to suck them out. They'd shared some interminably uncertain moments there, and a few hours after that until rescue crews in radiation suits arrived to join the local cops and firefighters who had met them, but there had been too much going on. Too many things with too many people. Their time had been emotional and brief.

Very brief.

Too brief.

"The trial broke early," Teddy told her, his shaved ice held between them. "I heard you're in Albany now."

Ariel nodded. "The SAC there requested me. Go figure."

"Not hard to figure," Teddy said.

Ariel reached up and brushed some hair from his forehead. "You need a trim."

"You in the business now? Second career?"

She shook her head, and he offered her his shaved ice. She took a taste and wiped her chin. "What are your plans, Teddy?"

"Me? A court date here, a court date there. Some time off. I don't know. I'm still getting used to being me."

She smiled at that and wondered if anyone other than he could comprehend what that really meant. "Are you still flying?"

"I can't stop doing that."

"You ever think you might fly up Albany way?" she asked and invited him concurrently.

He shrugged. "Right now, Ariel, I just kind of want to walk. Do you know what I mean?"

She thought so. "Do you mind if I walk with you?"

"I wouldn't mind that at all."

She passed back his shaved ice and he took some, then he passed it to her. They shared it all the way up Peachtree.